"Okay," said Barrin, "here comes the hard part." He took a deep breath and chose his words. "You, dragon, are a simulacrum. Master Urza here has created you out of raw mana using his rather impressive skills. You are designed to perfectly emulate a real dragon to aid Master Urza in his research. Since dragons are, of course, sentient creatures, he had to make you sentient as well. You are, in effect, a self-aware magical spell, cast by one of the most powerful planeswalkers ever known."

His assertion ended, Barrin studied the dragon's eyes earnestly, but found them impossible to read. The dragon blinked once, slowly, nictitating membranes gliding over the deep gold eyes like oil on water. Then, suddenly, the dragon laughed, and wisps of smoke spiraled in the air.

"Enough of this talk," it bellowed, "I hunger!" It looked at Barrin. "You will tide me over until I find some real food," it said. Its mammoth claw shot forth like a serpent and snatched Barrin out of the air. . .

Experience the Magic

Artifacts Cycle:

Masquerade Cycle:

Invasion Cycle:

MAGIC
The Gathering®

THE
DRAGONS OF MAGIC
A N T H O L O G Y

A MAGIC: THE GATHERING Anthology

Edited by

J. Robert King

THE DRAGONS OF MAGIC
©2001 Wizards of the Coast, Inc.

Distributed in the United States by Holtzbrinck Publishing. Distributed in Canada by Fenn Ltd.

Distributed to the hobby, toy, and comic trade in the United States and Canada by regional distributors.

Distributed worldwide by Wizards of the Coast, Inc., and regional distributors.

Cover art by Eric Peterson
Cartography by Dennis Kauth
First Printing: August 2001
Library of Congress Catalog Card Number: 00-190896

9 8 7 6 5 4 3 2 1

ISBN: 0-7869-1872-1
UK ISBN: 0-7869-2629-5
620-T21872

U.S., CANADA,
ASIA, PACIFIC, & LATIN AMERICA
Wizards of the Coast, Inc.
P.O. Box 707
Renton, WA 98057-0707
+1-800-324-6496

EUROPEAN HEADQUARTERS
Wizards of the Coast, Belgium
P.B. 2031
2600 Berchem
Belgium
+32-70-23-32-77

Visit our web site at http://**www.wizards.com/magic**

Table of Contents:

PART IV: WARRIOR DRAGONS

Dominaria Before
the Invasion

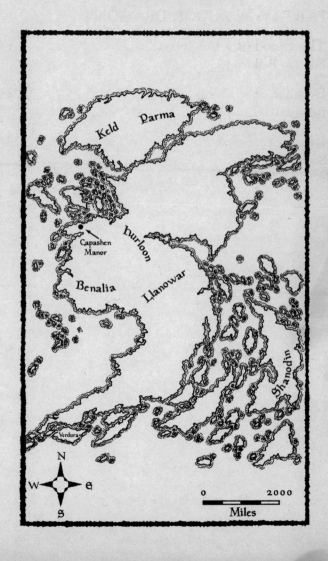

Keld Parma

Capashen Manor

Hurloon

Benalia

Llanowar

Shanodin

Verdura

N
W E
S

0   2000
Miles

Part I:

Lord Dragons

Dragons have always ruled us. Among all the clamoring nations of human and elf, dwarf and minotaur, a single dragon is a simple majority.

Just the sight of such a beast—its hackles lifting above a crag of stone and its neck uncoiling beneath a spiky head—sends us to our knees. We try to rise, to run, but realize this is where we belong. The languid stare of the beast passes across our bowed heads and burns into our souls. Talons shake the rock beneath us. Brimstone breath snorts over us. Then . . . oblivion.

Dragons rule us as does mortality itself.

First among our stories of lord dragons is a tale of a contemporary beast. This serpent rules plains that even the Phyrexians could not conquer. . . .

Then return to a time before the Phyrexian invasion, to a savanna half a world away, where a different sort of invasion occurs—a draconic one. . . .

Lastly, plunge to the deepest reaches of history, to a time ruled by the dragons Primeval. . . .

Dragon Lord

Vance Moore

The gliding monster flew high over the muted landscape, its brilliant marble-white hide lost against a backdrop of clouds. Two sets of massive claws lay curled against its armored scales. Eagyn, the last dragon of the order, looked through jade eyes on his dominion.

Like sails in a high wind, his outstretched wings rippled. The dragon turned, falling from the endless currents of the sky to the land below. Eagyn's nostrils dilated, taking in the scents winding through the quieter air—grass, pollen, and dust from dry land. Saliva poured into the dragon's mouth, as he tasted musk from herds that roamed the grasslands. However hungry he might be, it was an appetite for battle that set his wings beating, driving him back toward upper winds.

The Dragons of Magic

Eagyn had ruled for decades, but fierce northern warriors continually spilled into the plains. Raids were common as clan conflicts spun the losers off in search of better pastures. Though the order had driven the intruders back to the steppe, there was never a lasting victory. The barbarians thought the land, and the people on it, free for the taking.

When Eagyn first spread his wings, he had viewed the world in much the same way. For centuries, the dragon flew over the land as a lone predator. But the Phyrexian invasion had called him and others of his species into a united front. The catalyst of battle had changed him. Human nations became allies in a common cause, and Eagyn realized that the tiny builders of cities were more than just termites building their nests.

At the end of the invasion, Eagyn watched the expansion of settlements he had once raided. He looked to know more, and eventually the founder of the Northern Order agreed to meet with him. The dragon and the founder had discussed how his past depredations might be redeemed.

Eagyn was gradually convinced that the strong should protect the weak rather than prey upon them. The dragon had always thought people's antics entertaining, but after his meeting with the founder, he looked on the settlements as his own. Rather than raid the towns for food, he now demanded respect and service. After all, more meat and taste lay in a wild herd of buffalo or pigs than in an entire town. Though Eagyn needed no tribute of food, he directed the raising of walls to make lairs fitting for a ruler. Responsibility had driven him to protect the people of the plains.

Decades later, he flew on, looking for signs of barbarian devastation.

Smoke rose ahead, a marker of possible activity. Eagyn

winged toward the ribbon of black, thinking on what lay in this section of country. There was a farm at the edge of the lands he controlled. He was thirsty, and a draft of well water would be welcome before he turned to fly the perimeter. But the rising smoke grew wider as he approached. A building was burning, and he could hear screams. Vibrations beat against the skin stretched tightly over his skull. Eagyn flew faster. He heard the voices of women mixed with barbarian cries.

The dragon dived toward the fighting. Smoke rose over him like a cloud as he flared his wings.

Raiders ran among the outbuildings, the farmhouse, and the burning barn. They shouted with panic equal to the cries of women. The warriors ran for the wilderness and open fields as Eagyn came out of the sky.

He focused his energy and sent it forth like a shot from a bow. Magic spun off in small twisters, carrying messages and orders for his men. The smell of blood, sweat, and leather filled his nose, but cries from the farmhouse drew him toward the half-sunken structure. Some the farm inhabitants might yet live, though like a closing chorus, the voices fell suddenly silent.

A few barbarians were outside, one crouching by the stone wall of the farmhouse, under the thatched eaves.

Eagyn's breath hissed from his mouth as he lunged for the roof. The attack cracked stone and turned grass to crystal.

The barbarian froze solid and toppled to his side. His leg and arm stuck up in a bizarre salute.

Eagyn reared over the thatched roof. It was thick, and flowers peeked from the mat of compressed reeds. He could hear only the enemy, but perhaps some of his people still survived. He had to get inside. Claws sank into the thatch as he tore bundles away. A barbarian, seeing him occupied, ran to hamstring him. His tail batted the fool's head away like a child's ball.

The flowers and the smell of musty thatch covered the blood stench inside. He threw the woven reeds behind him in a spray. The house was as dark as a pit. The dragon forced his head into the structure. Thin shafts of light peeked from barricaded shutters and the door. The blood smell and noise were smothering as Eagyn peered into every corner of the house.

Warriors swung at his head. The dragon blinked rapidly, moving so knives bounced off his skull instead of sinking into his eyes. The bodies of women and girls lay on the dirt floor, blood from fatal wounds still spreading out and soaking into the earth. The warriors tore away obstacles they had placed only moments before.

Eagyn's breath lanced into the clump of men scrambling over the piled furniture. The back-blast of chill air beat against the dragon's closed inner lids. He peered through the transparent membranes. Men inured to the cold of the freezing steppe hit the ground, steel weapons shattering like thin glass.

Two barbarians stood before a large fireplace, throwing wood on the banked coals. Eagyn pondered their madness. Did they really believe the small blaze could armor them against the deathly chill? They tore open pouches at their hips and threw wads of paper into the fire. The dragon surged farther into the house, parts of the roof cascading over the bodies inside. He must stop the barbarians from destroying their maps and orders.

A thin wail from within the chimney told him the fire would burn more than paper.

Eagyn balanced his rear legs on the outside stone wall. Like a belt snapping at dandelions, he swung his head.

The larger barbarian raised a shield that split when the

7

reptilian skull slammed into it. Bones broke as the warrior hit the far wall and slithered to the floor. The smaller man swung a poker at the drake. Eagyn's strike catapulted him through a wooden loft into thick thatch. There he hung, blood raining down to mix with that of his victims.

The thin wail from the chimney was dying as Eagyn scooped coals out of the fireplace. A shower of flames exploded over fallen thatch. The steel grate pinwheeled across the room taking out a shuttered window. The maps had been soaked in something and were now only ash. A few pieces of paper lay in the back of the fireplace. The unburned papers seemed blank, but Eagyn hoped there might be hidden messages. Eagyn scooped the coals away, hoping to save something—or someone.

Terrified breathing came from above.

"Come out," Eagyn crooned, ignoring the embers embedded under his claws. "I am Lord Eagyn," he whispered, knowing the roar of his normal voice. "You need to come out, so I can protect you."

The dragon could catch the faint odor of terror as the chimney cleared of smoke. Perhaps he could still rescue someone from this massacre. The smell of hot blood reminded him of his early days as a settlement raider.

"Come out, child," he said gently, reining in his impatience. "There's none left to hurt you." Even as he spoke, the dragon saw a barbarian out of the corner of his eye.

The stealthy warrior pulled a sword from a dead man's hands. His swarthy skin paled as the warrior realized himself discovered. He wheeled to charge, drawing breath for a battle cry. Eagyn's left wing moved, shattering the man's lower legs. Before the barbarian could cry out, Eagyn brought his rear leg down, grinding the man's skull into the hard ground.

"Come out, or I will leave," Eagyn said, sounding as lonely and sad as possible.

He shifted his leg on the outside wall. Perhaps barbarians prepared to attack even now. His tail beat on the ground as he thought of raiders drawing near. His flanks were targets for any archer, and he drew himself the rest of the way into the house. Furniture and bodies settled as he rested his full weight on them.

"Don't worry," he said hurriedly over the noise. "I am just trying to get comfortable."

Soot sifted down, and a body shifted in the chimney. A small leg reached down to feel for a foothold but could find none. A young girl fell and lay sprawled in the ashes. She was covered in soot, and smoke had darkened her face to midnight. Her sides heaved as she took in gulps of fresh air. She could not have been up in the chimney long. Her bare feet, while terribly blistered, still looked like they might recover. The racking coughs made Eagyn more concerned over her lungs.

He carefully crowded closer to the fireplace.

The girl shivered as the dragon neared.

Eagyn coiled energy in and began to hum to distract the girl. Like cool waves of water, a healing spell lapped at her flesh. The blisters began to subside, though it was hard to tell under the layers of soot.

The child stopped shivering. She lay down, falling into a coma.

Eagyn poured energy into her young frame. His mind danced over her skin and felt for injuries yet unknown. The outside world receded as he devoted himself to healing. But the need for wariness gave him speed, and he soon finished. He could hear the barn burning and the girl's breathing but no other sounds.

Eagyn turned carefully in the confined space and raised his head over the wall. Only the dead lay outside, sprawled farmers and barbarians providing an audience for the burning barn.

He flowed over the wall to learn what he could before his men arrived.

* * * * *

"Lord Eagyn," the sergeant said, "we finished burying the dead." The soldier clenched his huge hands, tense knuckles the size of walnuts.

Sergeant Kort looked like a balding old man, a lean, impoverished grandfather. But his looks were deceptive, hiding his martial abilities. Bird warriors had come to Dominaria in the distant past, refugees from wars in other planes. Three races traced their lines back to flyers who settled in the north, making their home on the edge of the steppe. Soon they served in the armies that merged with the order.

The sergeant was of the middle race, the raypen—larger than the aven, whose small squat bodies and wings still allowed them to fly, but smaller than the huge elen, nine-foot-tall humanoids whose elephantine structure made them slow but powerful. Raypen warriors formed the backbone of the dragon's forces. They gave up their wings eons ago for the strength and toughness that fighting required. Though Kort's bones were solid instead of hollow, the fierce power that could lift a body into the air still remained. The sergeant and his men were a gift of the order to help Eagyn.

"Those animals killed everything and everyone on the farm. The men fell first, most of them before they could come in from the fields. The women tried to fortify the house, but the barbarians stove in the door with a post from the barn.

10

That must have been just before I came upon them," Eagyn said, growling with remembered rage and thinking of the time wasted trying to recover hidden messages from blank paper. "They headed northeast into the badlands as I read the tracks."

"They have several hours on us, sir." The sergeant sounded faintly scolding. His ashen skin flushed as he looked over his long nose at the outer lands. Kort's eyes were hawk sharp, but he looked in vain for signs of riders.

"They will travel through the gullies to stay out of sight, Sergeant Kort." The dragon's eyes slitted as he thought aloud. "They can't be more than ten or fifteen miles away. They may be even closer, thinking we cannot pursue. They hope we will stay here, looking after the dead."

A soldier, her hair tied up in a black band, walked past. She awkwardly carried the young girl. The only survivor was still fast asleep and clutched against the woman's shoulder, the ash from the fireplace soiling the clean uniform.

"How is she?" Eagyn asked.

"Asleep, Lord Eagyn. Her name is Pianna. I knew the family. Before our farm was burned out, I helped raise the barn." The young girl tried to snuggle closer into the enveloping arms, grinding more ash into the cloth. "She has no family now, my lord."

The sergeant grimaced as the talk interrupted the planning. "Leave her at the next farm we come to," Kort told the trooper. "We have greater concerns than the disposition of a little girl."

"We do *not!*" hissed the dragon. His anger made the topic of conversation stir uncomfortably in the soldier's arms. "We are honor-bound to protect everyone on my lands. The order put me in charge of the Northern Reach. I bear direct responsibility, and I will be her guardian." Eagyn turned his gaze

11

upon the soldier, who froze at this display of temper.

"She is your charge until we are back in camp." The dragon ordered. "She will be inducted directly into my household and will be a ward of the entire order. Now try to rinse that muck off her."

The soldier withdrew hurriedly.

Sergeant Kort emanated disapproval.

"We cannot forget why we chase the barbarians, Sergeant." The dragon said, watching the soldier haul her new charge toward the well. "You yourself are awaiting an addition to your family."

"That's true, my lord." Kort said reluctantly. "But I hope my son will always know and act on his duty. Saving a child is worthwhile, but how many more children are in danger? How many burnt-out farmhouses will we discover? Protecting your lands requires that we find the enemy. We can't spend much more time here."

"You are right, of course. Have the men mount up." The dragon looked out over the tracks. "We will continue into the badlands."

* * * * *

The land was dry, hot with summer. Eagyn glided, using thermals from the rocks below to carry him on. His eyes found traces of the reavers, and he swooped down to smell the odors his prey left behind.

For years the clans had raided, but now they struck deeper into Northern Order lands. The new leaders gathered horsemen to move into Eagyn's territory despite his fierce defense.

Suddenly, he could see the enemy in the network of narrow canyons below. They moved quickly, and Eagyn smelled lathered horses. Despite all their efforts, they had not traveled far.

Eagyn's men rode a more direct route to the steppe. They would soon cut across the raiders' trail.

The clan warriors were lightly armored, wearing shirts of horn scales. With lances ready, they rode small ponies up the draw. Composite bows rested in sheaths.

Eagyn winced at the damage they might do. Still, the men below had killed his people, and now they must die. He maneuvered to slow them down until Kort and the elite could arrive.

The dragon flew down to ground level and attacked from the side. He breathed a torrent of energy over the column point, seeing the surprised expression on the mustachioed man leading the party.

The warrior and his horse crashed to the ground, frozen stiff. Their corpses plugged the ravine mouth.

Eagyn climbed and turned. He popped up from the terrain to attack the rear of the column.

The warriors were ready. Magically charged arrows rose, impacting his flesh. Points penetrated. The power supporting the dragon faltered.

Winging toward safety, Eagyn tried to heal and armor his hide against the eldritch missiles. He dropped. His rear legs hit the side of the canyon with a bruising impact, shattering his concentration.

Eagyn pumped his wings hard. His muscles burned, mere sinew trying to replace the magic winds.

The barbarians turned, heading for another route to the steppe. More archers readied bows as they kicked their steeds into a gallop. A wide bowl of a valley lay not far away, down another canyon. The bowmen would be much more dangerous in open ground.

The arrows stung. Magic malevolence worked against Eagyn's body. His injuries were minor, but like porcupine quills to a dog, they dissipated his focus.

Eagyn flew back to his men, bellowing for Kort to meet him. He landed clumsily, snapping some of the arrows off against the ground.

Sergeant Kort's soldiers converged on the dragon, their horses lightly lathered but not yet blown.

Eagyn lay on his side, the broken shafts of arrows obvious against his golden scales.

"Cut them out!" the dragon ordered. Blood welled as the arrowheads continued to work against him.

His men fell upon him with knives digging into the dragon's hide. Eagyn trembled and tried to stay still.

Kort ran toward him, leaping obstacles in his rush to report to his overlord. As the tall figure stuttered to a stop, the dragon gave the orders for attack.

"Continue to the mouth of the canyon, and be ready for archers. I'll sweep them out in disarray. Be ready to charge if they reform, and remember that I want prisoners!"

As he spoke, the barbed heads of arrows were cut from his hide. Red blood colored his belly. A soldier still pursued one stubborn sliver of enchanted steel, his knife working deep into the dragon's body.

"Leave it!" Eagyn roared, turning over as the soldiers leapt clear.

The dragon ran, his wings working as blood poured from his wounds. Wind whipped the red seepage into a rosy spray as his wings filled and bones bent. Eagyn rose and circled, moving toward the raiders. His breath could freeze an elephant in its tracks, but he must be close to use it. The throbbing of the remaining arrow reminded him how dangerous archers could be. But Eagyn had other magic, and he climbed until his men were ants far below.

The clan members were nearly at the mouth of the canyon. Soon they would be on better defensive ground.

Eagyn called forth his energy and flung the wind beneath his wings. His body strained as he went into a steep glide.

It took hurricane forces to keep him in the air, and that power funneled down the narrow canyon. Riders separated from their mounts as the air blew them free. A few with shields were lifted, becoming kites before smashing into canyon walls.

Eagyn pumped his wings, slowing his fall and calling back his winds. Like a falcon, he rose as the barbarians tried to regroup. Once more he released his power.

Acting as a giant brush, wind scoured the warriors from the canyon. Magic spilled them onto open ground in a broad fan before the dragon's soldiers.

Eagyn's forces fell upon the dispersed warriors.

From a nearby ridge, Order archers fired at the few raiders still mounted, picking off those who had weathered the windstorm. Horses screamed as arrows sank into them. The mounts fell, twisting on top of riders whose luck had run out. Arrows hit like thunderbolts, Order archers enhancing the power of their projectiles. Barbarians hid behind any available cover, usually the bodies of their horses.

Eagyn flew to the rear of his own men to land, his wings exhausted from unaccustomed effort.

The raiders' leader screamed orders in a high tenor over the fighting. Enemy magic coiled, gathering power.

As Sergeant Kort took a group of mounted men onto the killing ground, Eagyn bellowed a spell. Power poured out of the elite Order forces, coating them in fiery gold.

Enemy arrows flew, charged with more than desperation, but broke against the magic armor. Maces and swords raised high, the elite met the circled enemy and began killing. Swords severed limbs, and mace blows shattered bodies. Kort and his picked team crowded against unhorsed men. The barbarians offered little resistance, and soldiers hewed their way to the enemy commander.

The energy pulsing from Eagyn's forces began to falter. The armor of squires and knights flickered as their power ebbed.

Enemy lancers turned pike-men converged on the weakest, a young squire only recently inducted into Eagyn's command. Long shafts plucked him from the saddle and dashed him to the churned ground. The scattered remnants of the enemy formation rushed inward to crush Kort and his men.

"Hit the left flank!" Eagyn bellowed, sending the rest of his men into the melee.

The elite joined the battle, but only a few were experienced in fighting in concert with a dragon.

Eagyn meanwhile attacked the right flank. Before him, barbarians scrambled for lances and bows, discarding the swords they had used to close with the sergeant and his men. Eagyn made for the bowmen first. His breath left them martial statues. He turned and blasted a group of lancers.

Cries of victory from the left told Eagyn that his forces were winning. Now all organized groups of the enemy were smashed, and only futile attacks by single warriors remained.

Tail strikes swept weapons aside as Eagyn tore warriors apart with his claws. He worked through the men in sudden lunges. Wings spreading, he turned left and began to kill his way toward Sergeant Kort.

Ahead fought the elite, most having exhausted their store of magical power and now relying on mundane armor and weapons. Sergeant Kort himself was surrounded. His horse went down. Clan riders raced toward him, only to die on the weapons of the elite. The look of anticipation was plain on enemy faces as they neared Kort. The sergeant threw himself in a high parabola over the warriors converging on him. He landed close to the enemy leader.

The warrior closed with Kort. The steppe rider was clothed in armor composed of small steel plates that showed no magic, but his sword was wrapped in power.

The sergeant slapped it aside, his hands grown huge and brilliant. He grappled with the leader. Kort gripped the commander around his chest and squeezed, his fingers long and slender but still strong.

Blood erupted from the clan leader's mouth. Ribs and organs collapsed. The enemy stood stunned, crushed like a tiny babe.

Raiders screamed, berserk in terror and grief. Ignoring their other foes, the reavers closed with Kort.

The sergeant used his dying opponent as a club, clearing men like a pack of dogs. He exulted as blood erupted with each strike.

* * * * *

The castle was gray and dirty in the overcast light. Squat and hulking on a small hill, it overlooked a village. The nearest fortress to the badlands, it had none of the majesty of other order castles, but it was Lord Eagyn's home. The huge drake dropped from the sky. Even the cattle in the surrounding fields were not disturbed. Eagyn hunted wild herds and left livestock for the people under his protection.

The trip had been long and arduous back from the

badlands. The arrow he still bore in his body limited his ability to fly. Eagyn had elected to march alongside his troops instead of ranging off on further reconnaissance. Only the proximity to home had lured him into the air.

Now he moved through the gates, his shoulders tensing as he strode under the portcullis. Spells preventing landings inside the courtyard were continually active unless specifically aborted. Mere personal convenience was no reason to weaken the castle's defenses. The courtyard was more open, a welcome relief after the tight fit of the gatehouse.

Ahead rose the main keep. A huge open balcony dominated one side. This glaring defensive weakness was somewhat mitigated by the murder-holes in the ceiling and thick doors leading to the rest of the building. Eagyn needed to be present at entertainments and feasts. The huge open room allowed him to interact with his guests as they sat at the tables of the great hall. A new fortified tower was rising beside the main keep, and the castle walls were being extended. The new tower was a second stronghold to which people could retreat since alterations had weakened the main keep.

The inspection of his dominion was interrupted as the war party followed him through the gates. Sergeant Kort rode in with a prisoner before him, carefully watching for any sign of self-destruction. The melee had proven deadly. Few of the enemy survived the fight and subsequent journey. Several injured warriors killed themselves rather than submitting to captivity. Eagyn watched as the sergeant ordered his men into the base of the new tower. The holding cells were dug deep into the building's foundations.

Eagyn's mood lightened as he saw the girl Pianna taken to the kitchens. The young orphan gave the dragon a shy wave and then turned to enter into her new life.

18

The world turned grim again when Sergeant Kort marched out of the tower to Eagyn.

"Sergeant, gather the men. As soon as you can get information from your prisoner, we will return to patrol." Eagyn had no interest in trying to extract the truth himself. As terrifying as many enemies found him, it was Kort who could dig out secrets. "I'll have the final arrow from the battle remove by the surgeon. Then I must feed. We'll investigate enemy movements after I get back."

Kort nodded and went into the tower, grim purpose showing in his stride.

Eagyn called for the surgeon and his arrow extractors. He lay in the courtyard as the man went to work. The blades and spoons dug deep, and only his will kept him still. Even as he ground his claws into the dirt, he heard cries of agony from the base of the tower. Eagyn could imagine the huge hands of Sergeant Kort handling the prisoner.

The arrow was barely out of the wound when he turned on his side and made for the gates. Humanity sometimes stank, and he needed the winds to carry him away to the wild herds.

Eagyn flew over several buffalo before falling upon a deer. His belly still grumbled as he digested the meal, but the dragon knew he would soon fly into battle. He needed hunger's edge to keep his mind sharp.

It was two hours before his return. Eagyn entered the castle and saw winged mounts being prepared for the elite. Sergeant Kort directed the packing of gear for aerial patrol. The bird warrior was still wet from a recent bath, and Eagyn's nose smelled no trace of the odors that saturated the prison.

The sergeant stepped toward the dragon and made his report. "He said the Kidring himself and his party were scouting the best routes for invasion." Kort said, showing contempt while he related the information he had extracted so easily. "There is a great deal of unrest among his warriors, and only the Kidring and his tribe support an out-and-out invasion." The sergeant waved cooks forward with more supplies to be loaded.

"The rest of the clans see no point to holding farmlands and believe in raiding rather than conquest." The sergeant paused and came closer. "If the Kidring should die on his scouting mission, most of the push for this invasion might die with him." There was a silence as if Kort invited comment. He continued slowly, "The steppe clans have always lacked unity, and an unfortunate death might stop or at least delay further incursions."

Eagyn turned his head and regarded the sergeant coolly. "Are you suggesting an assassination?"

Kort only shook his head sadly. "Of course not." The sergeant snorted. "We have no agents in place to kill the Kidring, and it would take months to recruit them. If he is to die, it will have to be in the field. You need to call for more men."

Eagyn shook his head angrily, pride driving him to repeat an argument he had made a dozen times before. "I can protect my lands without help from anyone." He looked sharply at the sergeant, so clean after his labor in the tower cells. "You and the elite are enough. I will not beg aid from the Order."

Eagyn turned and started out. He needed to be back in the air, alone with the winds.

* * * * *

The sky was pregnant with rain and lightning, and the smell of magic spread across the horizon. Eagyn flew over the heart of the badlands but could find no sign of a clan scouting party. Far behind, Sergeant Kort and the elite traveled in a slow aerial group. Eagyn depended on his own efforts to find the enemy.

The dragon flew lower and winged north, wondering if the enemy had outmaneuvered him. But no, there ahead moved horsemen and pack animals. The richness of one group told him he had found the Kidring. The color of their gear and clothes spoke of their access to the most expensive dyes and furs. Though no standards flew, the instant cohesion of archers and lancers as they saw him told the dragon they were crack forces.

Messages flew from Eagyn's wings in spirals of power, calling for the elite. As orderly as the forces appeared, Eagyn was sure Kort and his soldiers could take them. Even now, they would be converging on winged steeds.

The attack that struck the dragon was too quick to dodge. The landscape seemed to pulse. Energy leapt from the ground and impacted Eagyn's wing. Like paper in a fire, the thin flesh between the long bones flared and curled away. Pain shut down his mind. For precious seconds, he could not recover.

When Eagyn regained awareness, he was spinning viciously, falling from the sky. Instinctive cries for reinforcement spiraled away, only to be swamped in clouds of enemy magic. With one wing useless, the winds that supported him spun him wildly. He fought for consciousness as staunchly as he fought to use his power. Eagyn directed healing energies over his skeletal wing, washing away the pain but leaving him falling even faster. Golden armor began to grow over his limbs. Eagyn aimed his fall for a crumbling slope.

The land throbbed again, and another bolt leapt into the air. This time, Eagyn saw it coming. He spun around, the energy reflecting from his armored belly.

Enemy troops rushed to where he would impact. Eagyn used his remaining wing to direct his fall farther away. He raised the wind as best he could and then hit. The shock strained bones as the dragon tumbled down a slope of dirt and gravel.

Eagyn sprawled. Debris slid down around him. Dust rose in a choking cloud. The dragon tried to catch his breath, his muscles crying in agony. He tasted dirt. Every cough to clear his lungs jarred aching ribs. He tried to sweep the air clean with his winds, but they simply spun and raised more dust. The enemy still poured out power, confusing his magic. Eagyn's messages whirled apart into fitful knots of wind.

The dust settled, and warriors converged, their lances ready. Archers scrambled to reach higher ground.

Eagyn raised his head carefully.

Behind the men stood their leader, still young but a well-spring of orders to his warriors. He was drenched in flame-red cloth and drew the eye like a magnet. The man directed his warriors forward, holding his lance ready.

Eagyn knew the Kidring was the key to the battle.

"Scared to come at a cripple?" he cried, twisting to show his wing. Though clothed in energy, it was tattered, and Eagyn keened in pain as he tried to flex it. "A coward who hides behind a magician! The heroes of yore would spit on you, craven cur!"

Eagyn staggered backward, reinforcing the power of his limbs even as he spilled more curses at the enemy.

"Your songs have a hundred dragons dead at the hands of heroes! Perhaps your ancestors were liars and cowards like you!"

Anger filled the faces of the lancers. Arrows slid into dragon flesh. Eagyn's good wing was a waving shield, collecting arrows as he flapped it. The dragon raised more dust to beat against the faces of the closing men. It would be insane for one warrior to come against him, but his cries to racial pride goaded them.

A few men looked back to their leader. Here is a moment for the sagas, their eyes were saying. Where are you?

Eagyn could almost hear the sigh as the Kidring came forward. An advisor trotted beside him, dressed in the furs and leathers of a shaman. The dragon recognized his magical foe. Streamers of energy flowed from the magician's hands and wrapped over the leader's armor. The enemy grunted in unison. Flights of arrows died down as the main body of men closed with Eagyn.

He slithered to the side, keeping his head low.

A few arrows arched high over the men, and one penetrated at the base of his wing muscles.

Eagyn wondered if any of his men would arrive in time and moved to attack. The sweeps of his intact wing, tattered with arrows as it was, still drove dust and pebbles into the oncoming men and horses. He emitted a high, continuous scream that drove the horses to madness. Even as Eagyn scuttled forward, warriors threw themselves from their saddles. The legendary fearless ponies of the steppe reared and plunged, running from the dragon.

One warrior edged too far forward. A tail strike flicked in from the side, rewarding him with death.

Eagyn hunched up and let loose his breath. The men in its focus became grim warnings. They fell alive, shivering in the grip of frostbite and hypothermia. Still, the blast did not reach the Kidring. His shaman gathered a sea of power. It rolled in and smothered the glacial fury of Eagyn's breath. The dragon tried again, pushing harder than before. The air glistened in front of his muzzle. His attack met a mystic shield and snapped loudly enough to startle the few remaining horses on the battlefield.

Eagyn's energy sprayed back against the side of his head. His eye stopped working, and only the right jaw muscles closed as he snatched a warrior and worried him.

The man fell, a jumbled mass rather than separate pieces.

Eagyn retreated, snapping at the warriors. Each bite worked against frozen dragon flesh, and every flex of muscle was accompanied by the sound of fracturing ice.

A lance penetrated his belly, and he came down at an angle, snapping it off deep inside his body. The enemy closed faster, growing more confident as the dragon's blood muddied the ground. A warrior came from Eagyn's blind side, but the dragon heard him. The tail slammed him into the soft debris, burying him in a ready-made grave.

Eagyn lifted his head to locate the Kidring.

The leader worked his way forward, so swathed in magical armor he was distinctly rotund. His sword writhed as it moved through the air, forcing the warriors to give him a wide berth. Eagyn had never seen a more deadly weapon.

The dragon was beyond exhaustion now. His strikes no longer killed. His tail lay in the dust, and he could hear the cry of "Wurm" going up. There was still no sign of Kort and the elite. Eagyn was going to die here.

The Kidring came closer, a smile tugging at his lips as he saw Eagyn's ruined mouth. The battle paused. The two came face to face. The Kidring waved his men back and straightened to deliver a speech.

But Eagyn wasn't fighting for just himself. He fought for the lives of the people under his protection. The Kidring was the danger that threatened them.

Even as the Kidring began to speak, Eagyn unleashed his final magic—not at the man, but at the ground around him. The cost was great. Eagyn's wings withered, and his gifts dissipated. His breath and armor vanished in a wet bellow, and his wounds opened wide. Empowered by them, his will bored into the soft ground.

The soil under the Kidring boiled. He sank.

The shaman screamed, calling for warriors to save the Kidring. The magician unleashed waves of energy toward the dragon.

Eagyn let it strip away his hide as the last driblets of his magic worked at the ground. He was a bloody thing, stumbling forward, his remaining eye barely able to see. The Kidring lay under a mound of dirt.

Eagyn reared, ignoring the arrows that came, and hammered his front legs down on the mound. He reared again. A lance speared deep into his pelvis as he fell with his full weight. The ground settled, and Eagyn sprayed blood. He curled his tail around the sinking earth.

"This egg won't hatch," he whispered, knowing victory.

Eagyn never saw the lance that plunged through his eye.

* * * * *

When Kort arrived, the Kidring was out of the ground. He lay uncovered just beyond the battlefield. The man had smothered but, now cleansed, showed no mark of how he had died.

Eagyn showed every mark. Kort's master had become as hideous in death as he had been magnificent in life. Eagyn's corpse was a giant piece of meat, too large to carry without butchering.

In an unspoken truce, barbarians and order soldiers each paid homage to their fallen leaders.

The threat of invasion was over. Men broke off slowly from the Kidring's party, riding with shoulders slumped. Others wrapped the body of the Kidring and carried it away. The invasion would be buried with him.

Kort directed his squires and knights with weary precision. They dug into the side of the hill that Eagyn had hit in his fall. Kort's magically enhanced hands scooped tons of soil and triggered small slides. The ground slowly covered their lord. The sergeant directed the raising of a cairn to show the resting place of Eagyn.

The last enemies left, most of them belly-down on horses. The clans disappeared, and only the disturbed earth showed that anything had happened.

Sergeant Kort took a final look at the crude pile of stones marking the resting place of a hero.

"The last dragon in the Order," he murmured, still stunned.

He shook his head and waved his men toward their steeds.

* * * * *

The wailing of the castle's women echoed over the battlements. Sergeant Kort had said nothing on arriving, but his men relayed the news the moment their feet touched ground.

The bird warrior meanwhile stalked to the top of the wall and looked out to the setting sun. Kort wished that he had wings, that he might fly away.

Eagyn had been the heart of the Order for decades, and there was no clear successor. Dragons lived for centuries, and

Eagyn's death had seemed impossible to his followers. Now, like children mourning a parent, all the people were frozen with grief.

Only red light remained in the sky, the sun dead and buried under the horizon.

The clatter of kindling dragged Kort's eyes back to the courtyard. There by the woodpiles supplying the kitchen, the refugee girl Pianna gathered wood to feed the fires for the next morning. The sergeant's eyes picked out the tear tracks running down her face. Even as the last of the day died, the girl prepared for tomorrow. Kort thought of the fear that she must remember whenever she saw a fire. He respected her strength of will to feed the flames. Many would extinguish such blazes to allay remembered terror. The girl stumbled back into the kitchen with a full load of wood.

Kort thought of his own children and made his way to the courtyard.

Like Pianna, he began preparations for tomorrow's tasks.

Eagyn was dead, but the Order and the people it protected remained. The dragon's treasure was the people he had saved.

Kort vowed that he and his line would guard it.

Dragon of Jamuraa

A. L. Lassieur

It was a hot day, hot like all the other days on the savannas of Jamuraa. Above, the sky was clear, dotted here and there with small white clouds. Beneath this canopy of blue, the golden plains heat-shimmered in every direction like a dry sea. The surface of this soil-sea was broken here and there by small hills that seemed to swell and move like waves.

From the floor of the plain rose a red bluff, like the prow of an ancient vessel. A lone figure stood on the edge of the bluff. He leaned on a long, gnarled green staff set with a single white stone, which glinted in the harsh sunlight.

A feverish breath of savanna wind ruffled the figure's long robes, whipping the white fabric behind him like a restless tail. He stood erect and still as the wind pulled at him and tousled his short-cropped, curly black hair. His youthful face wore a calm demeanor as he watched the scene that played out on the plain beneath his feet. One side of his mouth moved slightly, rising into what might be a smile. His icy blue eyes remained hard and cold.

Far below him, two armies swarmed like ants. From this vantage, he could plainly see the ebb and flow of the battle. He watched the movement with the concentration of a game master viewing pieces on a board. Occasionally, the hot wind carried sounds of death—the screams of the maimed and dying, the final crunch of weapon against bone—to his finely sculpted ears. The sound soon drifted away, and the figure was once again surrounded by light and heat and silence—and the never-ending wind.

A new sound came on the wind, a low rumble that grew louder and became thunder. Hoofbeats approached behind him. He knew it was the commander of the Zhalfir forces and her officers. She was here to see a show, and he would give her one.

He waited until the tumult of hooves and neighs died behind him, and then spoke. His voice was rich and melodic, and anyone who heard him before they saw his face believed that he was a much older, wiser man. He knew how to use his voice for the greatest effect, and he did so now.

"The battle is uncertain. Your troops are evenly matched," he said to the wind, his back to the great commander. A muffled gasp from one of the officers made him smile. He knew it was a supreme insult not to face Qalhata when she approached, but he wanted to make sure everyone on the ridge knew exactly who wielded the most power.

The only sound was the whisper of the wind and the snap and billow of his white robes. Finally, he heard a slight movement of a horse, accompanied by leather shoes crunching on the gritty earth.

"Your attention is so deep on the battle, Majaliwa, that you cannot properly acknowledge me?" a light female voice replied. He detected an edge to the words.

"My apologies, Commander Qalhata," the wizard said, turning and bowing with one graceful movement. "I am focused on my task at hand, the spell that I promised you many months ago."

Qalhata approached, a proud, regal woman with clear eyes and a tall, lithe physique. She was clad in armor, but her muscular arms remained free. Her dark, oiled skin glowed with health and power. With the practiced ease of a seasoned warrior, she grasped a tall, effective-looking spear. The razor-sharp point winked in the sunlight as if to say that even talented wizards might feel its bite—should they anger its owner too much.

"Your eyes are sharp, wizard," she said, turning her gaze from Majaliwa to the edge of the bluff. "Femeref's troops are well trained, and we were surprised by the ferocity of the dwarfs who chose to fight with him. They wield battle axes with as much skill as they wield picks in the gold mines."

She turned back to Majaliwa. "I have heard much of your abilities," she said. "The tales of your talent rival those of my ancestor, the wizard Gazali."

Majaliwa's eyes widened. He did not know that Qalhata was of the line of Gazali, friend and confidant of the great Teferi. It was widely believed that Gazali had died centuries before in a great war, but whispered legends said that he had not died. They claimed his enemy, a wizard of Urborg, had cast Gazali into the darkness between planes. Whatever the truth, Majaliwa little respected Gazali—an old dotard, more interested in gardens than magic. He probably deserved his fate.

Majaliwa smiled and bowed. "Your ancestor was a great wizard."

Qalhata raised one eyebrow but said nothing. The wind had died down, and the sun felt hotter on Majaliwa's face.

"We have little time to waste on niceties," she said. "I have need of your skills, and you promised to help us defeat the Femeref army. Are you prepared to do this?"

"I am," he replied, taken aback by her commanding tone. He swallowed his displeasure at being addressed as a subordinate and forced a smile. "It will take a few moments for me to prepare. I would ask that you leave me to my work and return to the plain. At my signal, withdraw your troops to the south."

"What is it that you intend to do?" Qalhata demanded. "I must know what to expect."

Majaliwa hesitated. He wanted his first grand conjuring spell to be a stunning surprise, a sign of his power and skill as a wizard. But he could not refuse the commander. He gestured for her to come near. She leaned toward him, and they stood together, heads bowed. Slowly, Qalhata's eyes widened, and she looked at Majaliwa with open disbelief.

"Not even Teferi can do such a thing," she said aloud, straightening. "It is impossible."

A look of impatience crossed his face. "I can do this. That is a promise."

"If this works, you are truly a great wizard," Qalhata said. "If not, I will spit you on the end of my spear and hang your body from this very bluff. That is *my* promise."

Indignation rose like bile in Majaliwa's chest, but he held his tongue as Qalhata strode to her horse and mounted.

"You have half an hour," she said. With that, she galloped

across the top of the bluff and disappeared in a cloud of red dust.

"We shall see whose body decorates the next spear," Majaliwa murmured as he watched the horses recede into the dust. Then he turned and walked to the edge of the bluff. He planted his feet securely, closed his eyes, took a deep breath, and lifted his face to the wind.

Immediately, the world disappeared, and time ceased to move forward. He welcomed the darkness and relaxed, opening his mind to the energy of the land. At first, all he could hear were the sounds of the wind as it buffeted him. Other sounds slowly reached his thoughts: the rush of sand in dust devils, the howl of hot gusts in a storm, the sudden snap of a tent flap. He made these wind sounds louder in his mind until they resonated in one vast symphony.

Slowly, with his eyes closed and his body rigid in concentration, he raised his staff and pointed the gemstone to the sky. The whirling storm inside his head grew louder. Dim images rose from the darkness. He called on the power of beloved places: his home, the plains of his childhood, even the vast plain below him. Pictures swirled with the wind in his mind.

He opened his mind further, calling all the white energy of the land. A familiar jolt shook his body. Power channeled into him. Now began the struggle to control the energy that rushed through him like a river that has been suddenly undammed. The white gemstone in his staff began to glow. A low buzz issued from it.

From the time he was very young, Majaliwa knew there was something different about him. It was easy for him to pull energy from the world, much more so than for others. Power surged in his body like lightning. The feeling was both terrifying and exhilarating. As he grew, he became aware that he was more talented than other wizards. He used this knowledge to his advantage, pushing his mind into places that few dared to go. He realized he was skilled at conjuring and controlling creatures, and he concentrated his energies on this ability. Soon he was known throughout Jamuraa as one of the most promising adepts the land had ever seen.

But he had greater plans. An idea lived in him—an idea that would have stunned his teachers and his family. His burning ambition was to create a creature so majestic, so powerful, that no one would ever doubt his powers. For years, this creature had grown in his mind, until it had finally become as real to him as the ground on which he stood. It became his ambition, his all-consuming obsession, to bring this creature into the world. If he achieved this, he knew that his place among the greatest wizards of Jamuraa would be secured for all time.

Majaliwa took another deep breath and threw open his mind. The force of the energy that slammed into him made him stumble backward, but he continued to hold his staff high. Fiery white light from the stone snaked down the polished wood to Majaliwa's hand. When it touched his flesh, it burst forth, covering his body. His head throbbed from the buzzing, as if a swarm of angry flies tore his flesh. The wind swirled around him, pressing his robes about his body like a cocoon. Sand stung his face, but he did not feel pain.

The creature was coming.

The swirl and chaos of wind and images in his head had formed a narrow tunnel, sucking power through Majaliwa and sending it tumbling to the farthest reaches of the multiverse. At the end of the tunnel, no more than a tiny speck in the distance, something flew toward Majaliwa. He focused his mind on it, his excitement mounting. The creature grew larger. The howling wind became louder. Soon he could see its outline against the blackness. He gasped with wonder and fear.

The dragon was an enormous, majestic creature. It was almost invisible, with only a fine white outline to distinguish its sleek body and elegant, five-pointed wings. Within the outline, the dragon's form shimmered like a mirage, moving and swirling in the wind. Beneath the wings, the dragon had four legs, which it tucked into its body as it flew. Its long tail was covered with transparent spikes. Its head was narrow, with a wide mouth and deep-set eyes.

Those eyes held him spellbound. They bored like two points of hot light straight into Majaliwa's soul. Then, from somewhere far away, he heard a voice inside his head.

I have come to you, after these many years, it said. *What is your wish this day?*

"To defeat the enemies of Zhalfir," Majaliwa replied aloud. With great effort, he opened his eyes.

Suddenly the sound ceased, and the power drained away. Majaliwa gasped and fell to his knees, empty. Sunlight blinded him, and for a moment he could see nothing. He shaded his eyes with his hand and looked out onto the plain.

The ant soldiers still crawled, but their movements were now frenzied and mindless. Qalhata had begun to withdraw her armies to the south, but Femeref's troops bore down on them.

Majaliwa pulled his eyes from the scene below and looked up. In the distance, the clouds had swirled together to form a conic tunnel. From its depths the dragon emerged. In the sunlight it was all but invisible, but Majaliwa could see the outline of its body and its clear eyes. Wings rose and fell on the wind.

For a moment, the young wizard's heart stopped as he watched the powerful dragon approach. What have I created? he thought fearfully. What have I done?

You have made a marvel, a voice inside him replied. *No*

other wizard in Jamuraa—or in all of Dominaria—could have done what you have done today.

Overwhelmed with relief and arrogance, Majaliwa rose to his feet and threw his arms wide, laughing.

"Now we will see who is to be hung from a pike!" he shouted. "To war! You are to defeat the forces of Femeref this day. Attack! Fill their hearts with fear!" Majaliwa breathed deeply, feeling the rush of power from his mind to his hand. He pointed his staff downward to the plain and sent the command out to the dragon swooping upon the enemy.

But the dragon did not swoop or even change direction. To Majaliwa's utter surprise, the dragon seemed to smile. It flew forward with deadly grace.

I am ever at your command, master wizard, the voice said. *I will do as you bid. But you must come with me!* In a flash, the dragon arrived. It scooped the wizard up in its wide, invisible feet and deposited him on its back.

Majaliwa's concentration faltered. He looked down between his shaking knees and gasped. The armies and the brown grasses of the plain raced beneath him. The dragon's body felt solid, but its skin moved and shimmered like mist. Majaliwa's stomach lurched.

He flailed about for something to grab onto, and his hands felt something hard and smooth before him. Tall, spiny scales marched in two rows up the dragon's back from its wings to its head.

Yes, hold on. I will not let you fall, but we will be flying fast and hard.

Majaliwa grabbed on and took a deep breath. The shock of being lifted aloft by an invisible dragon was replaced by confusion—and anger. "How . . ." he began. "Why did you take me? Why did you not obey my command?"

The dragon soared upward and dived into a large cloud. Majaliwa was plunged into a wispy fog. It was almost as if the dragon did not yet wish to be seen.

"And how can you speak? I did not wish to conjure a dragon who could speak."

You did desire a dragon who could communicate. That was one of your chief goals, was it not?

Majaliwa started, remembering the long nights he labored over the spells that would create a creature who could communicate intelligently with him. The young wizard smiled at his own talent and began to relax.

Yes, you are indeed powerful. I am honored to serve you. And as for your other questions, the great beast glided lazily in a slow turn, *you commanded me to take you, so I did.*

"I do not recall that command," Majaliwa said with a hint of arrogance in his voice. "I did not ask to fly."

But did you not wish to make that impertinent Qalhata know who was really in command? Now you will fly into the thick of the battle upon the back of a dragon. We will be the doom of her enemies. No one who sees you will ever deny that it was you, not her, who won the day.

Understanding dawned on Majaliwa. Not only did his creation do his bidding, it could even read his thoughts. A thrill ran through the young mage. His eyes glinted with excitement.

"Then let us join the fray," Majaliwa commanded, pointing his staff to the ground far below. "Demolish my enemies and bring the Zhalfir forces to victory!"

Instantly the dragon dropped into a smooth, steep dive. Wind shrieked past Majaliwa as they burst out of the clouds and sped toward the battlefield. Majaliwa's head spun, and his stomach jumped violently as the ground raced toward them. He swallowed hard, gripped the dragon's back with his knees, and lifted his staff to the sky.

As Majaliwa and the dragon flew closer, the sounds of battle became louder. Qalhata's army, knowing they had to get out of the way of Majaliwa's grand, mysterious spell, were desperately trying to fight off the enemy long enough to escape. The moans of the dying were mixed with the shouts of the living. Dust billowed in great brown and red clouds like a gritty fog. It caused confusion in the ranks of both armies as they hacked at each other.

The dragon pulled out of its dive and circled the fray. Its eyes darted, seeking an opportunity to attack.

Majaliwa took a deep breath and surveyed the field. This vantage was much better than the bluff, and Majaliwa allowed himself a quick smile for his skill in creating such a marvelous creature. The dragon was exceeding his wildest expectations. Even he had no idea what this creature could do. The thought made him swell with pride.

They do not yet see us. We will introduce ourselves and show Qalhata—and all who see this battle—how powerful you are.

The dragon slowed to a stop. Majaliwa had the sensation of floating as the dragon hovered, its great wings beating slowly to maintain their altitude. He raised his staff, and the white gem gleamed. His eyes closed. Power surged into him once again. Wind rushed in his mind, swirling in a controlled chaos. Mana flowed from the land, through his body, and into the dragon.

Oddly, he did not feel the dragon draining away the energy he pulled from the plains. Majaliwa had expected a vast mana cost to maintain the creature. Instead he felt renewed, even invigorated, as he fed the dragon more power.

He leapt to his feet and stood on the back of the dragon, his robes whipping around his body as he held his staff aloft.

"Beware, forces of Femeref!" he shouted. "Majaliwa,

great wizard of Jamuraa, has created your doom!"

One by one, the soldiers looked up. The sound of battle faltered. The armies stood, stunned. They gazed with fear at the sight that hovered just above their heads.

A tall, white wizard seemed to be standing on air. He held a long staff in one hand and was enveloped in a white glow. The warriors shaded their eyes against the glare. Beneath him, so faint that it was not seen at first, was the white outline of an immense dragon. Majaliwa laughed when the faces of the enemy turn from puzzlement to horror. The battlefield grew still, the last sounds carried away on the wind.

All was silent. Majaliwa felt the dragon's great lungs fill and expand. Then the air stormed with heat and sound as the dragon roared.

A white-hot wind spewed from the dragon's mouth. The wind crackled and popped, enveloping one section of the Femeref army. In an instant, metal weapons glowed red. Wind ripped clothes and armor from the soldiers' bodies and reduced them to tatters. For a moment, the soldiers looked comical, standing naked on the bright, hot plain, bewilderment on every face. Their expressions changed to grimaces of horror and pain. Naked skin blistered and disintegrated. One by one, bodies thumped to the dust, little more than charred lumps of flesh. Pieces of blackened skin waved in the wind like strips of ebony cloth. When the last body had fallen, the plain grew still.

The warriors farther back stared in silent horror at the unholy spectacle before them. For a long moment, no living thing stirred. Then a light gust of wind ruffled the brown plain scrub. It was a small sound, almost silent, but it was enough.

Soldiers on both sides dropped their weapons and ran for their lives. The entire Femeref army, realizing that this doom was meant for them, scattered like frenzied ants. They ran in mindless circles, knowing they were dead but desperately seeking escape.

With a sound that seemed like a laugh, the dragon sprang into motion and attacked again. A second blast scorched the plain. Two dozen soldiers fell dead in their tracks, their bodies smoldering before they hit the ground.

The roaring wind consumed Majaliwa's thoughts. He struggled to control the overwhelming flood of power. He was so intent on harnessing and channeling the energy that he almost missed the voice. It whispered inside the tornado in his head. To Majaliwa it sounded like a sigh.

It is good to be free.

Another blast of the dragon's deadly breath sent a platoon of soldiers flying, their fiery bodies glowing like torches against the bright blue sky.

Majaliwa pointed his staff toward a knot of Femeref soldiers that huddled behind a small rise. The rise disappeared in a burst, burying the troops alive in an unmarked grave of sand and rock.

"Yes, I am glad that I freed you from my mind," Majaliwa responded as the dragon wheeled around. "You are the creature that I imagined from the beginning."

I know. I could be nothing else.

The dragon lurched forward and began chasing a lone rider that galloped desperately across the plain. The dragon easily flew above it, enveloping it in a wavering, almost invisible shadow. Majaliwa could see the whites of the terrified horse's eyes as the dragon reached down with its invisible paws and plucked the rider from its back.

The dragon shot upward. The captive, a Femeref officer by the looks of his uniform, struggled and kicked against the unseen force that gripped him. When they reached the clouds, the dragon loosed its grip on the officer. With a scream, the man fell.

The dragon paused. From far below came the sound of a body crashing to the ground. Satisfied, the dragon flapped its wings and headed downward once again.

"What do you mean, you could be nothing else?" Majaliwa asked above the tumult in his mind.

I am what you made me. But you are not the first.

"What?" Majaliwa gripped the air dragon's back.

It swooped down onto the plain, wheeled, and herded soldiers into a group. Then it blanketed them with another deadly blast.

"I conjured you in my mind. There is no such thing as you—I created you. You are the only one."

You believe this.

The soldiers burst into flame.

The voice came in a whisper. *You are powerful, young Majaliwa. Powerful and arrogant. I once knew another such as you.*

"Once knew?" A stab of fear and uncertainty cut into Majaliwa's chest. "Once knew?"

The dragon ignored Majaliwa. Instead, it chased down another group of riders, who had almost reached the northern edge of the plain. One blast felled them all. The stink of burning horseflesh broke his concentration.

Majaliwa felt the energy falter. He realized that his power was almost consumed. When it was gone, the dragon would disappear—and he would fall to his death.

Do not worry about your own death. You released me. I will not let you fall.

Desperate to maintain the power that kept the dragon in existence, Majaliwa forced himself to forget the enigmatic words of the creature and focus on the task at hand.

They were not finished, not yet.

Group by group, soldier by soldier, Majaliwa and the dragon destroyed the Femeref. Qalhata's forces had long since retreated to the southern boundary. They huddled there like insects, watching their foes be systematically decimated before them. Every once in a while, Majaliwa caught a glimpse of Qalhata's face as she watched the destruction. He smirked as her look of triumph changed to one of horror.

"Who wields the power now, Commander?" shouted Majaliwa as the dragon zoomed overhead. "Did I not keep my promise on the bluff?"

She is your adversary? Energy flows within her, from the line of mages that also begot Gazali.

"How do you know of Gazali?" Majaliwa sputtered. "You know nothing of this world."

Ah, but I know more than you believe. I know your every thought, your every wish. I came from you, and I made you. You despise Gazali, do you not?

Majaliwa said nothing. His mind whirled with the still-roaring sound of the wind and with the new, frightening thoughts that were beginning to form.

"*I* made *you*," he finally insisted, sounding more like a petulant child than a powerful wizard. "You know nothing of Gazali or of my opinion of him." Then a new thought dawned on Majaliwa. "I did not think of Gazali when I made the spells to create you. I have not thought of the legends until today, when I met the commander."

The two circled high above the ground. There was no other enemy to be seen. The plain was smudged with black spots. From this height, they looked like ink spatters on a creamy page.

The dragon let out a lazy blast of heat and energy, which

swirled the sand into a huge dust devil that skipped and bounced across the plain. Majaliwa could feel the energy draining from him. He had planned for this and called upon his last reserves of power to sustain the dragon until it could land safely.

Oddly, the dragon did not seem to be losing energy, as most conjured creatures did when the wizard's power waned.

Majaliwa closed his eyes and focused on channeling the last of the land's energy through himself and into the dragon. He once again saw the tunnel of swirling wind in his mind. In its center, far away, Majaliwa saw a face. A human face.

"Who are you?" he shouted.

You know, do you not? It is my master. The dragon landed gently.

Majaliwa peered at the face in his thoughts, struggling to recognize the long, gaunt features and the white hair that floated around his head like a mane. Slowly, the face became sharp and clear. Majaliwa shuddered.

"It is me, as an old man," he stammered.

The dragon laughed out loud, but the sound was not pleasant. The face in Majaliwa's mind laughed too.

In a manner of speaking, you are right.

The mouth of the face moved as if it were speaking, but the voice was the dragon's.

The man walked through the tunnel into the bright light of the plain. Majaliwa watched in wonder, thinking that he had somehow gained the power to call himself from the future.

Then the man's face contorted in a silent, terrified scream.

Majaliwa opened his eyes and blinked against the glare of the afternoon sun. He and the dragon were back on the bluff high above the plain. The wind kicked up swirls of red dust all around them. The clouds grew larger as the wind became stronger. Majaliwa squinted through the stinging dust at the dragon crouched before him. Its transparent body glowed with a faint reddish tint.

The dragon watched him with icy white eyes.

You are strong, yes, stronger than even you believe. I have searched for you for years uncounted. Have you not yet guessed my purpose?

"I conjured you to defeat the enemies of Zhalfir," Majaliwa replied, but he no longer believed it.

The dragon shook its head. Gusts of hot wind hit Majaliwa in the face.

Majaliwa raised his hand to shield himself from the painful blast.

And that I have done. My debt to you is finished. But yours to me has only begun.

The dragon took a step closer to the young wizard and touched his chest with the tip of its long, elegant snout. Majaliwa knew that one breath would kill him instantly. He lifted his chin and looked the dragon in the eye.

"I owe you nothing," he said.

Ah, but you do. Who do you think made you as powerful as you are? Do you really think that you, a young nothing from Jamuraa, could possibly contain such power?

Majaliwa remained silent, his mind quiet and numb.

The dragon laughed again.

You were born in a moment of great energy in the multiverse. The power found you and filled you. I saw this, and I watched. Yes, I watched you from the clouds, my prison for these many years.

"Then I did not imagine you, or create you," Majaliwa said in a dead voice. "You were already here."

Yes, and no. My creator lived centuries ago, and he gave me life. We traveled together, he and I, and our energies became as one. When he was cast away, I thought I was to be destroyed. But instead, I was locked in the sky, a prisoner of the air and wind.

The dragon raised his head and looked straight at Majaliwa.

For time uncounted I waited and watched. I knew that someday, someone would come that could release me from my jail. The descendants of my creator were powerful, but they chose different paths. They, too, knew that someday I would be released. Even now there are those who rejoice in my return.

And then you came. You were young, arrogant, and extraordinarily powerful. You would be the key. I whispered to you in the breeze as you played outdoors as a child. My voice filled your room when the breath of night blew past your sleeping face. Slowly, my image filled your mind, and you vowed to create me. Piece by piece, I gave you the means to unlock my prison. I gave you the spell.

Majaliwa's eyes glazed over. He began shaking his head. "No, no," he repeated. "This cannot be."

The dragon ignored him. Instead, it flapped its wings once and tucked them beneath its majestic body. The dust clouds around them swirled.

The path was long, and you resisted. But your pride carried you forward. You knew that if you created me, you would be known throughout the land as a powerful wizard. Power and accolades were what you craved. As it was with my master. You are much the same, you and he.

The dragon smiled, baring rows of teeth that looked like sharp white shadows.

You did not disappoint us. You had the power to release me. When you cast the spell today, my prison was destroyed. I was free.

"Why did you come to me then? Why did you not fly to freedom?"

The grin became wider.

Majaliwa shrank back. Fear gripped his heart. Until now, the dragon's story seemed benign. Yes, Majaliwa had been manipulated by this creature. The realization was bitter. But there was something more, something that froze his blood as the dragon's eyes glittered. The young wizard clenched his fists and waited.

Because my task was not complete when I destroyed the Femeref army. My purpose was not to obey your petty commands, although I was forced to do so as part of the spell you cast. I have a greater purpose.

The dragon raised his head and stared out into the red dust cloud. The cloud began to open. A swirling tunnel of wind and images from Majaliwa's life yawned before him. From the inside of this tunnel a figure appeared.

Suddenly, dizziness and nausea overwhelmed Majaliwa. He sank to his knees, gasping for breath. The air bore down upon him like a weight.

The figure stopped, but the mouth of the wind tunnel continued to stretch until it encircled both of them. As the walls of the tunnel moved around him, the world plunged into darkness. The wind roared and screamed. The edges of the tunnel clapped shut.

Majaliwa was immersed in blackness.

* * * * *

On the plain far below, the setting sun had begun to fill the sky with swaths of purple and pink. Qalhata stood before her troops and gazed at the red dust storm that sat, unmoving, on the edge of the bluff. She seemed to be waiting for something. Her troops were restless behind her. She ignored them.

Just as the last rays of the sun dragged their long fingers across the plain, the dust storm began to grow weaker. It diminished until it was little more than a red speck against the darkening sky. Then it disappeared with a puff.

Qalhata barked quick orders. She pressed her heels into her horse's side. The majestic beast leapt forward and carried her at a gallop across the plain.

The dragon was circling high above her. It bellowed and threw out a breath of wind. Its rider, clad in white, let out a yell. Qalhata slowed to a stop and waited, watching the graceful beast as it wheeled and soared in freedom.

Finally, the dragon landed before the commander. Qalhata dismounted and approached the beast, smiling.

"Thank you," she said. "I am in your debt—for many things."

You're welcome, Qalhata, lineage-daughter of Gazali.

The dragon bowed respectfully before the commander.

May we join one another again in battle.

Qalhata nodded and smiled.

The figure atop the dragon slid off of the creature's back and embraced the young woman. His white robes fluttered slightly in the evening breeze. The white gem atop his staff glowed. But there was a new, different gleam in his blue eyes. The icy arrogance had been replaced with a sparkle of laughter and freedom.

"Honor be with you, Gazali, and long life," Qalhata said.

The young man grinned. "And honor and long life to you," he replied.

They clasped hands. Then the young wizard climbed atop the dragon's broad back. The two eternal companions—mage and dragon—rose as one and left the battlefield far below them.

Qalhata mounted her horse and turned toward her army. A gentle breath of warm wind carried the sound of laughter. She smiled.

Somewhere in the blackness between planes, an imprisoned spirit, no longer arrogant, let out a silent, desperate scream.

Hero of the People

Jess Lebow

Mitrokin village was burning.

People ran from building to building. Villagers who had lost their loved ones in the press to escape the flames had abandoned civility, fighting to reach safety. Then chaos and panic turned to simple terror.

"Dragons!"

Leathery wings, and fangy jaws filled the sky above. Flames unrolled like giant lapping tongues from massive red dragons, igniting the entire market district. Groups of black dragons belched gouts of acid, dissolving fleeing villagers down to the bone, leaving bleached white skeletons to litter the streets. Some green and white dragons preferred a more direct approach, landing in the midst of the fleeing crowd and scooping up victims with powerful fore claws. The streets ran slick with blood.

Hunters unleashed volleys of arrows. Most of the flint-tipped weapons simply bounced from chitinous scales or were batted from the air like annoying insects. A few hit their marks, impaling eyes or plunging between ill-fitting scales. Still, the dragons continued their assault.

Farmers picked up pitchforks and scythes. Blades once used for harvesting wheat or tilling soil now dug into dragon flesh. The huge beasts seemed to laugh as they thrashed spiky tails at their attackers. Some farmers were thrown hundreds of yards, snapping their necks or spines as they crashed back to the ground. Others were simply impaled by the barbs and hooks jutting from tails, wings, and claws. Still more were crushed under thousands of pounds of flesh. The invading beasts stomped merrily down the streets of Mitrokin village, leaving only oozing, broken piles of bone and pulp.

The village militia and cavalry arrived, bearing lances and swords. They formed ranks at one end of the main thoroughfare, allowing fleeing citizens to pass and attempting to stop the dragons' marauding. As impressive as these soldiers were during the summer tournaments, they were puny next to the hulking, ferocious dragons.

Two hundred defenders on horseback charged first. Most were cooked alive inside their armor as a phalanx of red dragons swooped down and spilled flame across them. Horses stumbled. Riders fell to the ground motionless, smoke and flames rising from their metallic corpses. Still a few won through, charging valiantly on to certain death.

The remaining cavalry managed to skewer two smaller invaders before a large blue dragon alighted on the road before them.

One of the soldiers managed to yell, "Charge!" but that was all. The great blue wyrm reared back on its haunches and let out a hissing sound. The oncoming cavalrymen and their mounts stopped dead in their charge—every last one frozen stiff, though not by cold. They looked like the statues commemorating the dead outside of the city of Losanon. Now these living statues themselves would become the dead.

A group of ten smaller black dragons landed beside the statuelike cavalry and began devouring them. Between horse and rider, each of the dragons finished a pair in only three or four crunching mouthfuls. Though magically frozen, the cavalrymen and their horses were still aware of their plight. Screams and whinnies tore across Mitrokin village.

Citizens picked up rocks and debris off the streets, throwing everything they could find. Pitchforks, arrows, stones, and furniture hurtled through the air. Nothing stopped the feast. Militiamen formed ranks around the village, sealing off the town square from attacks on the ground. It mattered little. Huddling behind organized soldiers, the unarmed townsfolk were surrounded. To all sides, their village burned.

In the very center of the square sat a tremendous fountain. Named after the town's founder, Mitrokin fountain gurgled water. The falling streams splashed into a pool below; the soothing rhythm sounding the same today as it had on every warm spring afternoon.

A wall of water leapt from the fountain as a white dragon crashed atop of it, smashing the marble and stone into tiny fragments. This dragon was the largest of them all. With one foot, it had shattered the towering fountain. With the other, it had dug a crater larger than most farmers' barns. It stood on its back legs and stretched its wings, spanning almost the entire length of the town square.

Though fearsome, this dragon was also majestic and strangely beautiful. Its scales were alabaster circles, each overlapping another and creating perfect crescents that looked like the midseason moon. Its jaw was long and pointed, with whiskerlike appendages that twitched as the great dragon surveyed the cowering crowd. Its wings were massive and strong, yet delicate looking, as if they might easily tear. Its eyes were a calm, almost soothing blue. They peered across the faces of every villager in the square.

The white wyrm spoke. "Humans, I am called Pizoondertanx, and you shall consider me your ruler. You shall consider all dragons your rulers. The Primevals have decreed it so, and this plane, this world, belongs to us."

With pitchforks and large stones, several armed farmers charged the huge beast.

Smiling, Pizoondertanx watched them come. He flapped his powerful wings, unleashing a torrent of air. The flames of nearby fires rose higher with the violent gust of wind, and the charging villagers were lifted off their feet and sent flailing backward. They smashed against the wall of a burning smithy, and the building collapsed under the strain, plunging the defenders into an inferno.

More dragons landed on the outskirts of town, fully surrounding it.

Pizoondertanx spoke again. "I admire your spirit, preferring to die fighting rather than giving in to overwhelming odds. We shall give you a choice then. Bow to us now, promising loyalty and a live sacrifice at the turn of every moon, or we shall kill you all—old, young, man, woman, and child."

The great white dragon looked around at the thousands of villagers cowering in the square. The encircling dragons twitched and shook, rustling wings and grinding claws into the dirt.

When none of the humans moved, Pizoondertanx raised his head and let out a booming roar that shook the bricks of the square.

Slowly, the village militia dropped their weapons and fell to their knees. The farmers, blacksmiths, and merchants followed, and soon all of Mitrokin village bowed before the great dragon.

In the crowd, a man turned to his neighbor. "What do you think they intend to do with those who are sacrificed?"

"I think they will do the same with them as they did today with the cavalry. They will eat them alive."

* * * * *

Three Hundred Years Later . . .

Rokin struggled against the grips of the large guardsmen. Two armed village militiamen held him in place. Another was attempting to wrap his wrists and ankles with sturdy hemp.

The village clergyman tried to quiet the young man. "Be calm. Your sacrifice reserves you a place of great honor. Your name will be engraved on the Wall of Saviors." The middle-aged priest spoke these words as if he were bestowing on Rokin a fabulous gift. "Tonight, you will be in the prayers of every child in the village."

"Tell them to save their prayers," spat Rokin. "Tell them to pray that men like you stop cowering behind antiquated and barbaric laws. Tell them to pray that they do not grow up poor, so the merchants and village elders don't sentence them to dragon sacrifice."

The soldier who had been trying to bind Rokin's arms

and legs finally managed to loop the twine around his feet. With a quick pull, he tightened the knot and reached for an already immobilized arm.

"Maybe we should gag you as well," taunted the guardsman. "There is nothing in the law books that says a sacrifice must be able to scream while he is being eaten."

The other militiamen chuckled and began carrying Rokin up a set of weathered steps.

For over a century, the sacrifices from Mitrokin village had been brought to this same location. At the edge of a rocky field, the prone skeleton of a once-huge dragon jutted up out of the grass. Skin, organs, and wings had been worn away by the forces of nature, leaving only the rib cage to tower into the air. Vertebrae created bone steps up the gently sloping hill. Some of the older villagers claimed that this particular dragon was an outcast from the dragon nations, and this was its punishment for not bowing to the wisdom of the Primevals—the dragon gods.

Rokin wasn't the only villager to be sacrificed on this day. Another man was being forcibly helped up the dragon-bone steps. Rokin didn't know this man by name, but he had seen him sleeping behind the Dirty Flagon Inn and rummaging through the waste pile for bits of uneaten food. Rokin had lived an impoverished life, but that life appeared lavish compared to this man's.

Sun-bleached ribs created an archway under which the Mitrokin villagers passed—the living carrying the soon-to-be dead. At the top of the steps, in the middle of the spine, the guardsmen lashed Rokin and the other man to opposite sides of the dead dragon.

"If this is a sacrificial altar, why are there no bones or bloodstains?" Rokin asked.

"Perhaps you can ask the dragon when it arrives," replied the guard who bound his ankles.

"That's enough taunting, soldier," scolded the cleric. "These men are heroes to Mitrokin village. Show them a little respect."

"Yeah, right, heroes," responded another of the guards. He and his companions had almost finished tying the homeless man to the altar.

"They *are* heroes," insisted the clergyman. "Reluctant heroes, yes, but heroes all the same. Without these brave men, we'd all be facing the dragons' breath."

"How can you say that when the sacrifice we make is against our will?" Rokin spoke not out of desperation but out of the desire to be heard. "We're victims, not heroes."

The priest stepped up so that his face was directly in front of Rokin's. "Would you prefer that the whole town burn? That every living person in Mitrokin village be killed?" The older man stared for a moment and stepped back a pace. "Call it what you will, but when you are gone, like it or not, of your own accord or not, you will have saved thousands of lives. That, my son, makes you a hero."

The guardsmen finished tying up Rokin and the other man. They turned their backs on the condemned men and started down the steps out of the rib cage.

The cleric reached into his robes and pulled out a vial of crimson paste. Dabbing his finger in the vial, he began to anoint the homeless man.

"I draw upon you a circle, representing our home, Mitrokin village." The clergyman wiped red paste on the man's forehead. "From that circle I take away one life, your life. The circle is cleft, and we will mourn your loss." With a clean finger, he removed a small gob from the man's forehead, breaking the circle at the base just above the man's nose. "Our prayers will be with you. This night, your name will be inscribed on the Wall of Saviors, and Mitrokin village will give thanks for your sacrifice." The cleric stepped back and looked the man in the face. "Have you any last words to return to the village?"

During the entire proceeding, Rokin hadn't heard this man so much as whimper. He wondered if the man could speak at all. When he finally did, his voice was soft and quietly accepting, not harsh and condemning as Rokin's had been.

"I have no words for the village, but I have a question for you," said the condemned man.

"For me? G-go ahead, my son," replied the priest.

"Do you know my name?"

"I—I, I'm afraid I do not. . . ." The clergyman lowered his gaze, staring at the dragon's spine.

"Then I guess you won't be carving it on that wall."

Rokin could feel the priest's shame. He felt a similar shame at not knowing this man's name either, but Rokin hadn't been the one who condemned the nameless man to death.

The priest hurried through Rokin's anointing and left the two men on the dragon altar, too ashamed to ask the homeless man's name. He rushed to catch up with the militiamen who had started back to Mitrokin village without him.

When they were out of earshot, Rokin spoke. "I don't know your name, either."

"And I don't know yours." The nameless man smiled. "I suppose we'll be known as the unknown saviors."

Rokin chuckled. "It seems pointless now, but my name is Rokin."

The other man nodded. "I've been called many things by

people in that village—beggar, bum, vagrant, derelict—but rarely called by my name. I'm Jamar."

The conversation fell silent, both men realizing the futility in getting to know someone who was about to be eaten by a dragon. The sun set over the horizon. The moon had been up for some time, but now it lit the entire plain. Eventually, silence gave way to the sound of leather fluttering in the wind.

Two small black dragons flew in from the west, landing at the far end of the altar. On their hind legs, each was slightly taller than the bare ribs of the deceased dragon. Despite their size, these beasts were impressive. Their scales were very dark, and in the moonlight, their hulking bodies cast large shadows down the hill. Their mouths were open, exposing immense fangs and long, hideous tongues. After a brief moment, one of the dragons opened its wings to their full length and stalked along the outside of the altar, heading toward Rokin. The other dragon moved toward Jamar.

Rokin looked to Jamar, not knowing why he did but finding comfort in the fact that he wasn't alone. There was terror in the homeless man's eyes, and Rokin finally had the realization that he was at the end of his rather short life. He had been so busy being indignant that he hadn't thought about the moment of his death. Well, he thought now, there won't be much left to my imagination.

The first dragon moved directly behind Rokin, but his bonds prevented him from seeing the beast. The monster's panting breath reeked of rotten flesh. The second dragon moved in behind Jamar, and each man looked over the other's shoulder.

The beast behind Jamar leaned down, its mouth open, its claws closing in on its prey. It would be any moment now. Rokin winced. He certainly didn't want to watch Jamar be devoured. A claw tugged at the hemp holding Rokin to the rib cage altar.

Rokin closed his eyes. His heart pounded. He was sweating profusely, and he clamped his eyes tighter. Seconds seemed minutes. Minutes seemed eons. . . .

Finally Rokin let out a scream. "Hurry up and kill me, beast! Just get it over with."

The bonds holding Rokin to the dead dragon suddenly broke. He fell forward, his hands and ankles still secured. He opened his eyes, surprised that he wasn't dead yet.

"We're not going to kill you, human, but you may wish we had."

Rokin looked up at Jamar who was lying on his stomach in a similar fashion. Then he glanced back at the dragon. "You can talk!"

"Of course." The smell of decay accompanied the words.

Rolling onto his back, Rokin peered up through the rib cage at the black dragon. "I—I, didn't know."

"There are a lot of things you don't know about us," said the dragon, "but there is something you do know that will become very useful to you." The wyrm leaned down between the ribs of the altar and wrapped a cold, scaly talon around Rokin. Only his head jutted from the dragon's fist. "Fear," continued the dragon. "Fear us, for we are your masters, and your fate, your life, rests in our grip." The black dragon squeezed Rokin tightly as if to prove his point.

Rokin could only nod.

The winged beast looked up at its companion. "We're off." The black dragon lifted off the ground. In a few moments, both dragons were side by side, flying westward into the darkness, Rokin and Jamar in tow.

They flew for a long time and covered a lot of ground.

Eventually, they reached a mountain range. The dragons began to climb, staying close to the rocky ground but rising to avoid sharp peaks.

Rokin watched the cliffs and rocks fly by, and he wondered if he had been spared at the altar so the dragon could enjoy torturing him first. Every outcropping threatened to smash into the dragon's claw and crush Rokin. By the time they reached the central peak, he was sure his captor was looking for the best rock to smash him on, so he would be a more tender meal. The smashing never came.

Wind rose at the peak, and the dragons circled. They folded their wings and dived. The dragon holding Rokin tucked its claws up next to its chest, clutching its prey tightly.

The rocks and fissures rushed by again, much faster this time. Rokin felt his stomach rise as they descended in a free fall over stone points and precipices. The ground approached quickly, and the dragons opened their wings only long enough to dodge boulders and other obstacles.

Wind whistled in Rokin's ears. He could make out large boulders and fallen logs in the river at the base of the slope. The whitewater rapids came into focus next, and the dragons showed no sign of pulling out of their dive.

A wide, calm pool of smooth water came up fast. The surface hammered the side of Rokin's head. Stars swam before his vision, and he heard a loud slap before everything went silent.

Rokin was suddenly gripped in a bone-chilling cold. The world became thick and blurry. He reflexively tried to suck in air. His lungs filled with water, and his muscles clenched and spasmed, trying to cough out the fluid. He thrashed against the black dragon's hold. It was hopeless. Rokin began to lose consciousness.

All he could think before he passed out was, death is far more painful than I'd imagined.

* * * * *

Rokin awoke in a brightly lit cavern. He took in a breath and choked on a gout of warm water. He gagged and vomited. Judging by the smell, he'd been doing this for some time.

When he finally gained control of his breathing, Rokin glanced around the cavern. The ground he was sitting on resembled a dock or a port in a fishing village. Several fingers of stone jutted from one wall into a pool of water. The tops of those rock piers were flat and smooth as if they had been cut and polished. Rokin looked over the edge of the stone outcropping into the water below. He could see his reflection in the surface, but the bottom was utterly dark.

Where the stone fingers connected to the wall, a huge, rune-inscribed archway stood. The opening rose halfway to the ceiling. Beyond the arch opened an enormous, well-lit hallway that took a sharp turn, blocking Rokin's view.

The other end of the cavern was completely filled with water. Gray stone walls reached straight up out of the pool, coming to a conical point high above. From the vault hung large glowing orbs on heavy chains. The phosphorescent globes gave off a blue glow, bright but not harsh. None of the spheres appeared to flicker as would a candle or a flame.

Rokin remembered then that he hadn't been alone on the rib cage altar. He found Jamar laid out on the cold stone floor behind him, similarly covered in regurgitated water. He was breathing but not conscious. Rokin shook him.

Jamar opened his eyes and immediately began to vomit. Rokin moved to avoid the splash.

"Where are we?" asked Jamar when he finally emptied himself.

"I was hoping you knew," Rokin admitted.

"The last thing I remember was hitting the water in the river," said Jamar, glancing around the cavern. "The dragons must have left us here to revive or die."

Rokin shook his head. "I don't think they want us dead yet, but none of this makes any sense to me."

"Maybe they brought us here to be food for their young." Jamar shrugged. "I guess I understand now what that dragon meant about wishing I were dead."

Their conversation was cut short by a scraping sound coming from the archway. Around the corner, bathed in the same blue light that lit the cavern, came a large white dragon. Its wings were tucked, and standing on hunched legs, its head almost reached the top of the hallway.

The dragon entered the cavern and stretched its legs, lifting itself to its full height. The great beast eyed the two men lying in their own vomit.

"Stand," commanded the dragon.

Both men hurried to their feet.

"You." The wyrm pointed at Rokin. "Step forward."

Rokin did as he was told, moving down the stone finger toward the hulking monster. As he got closer, he realized that the dragon was holding something in its tremendous claw. It looked to be a stack of metal rings, each big enough to fit around one of the dragon's talons.

When Rokin was close enough, the scaly beast leaned down. It inspected the man like a farmer looks over a head of cattle, poking him in random places to test for firmness.

Then the dragon stood upright and pulled one of the metal rings from the stack in its claw.

"Lift your arms," commanded the dragon.

Rokin complied.

The dragon placed the single ring over his head, maneuvering the metal band down to his waist. The wyrm lifted Rokin's still-wet shirt, exposing the metal ring to his flesh. It was dull gray in color and unexpectedly warm against Rokin's skin. The band shrank to the exact size of Rokin's belly. It expanded as he inhaled and contracted when he let out a breath. Rokin watched the metal ring grow and contract several times before reaching down and tapping it with his finger. It was hard and made a slight ringing noise when he hit it, yet it moved with his body as if it were a woven cloth. Rokin's inspection was interrupted by the dragon's voice.

"You." The dragon pointed at Jamar. "Step forward."

Jamar had witnessed the procedure already and stepped forward confidently. The dragon leaned down and poked at him the same way it had with Rokin. This time the examination took longer, and Jamar was made to turn several circles before the inspection was finished.

The dragon stood up and considered the two men for a moment. Then it barked out several loud syllables and reached down toward Jamar. It placed a single talon on the man's forehead, and a ghostly vapor surrounded Jamar's entire body.

Rokin expected his fellow captive to vanish or turn into some sort of hideous monster.

When the cloud cleared, though, Jamar still stood on the stone floor beside him. The man wasn't moving, and his eyes were wide open—not blinking.

"You will follow me," said the dragon to Rokin. It reached

down and picked up the lifeless Jamar and headed down the hallway.

Rokin followed. Neatly worked walls of stone headed around one bend and then another. Suspended blue orbs, these smaller than the ones in the cavern, lit the way. The dragon had to crouch to avoid hitting the ceiling with its head, but it made good time through the passage. Rokin had to hurry to keep up.

They followed a series of turns, all of polished stone and all lit by the same glowing spheres. The hallway slanted downward, and the air grew cooler. After some time, the dragon stepped out of another archway, and Rokin got his first glimpse of the dragon city.

The cavern he had awakened in was but a bird's nest compared to this chamber. Overhead, dragons flew circles above dome-shaped buildings and an intricate series of waterways. Bridges crossed the rivers in regular locations for as far as Rokin could see. Flat-topped spires reached into the sky from some of the larger buildings, and tall pillars billowed steam into the air. Dragons of all colors, sizes, and shapes walked casually through streets like those in Mitrokin village—only much larger.

"They live as we do," Rokin said under his breath.

Huge glowing blue orbs, just like the ones he had seen before, were suspended in the air. Past the orbs, Rokin could make out only darkness. On the street level, posts jutted from the ground with other, smaller orbs stationed on top. The whole city was lighted with these strange creations.

To the left of the archway, a series of rock steps led up to an overhang several hundred feet from the ground. The dragon continued up the steps, and Rokin followed.

The steps were large enough that the dragon could place

one foot on each, making a slow but steady climb to the overhang. Rokin had some trouble, for the rise from one step to the next was formidable. He had to hurry to keep up.

At the top of the steps was a vast platform with many red clay mounds. There were several rows of these structures, and they ran from the end of the steps to the far end of the platform, looking like giant pottery baskets. The white dragon stomped casually down the first row of mounds. As he walked, Rokin could hear movement inside the structures—scratching and a strange, high-pitched whine.

The white wyrm stopped at a basket in the middle of the row and held out its claw. Jamar's still-stiff form dangled from the dragon's talons.

Rokin paused in midstride and watched in horror.

A small, scaleless dragon lifted its head out of the clay mound, snapping at Jamar's heels.

The white dragon let out a series of barking sounds.

Jamar blinked. He shook his head, looking around at the city and then at the baby dragon below his suspended feet. The helpless man let out a shrill sound that could only mean he knew what was about to happen.

The white dragon released him into the clay nest.

Jamar screamed for a few short seconds, the sound drowned out by the squeals of young dragons fighting over and devouring him.

Rokin lost his balance. He went to one knee to steady himself against vertigo and nausea. In the next moment, he felt only anger. He stood, using his hatred against this act of sheer cruelty to support him. He glared up at the white dragon, knowing he was at the creature's mercy but feeling righteous indignation toward the beast.

The dragon looked down at him and said simply, "There

are worse ways to die, as you will find out if you don't follow the wishes of your masters."

The scaled creature scooped up Rokin in its mighty claw and leapt out over the edge of the overhang. Rokin's anger was momentarily replaced by the rushing fear of falling. The dragon opened its wings, and they glided out over the city.

The domed buildings below contained intricate carvings of five colored dragons. Each picture depicted the dragons in a different pose but showed the same five dragons. One dome showed the dragons in a circle, joining claws in the center and holding up what looked like a small blue globe with large brown patches in irregular shapes. Another depicted the five different colored dragons each sitting in thrones and holding scepters. Still another showed the dragons in battle, each devouring a large section of what appeared to be a human village.

Also from this height, Rokin could see that the flat-topped spires allowed the dragons easy access to the buildings via the air. They must have huge doors on the ground level and platforms on the roofs, thought Rokin. It made perfect sense for a race of creatures that could fly.

At the center of the city was a large arena. Dragons of all persuasions sat in oversized stands watching some sort of contest below. As the white dragon flew over the top of the stadium, Rokin caught sight of the first humans he'd seen in the city. They were standing in the middle of the arena. Around them circled all manner of nightmarish beasts— tigers with huge fangs, carrion crawlers with gaping circular mouths and groping tentacles, giant lava hounds with huge fangs and molten red eyes.

Rokin lost sight of the coliseum as the dragon rose to avoid a pillar belching steam. The beast dived toward a flat-topped spire, alighting on the surface and dropping Rokin in the process.

Torches burned around the perimeter of the clay surface, not the glowing blue orbs that lit the rest of the city. At one edge stood two black dragons side by side. They bowed and stepped apart. The white dragon walked between them onto a stone platform that extended off the edge of the spire. Rokin trailed behind.

The stone was the first of many spiraling steps that led partway down the side of the tower and into a large archway. Inside, the building was hollow. A narrow stone ledge circled the space. Beyond it, a drop off fell hundreds of feet to the floor below. At the bottom of the tower sat a circle of huge dragons—each larger than any Rokin had seen before. The white dragon pointed to a human-sized ladder at the edge of the circular pathway.

"Climb down," it commanded.

Rokin stepped onto the first rung and began his descent. The stone entryway was the only one in the entire building. The rest of the structure consisted of a seamless stone wall that reached from the floor to the top of the ladder. Painted pictures of dragons covered the curved rock. The dragons in these pictures, however, were different from the ones he had seen on the domes. These creatures seemed less grand. Some scenes even depicted humans in powerful positions over prone dragons. As Rokin got closer to the ground though, the paintings regained their triumphant flavor.

Eventually he reached the floor. The space at the bottom was large enough to comfortably fit hundreds of dragons, but only five were present. Stationed around the circular room on huge pillows sat five very large, very old dragons.

To Rokin's left sat a red dragon on an embroidered orange

and yellow pillow that was easily twice the size of the dragon itself. The beast's tail wrapped its body, and its wings tucked up against its sides. A second enormous pillow rested near the center of the room, and the scaly giant had laid its chin there. Its eyes were barely open, but Rokin could tell that the creature was taking his measure.

Arrayed around the red dragon were several humans, some male, some female, each with a silver belt similar to the one Rokin himself had. To the right of the great dragon's head, two women bore the hilt of a giant fan, waving it lazily over the slumbering beast's ears. To the left, two men worked in tandem, grooming the dragon's razor sharp talons.

The next dragon in the circle was green, and it lazed about on an emerald pillow. This one's snout was longer than the red dragon's, and its eyes were a pale yellow. It had a long tongue that it whipped about, tasting the air in a huge circle around its head.

There were human servants surrounding this dragon as well. A group of six gathered around a huge pack animal, and two strong-looking men dismantled the beast with sturdy two-handed axes. The green dragon looked on in anticipation.

To the left of the green dragon sat a white dragon, the largest of all those in the room. It looked very old, and it sat back on its hind legs, smoking a large glass pipe that was manned by two servants—one who filled it with bushels of tobacco and another who held a torch to the brown leaves. This dragon had the fewest servants and seemed the least distracted of the bunch, intently watching Rokin from the moment he had entered the building. Its whiskers twitched as Rokin examined the pipe, the servants, and the snow-white pillow that the great wyrm was perched on—which easily weighed more than the dragon itself. The dragon blew out a large puff of smoke.

"What is your name, human?" It looked Rokin up and down, seeming to stare right through him.

"Rokin," he said, not intending to speak more than necessary.

"I am Pizoondertanx, eldest of the dragon chiefs and leader of the white dragons." Pizoondertanx pointed to a blue dragon to his left. "This is Varuna, eldest of the blue dragons."

Varuna lifted her long thin jaw from the sapphire pillow. Her body was covered in feathers instead of scales, and she wore a silver torc around her downy neck. The blue dragon narrowed her eyes in introduction and examined Rokin as if trying to decide if he would be a good snack.

"To her right is Macumba, champion of the black dragons," explained Pizoondertanx.

Large piles of precious metals and all colors of gems sat at Macumba's feet as he lounged on his obsidian pillow. Human servants scurried around, organizing the treasure into neat stacks as the huge serpent shifted in place, knocking the coins and stones across the clay floor.

The great white dragon turned his head to face the red and green dragons.

"This is Heptane, speaker for the red dragons," said Pizoondertanx, pointing to the red dragon, who blew smoke from her nostrils and replaced her head on her pillow, closing her eyes. "And this is Siliq, chief of the green dragons." The emerald wyrm was busily devouring the meat her servants had neatly dismembered. She paid no attention to Rokin.

"Now that you know our names, it is time you know who we are. We—" as he spoke, Pizoondertanx swept his arm out to include the other four dragons—"are the greatest dragons in this land, second only to the Primevals themselves. But we are even more than that to you." The great white dragon leaned down and put his face right in front of Rokin. "We are your masters, every dragon is your master, and you will obey our every whim." Pizoondertanx sat back. "Or you will die."

The dragon elder pointed a talon at Rokin. He felt a searing pain from the strange belt on his belly, and he was suddenly unable to move or squirm. He stood motionless but in excruciating pain. All he could do was close his eyes. He held them shut for what seemed an eternity, trying to keep a grip on his sanity.

Then the agony stopped, and Rokin could move. He bent over and steadied himself against the ground. When he had caught his breath, he looked up.

Pizoondertanx was smiling, obviously amused by the torment he had caused.

Heptane sat up then and raised a single talon. Rokin's belt turned red hot and seared his belly. Falling to the ground, he worked furiously to get his thumbs under the belt, trying to get the metal band to release him. It was no use. The gray ring had turned bright red. It burned both his stomach and his thumbs. He thrashed against the pain.

Rokin passed out.

He awoke in the middle of the dragon chiefs' sanctum. His thumbs were scorched, and his belly was badly blistered.

"Stand," commanded Pizoondertanx.

Rokin closed his eyes and gritted his teeth against the pain. He climbed to his feet.

Macumba was next in line. With a sharp command, he set Rokin in motion. In one moment, the helpless man lost all control of his body, and he slumped to the floor. Then he rose, his arms and legs moving him all about the room without his willing them to do so. He began to climb the ladder to the circular platform. Rokin struggled but could not stop himself from continuing up the rungs.

His limbs paused after he had climbed over fifty feet from the ground. Then his hands simply let go of the ladder, and he fell. Rokin watched the ceiling rise away from him as he plummeted helplessly to the ground. He landed flat on the clay surface and struggled to breathe.

Gasping, Rokin looked around the room for an escape. There were no openings on the ground floor. The only way in or out was the archway above. A human could exit the building only by being carried by a dragon or by climbing the ladder and dropping to the ground from the stone platform. Falling from that height would surely kill anyone who tried it.

Rokin would either live through the dragons' hazing or die in the process. Either way, he wasn't looking forward to the rest of his day.

Varuna took her turn next, lifting Rokin high in the air with only a swish of her claw and moving him about the circular room by simply pointing. The blue dragon delighted in watching Rokin bounce from one wall to the other. She bashed him against the paintings along the internal curve of the chamber until his blood added accents to the artwork.

Rokin hit the clay more softly than he had the previous time, but a puff of dust jumped into the air as he landed. He coughed as the loose clay settled on his prone body. He couldn't move, and he wished these dragons would just kill him and get it over with. There was only one left who hadn't had an opportunity to show Rokin what he would get if he stepped out of line, but the lessons were getting harder to live through.

Siliq whipped her tongue out toward Rokin. The metal

belt unfurled from his torso, transforming into a leafy vine before his eyes. The vine grew, sprouting leaves and sharp wooden thorns. It climbed toward the ceiling and lashed. A curved wave leapt from the very end, heading down the length of the vine at Rokin. When the wave reached the prone man, it whipped him and sent him rolling across the ground. The vine wrapped itself around his body in the process.

Multiple thorns punctured his skin, and the more he struggled against the vine's grip, the deeper the spikes worked themselves into his flesh.

Rokin suffered agony. His eyes clenched shut, his teeth gritted, and his fists knotted tightly. His whole body burned with pain, and he wanted to die.

Pizoondertanx spoke again. "Do you see now, Rokin, who we really are?"

Rokin couldn't unclench his jaw enough to answer, nor did he know what to say. He smelled the rotten scent of dragon breath and felt something touch his forehead. A loud squealing sound echoed above him, and the pain stopped.

Rokin opened his eyes. The vines were gone. He was on his back facing the ceiling. His body was whole, healthy, and scarless.

Pizoondertanx hovered over him, smiling.

"We are your gods," continued the white dragon. "We own you. We control you. We created you, and we can destroy you." Pizoondertanx leaned back. "Do you understand?"

* * * * *

Rokin was put to work as a messenger for the council of dragon elders. This was a challenging task since the only way into the council chambers was to be flown to the top of the flat-topped building by a dragon and climb down the ladder on the inside.

The black dragons guarding the entrance to the tower were tasked with flying Rokin the length of the tall building, allowing him access to and from the council chambers when he was delivering messages. The dragons didn't like that they were required to ferry a human up and down the building, but the flight never lasted long, and they were forbidden to harm Rokin because of his status as a runner for the council.

It took him a while to get used to being carried by a dragon. His first few encounters weren't very pleasant, but after some time, he began actually to enjoy it. The experience of flying gained something when he didn't fear he would be eaten or bashed to smithereens. All in all, his life was relatively easy as a slave to the dragons.

Any dragon in the city could give Rokin an order, and he was required to obey, but being a messenger to the dragon council had its privileges. If Rokin was on official business, he was left alone. The council had given him an official seal that he carried with him to validate his status, and no dragon dared harm him while he was delivering a message for fear of retribution by Pizoondertanx. Life as a slave was not great, but in his position working for the council, Rokin could see how it could be a lot worse.

The streets of the city bustled. Most of the hauling and building was done by human slaves. Humans prepared food, disposed of waste, performed routine maintenance, and ran messages.

The most important job done by slaves, however, was the daily upkeep of the Obsidian Well. Every blue orb that lit the city was magically linked to this ancient artifact. When the city had been built, a huge stone well had been constructed over an open geothermal vent. The rising steam moved gears, paddles, levers, and pulleys, providing enough power to light the entire dragon city. Without this well, everything in the dragons' domain would be dark. Over the centuries, the well had been adapted also to control a series of drains and flood gates that maintained the water levels in the rivers and waterways. Without the well and its regular purging of excess water, the city would flood.

Dragons did nothing in the way of supporting or maintaining their own basics needs. If a human could do the task, a human did the task, leaving the dragons to pursue leisure activities like art, sport, philosophy, and magic. The only dragons who worked were the ones who did so out of service to the dragon council, and they were rewarded handsomely for their devotion.

Many dragons enjoyed watching blood sports in the central arena. Rokin had glimpsed these games the first day he was in the city. Now that he'd had some experience with the dragons, he scoffed at calling what happened in the arena a sport. Humans were herded into the center of the floor, and dragons in the audience would summon all manner of beasts and monsters. Other members of the audience would place bets on how long it would take the creatures to completely devour all of the humans. They weren't even given weapons to fight back. Then a new group would be ushered in, and the games would resume.

* * * * *

Fire rose from the eastern quarter of the city. Rokin headed toward it, carrying a message to the sewage facility. There had been a slave uprising, and Pizoondertanx

71

wanted a report from Varuna, who had gone to squash the rebels. Rokin was to find the eldest of the blue dragons and discover why the slaves had become so bold.

Rokin himself was interested to hear what the dragon elder had to say. He had been personal witness to the punishments dished out if slaves disobeyed. During his enslavement, he hadn't heard of a single slave ever outright defying his or her master. The punishments were too great and the rewards too small. Besides, if a slave did as he was told, he lived a fairly decent life. Why risk punishment and destroy a good thing? Rokin wondered. Something had happened to make these slaves think otherwise.

He arrived at a building in chaos. Dragons of all colors and sizes arrayed themselves around huge detoxification pools full of excrement. Hundreds of human slaves writhed in pain inside and outside the pools as the dragons unleashed lengthy barrages through their slave belts. Some workers were caught between the wrath of more than one dragon. They thrashed even harder. Their belts boiled their skin and froze their bones and tore their eyes out of the sockets with recently formed beetle pinchers—all at the same time.

Rokin could barely stand the sight and smell of the carnage, but he pressed on to find Varuna. She was perched beside several other dragons who tortured renegade slaves. By the look on her face, Rokin guessed she quite enjoyed what she was watching. When he approached and conveyed his message, her pleasant look faded. She ushered him outside to give him a report for Pizoondertanx.

"You, slave, will die a terrible death by my own hands if this message is heard by anyone outside of the council hall." Varuna leaned her face into Rokin's and breathed heavily on him. "Do you understand?"

"Yes, my master," replied Rokin.

"You will repeat my words as I say them," commanded Varuna.

Rokin nodded.

The great dragon began, "One of the Primevals has fallen. I have scryed the globe and found this to be true." Varuna looked around to make sure no one else was listening. "The circle of five has broken. We must take measures to insure the safety of the city. Call the council to chambers. We will meet when I return." The eldest blue dragon leaned away from Rokin, a worried look on her face. "Go, human, go now!"

Rokin took off toward the council chambers at a run. He didn't understand Varuna's message, but perhaps he would discover more when he reached the dragon council tower.

One of the black dragon guards was waiting for Rokin when he arrived at the council chambers. Evidently word had spread about the slave uprising, and the dragons were worried. Even as powerful as they were, there were far more humans than dragons in the city. The guards wanted to hear the word from Varuna as much as the other elders did, and Rokin's arrival was much anticipated.

The black dragon flew Rokin directly inside the building and down the empty chamber. He was placed carefully in front of Pizoondertanx, who lounged on his opal pillow, smoking his pipe.

"What have you to report, human?"

"I bring a message from Varuna. She bid me to repeat these words to you." Rokin cleared his throat and then repeated, verbatim, what the blue dragon had told him.

The great white dragon stopped puffing his pipe and looked up to the black dragon guard.

"Find Macumba," he barked. "Go, now!"

The younger dragon did not hesitate. In a rush of wind and sheer force, the guard leapt from the floor into the air.

Pizoondertanx looked to Heptane and Siliq, who sat up stiffly on their enormous pillows. "The circle of dragons has been broken," he said. "I truly thought this day would never come."

*   *   *   *   *

In the following weeks, slave riots broke out regularly. The hold the dragons had over their human slaves was beginning to slip, and people were dying by the hundreds every day in retaliation. Rokin tried to keep his head down and follow his orders. He would of course rather be free than enslaved, but his existence as a slave hadn't been bad, and he didn't want to die either, so he maintained his loyalty.

With all of the elder dragons in the council chambers, Rokin was temporarily without messages to deliver, so he had been relegated to filling Pizoondertanx's pipe with huge armloads of tobacco. The great white dragon puffed on the pipe as he listened to the other dragon leaders.

"Another of the Primevals has fallen," reported Varuna. "The humans on the surface have formed alliances with the elves, orcs, cat people, and even our cousins the lizard men. They threaten the rule of the dragon gods. Our hold on this city weakens daily."

"We do not need the Primevals to rule our land. We are dragons." Heptane blew out a fiery breath to punctuate her point. "We are more powerful than any other creature on this plane."

"The circle of Primevals is the magical center of all dragon power," explained Varuna. "Without them, all but a few of our kind will lose their magical abilities. We will lose control of the slave belts, and our city will suffer."

"Surely we can control the renegade humans through simple fear," interjected Macumba.

"Control of a few does not worry me," said Pizoondertanx. "Controlling them *all* does. The Obsidian Well requires constant maintenance by hundreds of slaves. The upkeep of the city and the means of production are entirely in the hands of the humans. Without them, the city would go dark, and eventually the cavern would flood—"

A large crash shook the tower, and a huge section of the wall disintegrated. Stone and clay blasted into the council hall, and a giant dust cloud plumed out, covering the outside city from view.

Dark shadows formed inside the dust and began to grow. Then the first humans burst out of the debris, carrying hunks of rock and broken bits of wood. Some even had talons or teeth wrenched from dead dragons. They charged en masse toward the dragon lords.

Heptane was the first to strike, leaping off of her pillow into midair. She blew fire from her mouth and each nostril. Humans turned to ash in one incinerating blast. Despite the flames, the tide of slaves grew.

Pizoondertanx waded in next, linking directly to the slave belts and trying to freeze the invaders in their tracks. Nothing happened, and the council chambers filled with running, armed slaves.

"The third Primeval has been captured," screeched Varuna over the growing chaos. "The belts are useless."

"Then we shall destroy them on our own," interjected Siliq, who had joined Heptane in the slaughter.

The green and red dragons hovered above the ground, killing humans by the handfuls. Heptane was blowing fire and scooping up the renegade slaves in both talons, crushing them in her powerful grip and not bothering to scrape off their remains before grabbing for another clawful. Meanwhile, Siliq was slapping the invaders with her long, whip-like tail, sending twenty humans at a time smashing into bloody puddles against the walls of the chamber.

Macumba had stepped up to defend the inner council as well. Unlike the other dragon elders, Macumba had some real magic of his own. A ghoulish howl issued from the black dragon, and a legion of dead human slaves stood in the center of the room. Many had been broken quite badly, but Macumba's magic held them up. They marched, limped, and crawled toward the living slaves, fighting their onetime allies.

Varuna had no magic of her own, but she did have a stash of ancient and powerful artifacts. With a tremendous screech she pointed a sapphire-tipped scepter at the charging slaves. Many of them stopped running and turned on their peers, cutting them down. Still others simply disappeared midstride.

All this happened in a matter of seconds.

Rokin stood stunned, clutching an armload of tobacco. They had done it. They had breached the council chambers, but would any of them live through the day? Other inner council slaves had already taken sides, most of them fighting to save the lives of their dragon masters. Already, two of Siliq's personal slaves chopped the rebellious rabble with the two-handed axes they used to dismember cattle. The poorly armed rebels were quickly cut down.

Only a few of the elder dragons' personal servants joined the press of slaves, choosing to risk their lives for the freedom of all the humans in the city. They were soon lost to view, killed by their irate masters or disguised among the still-growing throng of rebels.

Standing in a pool of human blood, Pizoondertanx turned away from the battle and looked at Rokin. "Fight, slave! Defend your master!"

Rokin dropped the tobacco he was holding and stared at Pizoondertanx. He hesitated for a moment, cleared his throat, and replied, "As you wish, my lord." He rushed toward the crowd of slaves.

Pizoondertanx smiled and turned back to the fight. A band of rebels used sticks and debris to chop at his claws and wings. He opened his wings to their full length and swung them inward, creating a huge gust of wind that knocked the slaves in front of him to the floor.

"You insolent humans will pay. Every one of you will die a hideously painful death. Do you realize what you have done? We are your gods. You have angered your gods, and now eternal damnation awaits you."

The giant white dragon leaned down to devour the prone slaves. Pizoondertanx opened his great mouth, and it slammed shut—but not by his own accord. Something huge had hit him on the back of the neck, and it pinned the great wyrm to the floor.

Rokin stood behind his dragon master. With the help of hundreds of slaves, he had heaved Pizoondertanx's pillow on top of the elder dragon. His wings were spread wide, and the heavy cotton inside the pillow was too much for him to lift.

All through the council chambers, groups of rebels clubbed the other dragons in a similar fashion.

"Light the pillows!" screamed Rokin. He carried the torch used to light Pizoondertanx's pipe. Now he was going to light the dragon himself.

The gigantic pillow ignited quickly, and its massive bulk held its owner to the floor. The room quickly filled with smoke as other slaves followed Rokin's example.

Heptane and Siliq avoided capture by the crowd of slaves, but smoke and flames forced them to flee the building.

The humans began to vacate. Rokin crouched down to avoid rising heat and crawled on his hands and knees to the opening in the wall.

Outside, former slaves ruled the streets, and in all directions, buildings burned. Dead dragons littered the ground. Live dragons flew overhead, spiraling up to escape the flames and the angry slaves.

The giant globes that had lighted the city suddenly went out, and a tremendous cheer rose on the air.

They had shut down the Obsidian Well. Rokin smiled. He could see the city only by the light of the fires. He looked up, watching dragons circle above—Heptane and Siliq among them. With the light globes extinguished, Rokin could see the ceiling. Light glimmered through a large hole in the top of the cavern, and he realized that the dragons were abandoning the city, leaving through the opening.

Rokin looked around at the ruined city. In a few days, the cavern would flood and wash away any evidence of what had happened here.

He frowned, thinking of Jamar and of the priest who anointed them both at the rib cage altar. The old cleric had called the two men heroes. Rokin thought about how he had scoffed at that, how he had accepted his life as a slave. Now, in the aftermath of the slaves' uprising, in the aftermath of the decisions he himself had made, Rokin thought perhaps the old priest had been right after all.

Turning to follow the crowd out of the city, he wondered if it was too late to get Jamar's name inscribed on that wall.

Part II:

Slave Dragons

Since the fall of the Primevals, dragons have not so certainly ruled mortals. Many dragons live enslaved by the creatures that chained their gods.

One cannot speak of gods and slavery without speaking of Urza Planeswalker. Twice he has captured dragons to serve him on Tolaria. Those stories begin our section.

In the first tale, Urza presides over the Tolarian Academy before time ripped it to pieces. He seeks to build himself a perfect dragon engine. To do so, he summons a magical construct, a dragon he can study. Urza is surprised to discover that his creation ardently studies him. . . .

The next story moves far ahead in time, past the Tolarian explosion, past even the collapse of Serra's Realm. Urza builds new defenders, armies of meat and bone that he will name the Metathran. He imbues them with the essential strengths of numerous beasts, and what beast is stronger than a dragon?

Finally, we read of a subtler enslavement, the tyranny of one color over another. When a white dragon crashes from the skies into a druidess's garden, it may find nurture, but can it find freedom? And beyond the green enclave, do worse slaveries await?

Dragon's Paw

Edward Bolme

"Who am I?"

The question echoed in the large, open chamber. No answer came.

"Who am I?"

"You are a tool."

The tool considered this.

It was clearly alive; this it knew instinctively. It was conscious, because it was thinking and aware. A moment earlier it had been neither of these, only this immediate moment was the entirety of its experience, it thought nothing of the fact that it could reason, let alone speak.

It looked around, and its slitted eyes darted methodically, carefully cataloging rack after rack, wall after wall of implements, hardware, mechanisms, apparatuses, and artifice. Those, it thought, are tools.

It turned back to the creature that had given the answer.

"I asked '*who* am I,' not '*what* am I.' I ask once more—who am I?"

A shrug. "You are *my* tool."

A span of three breaths passed as the tool considered this. Then: "Who are you?"

"I am your creator."

The tool considered this also. It looked down at one of its limbs. The paw was robust, well formed, dynamic of shape and potent of function. It flexed, and brutal virgin claws slid forth from concealment. For a moment the tool could almost imagine what it felt like to use those claws, the power, the blood, the . . . the . . .

The moment passed. Still, the tool enjoyed having claws. It popped them out a few times, experimentally, not noticing that its creator raised one eyebrow as he watched. It stretched and raked the claws across the stone floor, leaving incidental furrows in the flagstones.

Then it looked down at its creator. He had upper and lower limbs, not fore and rear. His paws were weak, covered with pallid, naked flesh, not armored with glistening scales. His claws were laughable, blunt, rounded, incapable of gutting even a small rodent. And, the tool noticed, he was very small. He stood almost beneath the tool, gazing up, one hand holding his chin, the elbow supported by the other arm across his chest. So small, hardly a mouthful. And yet the tool did not even consider shredding the creator, though its claws were fully as long as his forearm.

The tool lowered its head on its long, sinewy neck, lowered it almost to the floor to look its so-called creator in the eyes.

The creator's eyes were as chips of stone: bright, polished, powerful. Emotionless. The tool could see its own slitted pupils reflected in their pupil-less surface.

"You are a planeswalker," it said matter-of-factly. "But you are a human as well. You did not beget me, and no one could create a creature such as I."

"Of course I can. I can do what I want."

The tool grinned mirthlessly. "I do not believe you."

The creator made a curious gesture, and there was nothing more.

* * * * *

"There," said the small human. "I have just unmade you and created you anew. Do you acknowledge me as your creator now, tool?"

The tool ignored this. "Who am I?" it said.

The creator's head sunk into his hand. As he rubbed his forehead, he made a curious gesture with his other hand, and there was nothing more.

* * * * *

The great doors to the central laboratory opened as if of their own accord. As they swung apart, a figure passed between them. His expensive silken robes swishing easily with his stride. Hands clasped behind his back, Barrin, the second most powerful mage in Tolaria (as well as the best dressed) strode in. His easy brown eyes scanned the collection of vast metallic limbs arrayed about the cavernous room. He strode past a reptilian arm, the scaled chain-mesh skin flayed open to reveal an incredibly intricate mechanism of cables, gears, pulleys, pistons . . . and there, ready to run out on a heavily reinforced spiral gear, a three-foot-long blade of razor-sharp titanium, ground to a mirror polish. It had a copious blood gutter to allow—well, best not to think of such things.

He strode past the paws, briskly along the length of the forearm, and around the elbow. He passed beneath the upper forelimb where it leaned lazily against the leviathan haunch, which was itself set upright, so it nearly reached the ceiling.

There Master Urza stood, staring vacantly with his chiseled eyes into the empty half of the laboratory. One arm was crossed over his chest, supporting his elbow. The other hand idly held his sandy beard, with his index finger rhythmically tapping his lips.

"Troubles, my friend?" asked Barrin. He knew the look. When Urza tapped his lips in a complex mathematical series, it meant a real puzzle.

"Yes," came the reply. When around Barrin, Urza rarely bothered to look or move his lips, or breathe, or otherwise act mortal. Though Barrin had learned to expect such an immortal display, somehow, on some instinctive level, Barrin found the habits of the planeswalker bothersome. It was as if Urza found human existence negligible and retained his human shape the way that Barrin kept cracking his knuckles. Unconsciously, habitually. Something to be readily dropped if only one would bother to spend the attention on such a trivial matter. Every so often, Barrin felt like he was in way over his head.

But someone had to be there for Urza. Might as well be him. "What are you doing?" he asked.

"Working."

"I knew that, but—"

"Then don't ask."

Barrin rocked on his feet for a moment before formulating his next question. Urza continued tapping his lips.

"What manner of artifact are you currently creating?" he asked directly.

"A dragon."

"It looks like you have finished the parts," he said, turning in a slow circle. "Skeletal structure looks sound. The skin, by the way, looks excellent, good fine chain mesh you have, and those barbed scales are sure to prove their worth in—"

Urza raised a hand, the first movement other than the tapping finger. But he still didn't bother to move his lips, or turn his head toward Barrin. "The chassis is indeed complete. I based it on the autopsy."

"You mean Mg'razzgh?"

"Hm?"

"You know, Mg'razzgh, the Shivan dragon that terrorized the North Coast."

"Yes, certainly, whatever," said Urza, resuming his lip-tapping. "Back to what's important. The machine is nearly complete, but I lack a control system, which has proven to be somewhat difficult to manufacture since Teferi disintegrated the carcass' head."

"Ah. You need a dragon's brain."

"A control system. Right."

"And without a sample, how will you gather your research material?"

"I have conjured a dragon, but—it proved unsatisfactory."

"Show me," said Barrin amiably. "Perhaps I can help."

There was a sharp sound, a near-crack, almost like the sound of lightning. From the center of the vast, open portion of the lab, feathery light swiftly flew in all directions, too fast for any but the trained eyes of the master mage to follow. In the phosphorescent wake of the spell, there it stood, the dragon. The flagstones creaked in protest at the sudden return of such imponderable bulk.

Barrin eyed the dragon critically. It was an excellent example. One thing about Urza, he thought, he can execute the details. If only he wouldn't keep letting the details obscure the concept.

The dragon's head swiveled, sweeping across the room on its serpentine neck. Finally, it spoke.

"Who am I?" it asked, and its bass voice rumbled through the room like boulders down a mountainside.

Urza turned toward Barrin. Not like a mortal would, of course. He simply rotated without moving.

"You see," he said. "It's dysfunctional."

"How so? It looks rather fine to me."

"Watch," Urza said. Then, louder— "You are a tool. I am your creator."

The dragon lowered its head to peer down at them from a height of a mere fifteen feet. Its whiskers grazed the ground as it sniffed at them. Barrin felt his robes being tugged, fluttering toward the gargantuan snout. The air reversed itself, and a waft of sulfurous stink suddenly assailed his nostrils. He coughed reflexively.

"You are a planeswalker," the dragon said. Urza gestured to Barrin as if he should understand the significance of that statement. "But you are also a human." The dragon studied them some more, and then raised its own paw. It rotated its paw palm up and extended its claws in a smooth and almost hypnotic motion. It bared its teeth in what Barrin hoped was a smile. "A human cannot create a dragon, nor beget one. I do not believe you."

"You see?" said Urza. "I created it, dispelled it, created it again, dispelled it again, and then just now I created it yet again. You saw me. And yet its inherent failure to acknowledge its own creation proves its cerebral cortex is a flawed system, and therefore an unsuitable model for mechanical replication."

"Well of course, it doesn't believe you."

"Exactly. Failure to provide output consistent with reality is a sure sign of an inherent cerebral flaw that—"

"No, no, no, no, please, let me speak." Barrin paused and marshaled his words. "It's not flawed. It simply doesn't believe you. You didn't create a machine, here. You created a conscious being. It has the data, at least all the data it has gathered in the last minute or so. It chooses to disregard them because they don't fit. They don't, you know, work with . . ." Barrin waved his hand vaguely, stumbling over the words, ". . . whatever internal . . . draconic concepts . . . preconceptions, whatever, dragonkind has." He shrugged. "By the looks of it, you've got a fully grown Shivan dragon here, so of course it has ideas of its own."

Urza scowled, looking somewhat affronted. "Very well," he said at last. He rotated back to face the dragon, which studied the two wizards suspiciously. "You are a tool. Specifically, you are my tool. I created you. These data are facts and cannot be refuted. Make those data a part of your function."

"No," the dragon said with a slight chuckle. A small gout of flame flicked out from between the spiked teeth.

"Master Urza, let me try," said Barrin. He levitated himself up to the height of the dragon's eyes. "Tell me," he inquired, "what do you think that you are?"

"Can you not clearly see that I am a dragon?" the beast

asked with a rumbling voice. "And yet, I do not know who I am. I am easily a hundred years old, based upon my scales, my claws, and the size of my body. Yet I cannot remember . . . I can almost . . . I lived—live in a mountain, near the north coast. . . ."

"Okay," said Barrin, "here comes the hard part." He took a deep breath and chose his words. "You, dragon, are a simulacrum. Master Urza here has created you out of raw mana using his rather impressive skills. You are designed to perfectly emulate a real dragon to aid Master Urza in his research. Since dragons are, of course, sentient creatures, he had to make you sentient as well. You are, in effect, a self-aware magical spell, cast by one of the most powerful planeswalkers ever known."

His assertion ended, Barrin studied the dragon's eyes earnestly but found them impossible to read. The dragon blinked once, slowly, nictitating membranes gliding over the deep gold eyes like oil on water. Then, suddenly, the dragon laughed, and wisps of smoke spiraled in the air.

"Enough of this talk," it bellowed. "I hunger!" It looked at Barrin. "You will tide me over until I find some real food," it said. Its mammoth claw shot forth like a serpent and snatched Barrin out of the air.

Startled, the mage barely had time to call forth barbed armor from his skin, which strained against the idle strength of the dragon's paw but kept the mage from being crushed outright.

"Are you going to eat him next?" Barrin asked quickly, nodding his head toward Urza.

"No."

"Why not? Free food, right there. If you're a dragon, why not eat him?"

The dragon paused to consider this, but it could find no answer.

"You want to know why? You can't eat him because he summoned you."

The dragon narrowed its eyes, stared at Barrin, then turned its head again to look at Urza. Still, it refused to believe. "Why, then," it asked, though Barrin could see its confidence had been shaken, "do I remember times past, if indeed I was just created?"

"You were created based upon our observations—rather close ones, I might add—of a living dragon. Master Urza used those memories as his basis for constructing you. Since Urza wants you to know what the dragon knew, though of course he doesn't know what all that might be, it's not unreasonable that the shades of some of the memories of the real dragon might have found their way into you." Barrin thought for a moment. "Look," he said, "I might have a solution. Urza, you cast this spell, why don't you unravel it? Only undo it slowly and carefully," he added, patting the thick scales that covered the mighty paw that held him, "so you preserve the central consciousness of this here dragon. That way, it'll experience being unmade almost to nothingness. Then you reconstruct the spell, and it'll know what it feels like to be created. That ought to settle the debate, hmm?"

The dragon looked suspiciously at Barrin, and its tongue licked out across its teeth. "Submit myself to a spell? I think not. Rather—"

"Oh forget it," said Barrin, irritated, "I'm sick of this debate. You're a spell for goodness' sake! Just do it, Urza, and show this spell who's boss."

There followed a very long time, a seeming eternity, in which the dragon almost died. It could feel itself dissolve away, like melting in acid but without sensation. Instead of pain, there was only an emptiness, an emptiness that grew, yawning like the void, slowly drawing in its wings, its legs, working up its pelvis, slipping the very organs from within its torso. It felt like its body was being exhaled.

The emptiness grew all around it as its head was slowly unraveled. Without ears, it heard nothing. Without eyes, it saw nothing. Dissected to the barest essence of its being, it huddled, naked, powerless, yet aware, aware of its pathetic state and that something, somewhere beyond reach, could crush out the last precious and essential spark of its being.

Yet in this darkness, with no other distractions, the dragon found its existence. The purity of that fragile flame burned itself into the dragon's memory, never to be forgotten.

* * * * *

Again it was alive, and what a beautiful gift! Existence had returned like a breath of fresh air into suffocating lungs, like a sudden dawn after the endless night of the arctic. The dragon flexed its paws, felt the blood coursing through its veins, the tightening of the sinews. It spread its wings to feel the membranes ache with tautness and the pectoral muscles stretch invitingly.

Although life had returned, it brought with it also the undeniable fact that Master Urza was its creator, and the dragon was as nothing. Nothing, that is, in the minds of Master Urza and his associate. . . .

"I am who I may be," said the dragon, cocking its head to one side, "but you have demonstrated that I am indeed your tool. In what manner shall I serve you?"

"I need reports on your function," said Urza peremptorily. "I need an accurate diagram for my work."

The dragon bridled. Having been nothing, even though temporarily, it disliked the creator's disregard for its newly returned vivacity. For all the life that coursed through its body, for all the essential energy, it was still a tool, a simulacrum, a mere spell. It felt like so much more.

The dragon exhaled mightily, though if Urza noticed the sudden violent billowing of his robes or the collar flapping in his face, he gave no indication.

The dragon narrowed its eyes and lowered its snout as it spoke. "If you wish accurate reports, creator, you must give me . . . more data." It gritted its fangs as it continued. "Without providing me proper parameters for functional analysis, the data I provide will be meaningless and useless to your experiment."

"Naturally," said Urza, though it was clear by his brusque reply that this had not occurred to him. "I have here the pieces of an artifact dragon. This dragon I shall assemble, once I have completed the control mechanism, which shall itself be modeled on your brain. The dragon's purpose is to protect this academy from attack, which shall most likely be in the form of a Phyrexian invasion. Thus I need to measure the operation of your brain, abstract those indices into equations, and construct an analog."

"Ah. You are creating a fighting machine."

"Yes. Fighting is what a dragon does."

"Well," demurred the dragon, "that's not the only thing a dragon does." But, it added silently, it is the most enjoyable.

"Humph. Fighting is all I am interested in."

"Why not just use me to defend?" asked the dragon hopefully.

"Bah. I couldn't be bothered with maintaining you," said Urza, oblivious to the way the dragon's eyes narrowed.

"Furthermore, spells can be dispelled, undone, or blocked with protections. They're very ineffective compared to a good, reliable engine. Well, enough of that. Sit still and think violently. A Phyrexian walker approaches you, with flames coming from a large caster. Do you—"

"One moment, please," said the dragon, holding up one forepaw. "You created me from your memories of a dragon you fought. And while I'm sure that your opinion of a dragon is, shall we say, complimentary, we all know that a human's perception of a dragon's ability cannot compare for accuracy with the dragon's own personal experience."

Urza stared blankly at the dragon, an easy expression considering that his eyes were chunks of stone.

"Let me rephrase," rumbled the dragon, narrowing its eyes. "I sugg—no. You would be best served if you put m—ah, your tool through practice trials. After all, if you want to understand the combat capabilities of your construct, it is far better to base your analog on operational parameters instead of theoretical processes, correct?"

"Ah," said Urza with sudden understanding. "I collect field data as you kill people, break things, and destroy the countryside. Very well. That would provide me with a far better example. There, I have set some tracking spells upon you so that I may gather data from afar. Inform me if your brain is incapable in any way. Begin!"

With a feral smile, the dragon turned. Urza waved open a great portal in the laboratory. With a powerful war cry, the dragon shot into the sky, a contrail of fire streaming from its mouth. The experience of freedom flooded into the dragon's soul as it felt the air beneath it. Though it had spent all of its short existence inside the laboratory, the memories of freedom still echoed in its mind. Its body and mind were based upon a dragon that had once terrorized the lands.

The dragon's ascent took it over the edge of a steep mountain slope, and it dived, followed the talus downward. The dragon did a barrel roll, a maneuver made all the more terrifying by the huge bulk of the beast and the agonizing slowness with which it rolled. Animals and humans alike scattered as it flew, death and thunder on the wing.

At the foot of the mountain, it leveled out, ripping a mere thirty yards above the treetops. Draconic wings buffeted the palms, leaving a veritable cloud of small branches, leaves, and dust in their wake. It wove back and forth, and the twining slalom proved an enjoyable challenge for the beast. Though it knew how to fly, it had never actually done so before.

The palms ended, and the beast streaked across the beach and over the ocean. Straightening its neck into a trumpet, it gave a great bellowing roar, and it was pleased to see the sound waves rippling the waters in front.

After a few dozen miles, when the dragon had exhausted its initial surge of excitement, it rose higher in the sky and turned toward familiar terrain, which instinct said was far to the east. For hours, empty ocean waves rolled beneath its watchful eye. Ocean gave way to unfamiliar land, and the dragon turned to follow the shore. Occasionally it swooped ponderously toward the rolling plains to snatch a small, screaming snack.

But when the dragon at last reached the regions near the north coast, its smile widened. He'd visited these lands before only in dreams. The terrain was tantalizingly familiar, though many memories were tainted by the ground-walking human perspective. It circled the countryside in a great arc, its sharp eyes carefully scanning the land, reacquainting itself with the area, plotting its reign of terror.

It practiced effective use of its claws, giving special attention to those tricks that had almost saved its progenitor. Its flaming breath drew great arcs of blackened agony across the fields, and its wings beat the air with the sound of a hurricane. There was much to be learned and oh so much to be enjoyed. It had been ordered to research these things, and research them well. . . .

* * * * *

A week later, as it lay among the smoking ruins of the fifth castle it had destroyed, the dragon stopped to ponder. Life—well, existence as a simulacrum of a living creature—was good. It had hunted, and it had gorged itself upon the charred corpses of the population, delicious with the tangy flavor of fear. Somewhere between the ragged pain of exhaustion and the soothing embrace of gluttony, it took a moment to think about all that it had done. It had experiences now, real experiences, and the dragon compared those to Urza's somewhat fuzzy memories of the other dragon—the real one, it thought in annoyance.

The comparison brought a decision. The dragon rose slowly on its wings and flew back to the Tolarian Academy. Eventually it glided through the great portal leading to the laboratory and landed on the flagstone floor.

Urza stood beside the great mechanical arm, which thrashed viciously.

"It works well," said Urza. "Even better than yours."

"I know," said the dragon. "I need to be bigger. I was not as effective as the dragon you fought. If you want better data, I need to be a better dragon."

"No. You are not less effective. I make no errors in my spells."

"Oh, I'm casting no aspersions upon your ability, creator," said the dragon smoothly. "It's simply that, well, to a planeswalker, very little is a challenge. You defeated the dragon rather easily, hence, in your eyes, it was not nearly so great a creature, and you patterned me after your memory of it. Thus you only created me to be as great a threat as you perceived the dragon to be.

"However, consider the castle at Rushlim, latest of my . . . shall we say, tests. It took me a full five hours to lay waste to that castle, but it should have taken me less than four."

"How do you know that?" asked Urza, confused.

"You created me from your memories of that dragon. I have your memories of its abilities. I know that you helped rebuild the wreckage of that castle, and all the while the annoying silver-haired demagogue told you of the attack. He said it took the dragon less than four hours. I required five."

Urza pondered for a moment then raised one hand toward the dragon.

To the dragon's eye, the world shrank just a little. This was the right size. It felt right. It matched the memories. But the dragon licked one lip with a cloven tongue, looked back at Urza once more, and said, "Bigger."

"No, it wasn't."

"I was that dragon," said the creature. "You made me so that I would be. And I have the objective view here. Yours, planeswalker, will always be subjective, and I will always be made too small, for nothing is a threat to you. If you used the descriptions of that castle's ruler, however . . ."

"Very well." And the world was smaller yet again.

The dragon studied its claws. "Close enough," it said, pursing its lips.

"Humph!" snorted Urza. He waved his hand once more, and the dragon felt itself grow again.

"That feels good," purred the dragon, for indeed it did.

Real or not, it was now a good deal larger than its predecessor. "However, there is one other minor detail," said the dragon quietly. "I need to be smarter. It takes me too long to plan attacks and too long to spot weaknesses in my foes. This will, of course, diminish your measurements and make your machine somewhat less than adequate to the task. It will be too slow. Unless you want to pattern your greatest creation after a second-rate dragon."

Urza scowled. "Done," he said.

The dragon smiled, for now the world was a clearer place to live in. "Excellent. Now I must go to test myself again."

So saying, the dragon rose once again into the sky, but this time, it turned west, toward new lands. It flew through the night, pushing itself hard to make sure that it worked up a good appetite.

Over the next ten days the dragon fully destroyed a kingdom. The smoke from the burning cities and forests were as black as a funeral shroud and higher than mountains, and fear struck every soul for hundreds of miles in every direction. In the center of the pyroclasm, the dragon drank deeply of the wine of carnage, and explored every portion of its draconic soul as fully as it could. Amid all the gluttony and wrath, the carnage and terror and wanton destruction, the dragon realized that there was yet one draconic vice unexplored.

Again it rose into the sky, leaving behind a raging forest fire and a half-plundered city, sick with the smell of death and filled with the wails of the wounded.

Again it flew across the sea toward the place of its magical birth, and returned to stand before its cuckold father.

"Most excellent," said Urza as the dragon landed. He was standing in the mechanical skull of his unfinished creation. Tools hovered about him or moved of their own accord, inserting gears, wires, levers, and powerstones from the cloud of parts. "I have gotten some excellent data. I think that about wraps it up. Is there any additional data you need to impart to me before I dispel you?"

"Yes," said the dragon. "You don't have complete data yet. The more I do, the more I remember. . . ."

"Impossible."

"Not so, great planeswalker," said the dragon soothingly. "Your powers are almost limitless, and when you created a dragon to the best of your abilities—me, that is—you apparently filled in the gaps in your understanding. Such is the power of a wish. You created a better dragon than you knew how to create, simply because you wanted it to be better, hmm? But now I know that I am not yet a true dragon." It paused and gazed humbly at the floor. "You see, I have no gender."

Urza gave the dragon a blank stare.

"Surely you understand what an impediment that is? Or have you forgotten, planeswalker, what it is like to be mortal?"

Urza's stare didn't change.

"Permit me to explain. For a great and powerful creature like a dragon, to have no gender is an embarrassment, an embarrassment that impedes performance. Like all living creatures, we—er, dragons have hormones. Nothing puts the edge on a fighting machine like a good dose of hormones. It hones our reflexes, reinforces our will, enhances our viciousness. I need a gender. You must grant me a gender if you want to measure my peak performance."

Urza pondered for a moment, as the tools and gadgets continued their work on the mechanical brain. "I do not know how to make that happen. I admit, I am out of practice in the whole reproductive arena. And I have never been versed in draconic anatomy."

"That's not difficult," the dragon said reasonably, as its claws slid out. "I *do* know. You made me to be a dragon, and I can sense where the . . . where the oversights are. I can explain it to you, but it would be far easier if I were just to do it myself. I know how I should feel, and I can make that happen. Just give me some magical power, and I'll take care of it for you."

"Very well, then. A self-repairing tool you are."

The sense of mana filled the dragon's mind, expanding the world of possibilities. The dragon flexed its spirit and reached out with its soul and touched a thread.

"Oh, I need more power than that. You're asking me to repair a planeswalker's spell. That requires real power. For that matter, dragons are very powerful practitioners of magic. Some are almost as powerful as planeswalkers. An artificer as clever as you could find some mechanical means to reproduce the magical abilities of a dragon, given the best set of data and measurements to calibrate your devices. I am prepared to give you the best data you could want. Think of the machine you'd have then—large, powerful, keen with analog hormones, invincible with technical magic. Now that would be a true artifact dragon, and would make this place impregnable!"

"You are correct," said Urza, and it was so.

The dragon screamed with fear, hysteria, joy, and pain as vast power flooded into it. It could feel itself unraveling. Its spell-flesh threatened to burst, but it turned the power inside out and contained it.

Urza watched as the dragon's scales became even more refined, with barbs covering the surfaces. The fire in the eyes grew hot with fury and cold with hate. The whiskers wafted in an unseen breeze. And the dragon's shape . . . changed. The dragon now had gender.

"Your tool thanks you, creator," said the dragon, bowing

his head, "for now you have imbued him with everything he needs to show you a dragon's true capabilities. Behold!"

The dragon reached out with an etheric paw and snatched up the fragile thread of its existence, stealing the spell for its own. With a mighty swipe of its tail, it struck Urza's mechanical monstrosity squarely in the torso, rending the abomination in half. Tools and parts scattered about the room.

Surprised, Urza hung impossibly in the air.

The dragon opened its mouth. A huge gout of flame burst forth, mushrooming out and searing the entire inside of the laboratory. The vast space filled with white-hot gases. By the time the flames cleared, the dragon was already flying away as fast as possible, flying south to find new lands to conquer.

Urza smiled at his success and started to track the dragon's progress. He frowned. His spell of observation had been removed. When he moved to dispel the dragon, he found the spell was gone, no longer his to control. The spell—the simulacrum—was now supporting itself. *I wanted to create a dragon,* thought Urza, *and indeed I did.*

He looked down at his mechanical dragon, now wrecked and fused together in a heap of slag.

Rapid footsteps approached the laboratory, and the doors swung open. Barrin rushed in. He looked up at Urza, still hanging in the air.

Urza turned back toward the great portal. "It is against monsters such as these that the academy needs protection."

Barrin looked at the damage the dragon had caused and then back at the one who had summoned it. He stared at Urza for a long time.

"Indeed it does," said Barrin quietly as he turned away.

Of Protectors & Pride

Steven E. Schend

Heed these words, whether ripples or waves of days separate us, for these are the teachings of Eadyyr, he who rides the tides that others may never swim or scent, a voice and mentor to Taanan the Pupil. Let this sacred tale grace the waves within the Coral Caves above our home, a song that each voice must learn to understand how life is to be.

I sing of Maraavis and the tide when the Protector begat another—the last, yet the first of many who protect but are not Protectors. This song spans the depths and the beyond above. It spans my now and the nows of voices to come. . . .

* * * * *

Steven E. Schend

Bloody claws rose to bloodied fangs time and again. The dark crimson of drying gore stained the dragon's azure talons. The tongue lashed the claws clean, and then the teeth, and yet worked at another unseen target. The battle within its jaws continued as the dragon reared back and spread its wings wide. She took to the air effortlessly and almost silently.

"Curse it." Speaking to herself over the crunching of bones and the dying cries of her prey, Maraavis chided herself. As much as she loved fresh mutton, it would take forever to pick the bones out of her teeth. Still, the herd had been a tasty rarity, and she happily winged her way back over the waters that were her home.

Few along these coasts had ever seen a creature such as she. Her breathtaking splendor and power had frightened a herd of sheep and caused its shepherd to faint dead away, much to her amusement. More than a score of yards in length from snout to tail, Maraavis knew herself to be an impressive dragon. Scales sapphire-bright along her back darkened to a deeper, midnight blue along her belly, jaws, wing membranes, and claws. Like her mother before her, Maraavis had eyes that were kaleidoscopes of turquoise and sky blue. They entranced her past two merfolk priests. Spreading her wings wide, the dragon picked up speed in flight. Her grace and silence belied her size.

Maraavis looped high into the bright sky, closing her eyes and relishing the warmth of the sun once more. She then turned nose to tail and dived sharply toward the waves. As she clove the water's surface, the muted bark of her dive made only the slightest splash. The waters closed behind her. Her hind legs pressed tightly against her tail and moved in unison to propel her through the depths. She swam along the shallows, heading for the deep reefs that marked her domain.

With a blasting breath, she expelled the air from her lungs. It scattered a hunt of sharks fin-over-tail in a flurry of bubbles and noise. Drawing water in through her gills, Maraavis welcomed the cool salt tang and smiled as she made her way home.

She swam steadily, growing ever closer to her lair deep within the Fourth Reef of the Cosiman Tribelands. Still, Maraavis knew something was amiss, a slow skitter of dread crawling across her scales.

Everything seemed normal. Coral merfolk tended the upper kelp fields or secured and cleaned their latest catch. They smiled or cheered at Maraavis's passing, for to them she was goddess and Protector. Careful not to swim too close to the sloping ground and disturb the silt fields, the dragon trumpeted an acknowledgment of her worshipers. She swam on.

"Why are you so pensive, Maraavis?" she asked herself. "You've fed well and will properly nourish your young one upon her hatching. She lies protected by many veils and many who would trade their lives for hers. Peace has nestled in Cosiman's waters for decades. Enjoy the swim. A mother rarely gets these luxuries."

She took in the sights of the multicolored coral walls that separated the kelp fields, all awash in dark greens and blacks and browns. She skirted the upper slopes before descending beyond the plateau to the lower reefs of the tribes.

A surge of magic and emotion hit her like a riptide. Atadon, her elderly merman friend and high priest, spoke into her head.

Maraavis paused to weave a manipulating magic that amplified the hastily cast spell. With her aid, his message became an image of him, as if he stood before her despite the leagues between them.

Atadon's image bobbed near a coral shelf, the waters around him much clouded with blood. "Mistress Maraavis, aid us! One from above seeks to take the Next Protector. We have fai—" the image lurched and twisted horribly as a massive pike erupted through Atadon's chest.

"No!" Maraavis whispered sharply. The mental bonds of the spell transferred Atadon's own pain and panic to her. Shock turned to grief and became anger in short order. "My child—my children! No!" Her cry echoed off the shelf and boomed through the water, melding with the growing sounds of the battles drifting up from below. Rising currents bore the scent of blood.

Maraavis's snout flared, and she opened her wings.

Need to calm myself . . . I must summon my magic, and for that I need inner peace.

Maraavis fought within her mind and heart, willing herself to be calm despite her dread. Her neck gills flaring, she tentatively spread her claws and wings, reaching out for mana from the waters around her. Sensing the aquatic and magical worlds as one, she opened her eyes and saw the eddies and tidal flows of the mana-rich water. With subtle flexes of her talons and wing membranes, Maraavis manipulated the currents and directed their power as she willed. She flapped wings and tail in unison to establish a strong undercurrent, roaring a word of power. Dragon and sea united. She dived willfully into the flow of power she began, and Maraavis dissolved into the waters below.

Rarely used, the tidewalk enchantment had many dangers, all of which the dragon feared less than the dangers that lay ahead. Melting one's body into water to reform it at a familiar place along its currents required much concentration, both to control the currents and to restore the body at travel's end. Maraavis willed herself along the mana-charged waters. Nearing the mouth of the coral cave she called her lair, she drew herself back toward hard flesh and sinew and gem-hard claw. While less than solid, the sounds and scents of battle had grown muted in the rush of power, but returning to a more substantial shape brought grim reality into loud focus.

Coral that had been carefully shaped and tended over centuries lay shattered. The bodies of merfolk soldiers and priests littered the ruins, and the stench of fear and blood filled the water. Echoes of struggle remained, as did vibrations of foreign magic. Shields of white magic glowed brightly in her mana-sight, but buckled against her watery form's pure blue mana. The telltale shimmer of summoning mana highlighted the waters where the intruder's servitors once swam.

Maraavis took all this in as she reformed her body and swam through her lair's shattered defenses. She chided herself for complacency. Her real and illusory fortifications were far too weak. She reached the main chamber almost instantly, finding her fears realized.

A human stood among the fragments of the heat illusion she had woven over her egg. Dragon and mage gasped in unison.

Maraavis snapped her wings forward, hoping to stun the intruder and knock him away from her nest. She dared not unleash an attack where the egg might be harmed.

The human swept his arms downward, his hands trailing green sparks. In answer, the coral stalactites on the ceiling grew and thrust into the floor before her. The slender pillars blocked one wing and painfully pierced the membrane of the other.

Maraavis screamed in rage as much as in pain.

The human wordlessly threw himself onto the egg, which was more than half his size.

Maraavis lunged forward frantically, shattering the coral jail but landing a few feet too short.

In a whorl of white mana, the human and the egg swirled through a portal and disappeared. Maraavis struggled to follow, but the aperture instantly slammed closed on one of her claws. The portal sheared her talon off nearly at its root, leaving a clean stump as if a giant had trimmed her claw.

Maraavis growled, but the sound soon broke down into ragged sobs. The cave filled with the briny tears and shining blood of a mother, wounded and bereft of her child.

* * * * *

"But Master Malzra, you said the egg's mother had abandoned it . . . that it would go unhatched if left within that reef." Riand's mind raced as swiftly as his pulse had after escaping the dragon's attack only scant hours before. "I never would have—"

A sonorous voice interrupted, as if its owner were unaware Riand had been speaking. "You have done well, Riand. As a student and mage, you show much promise. However, you fail to grasp the sacrifices necessary for our work here." Ash-blond hair flowing well past his shoulders, the older man only showed his broad, blue-robed back to the boy. Master Malzra, head of the Academy of Tolaria, demanded much from his students, yet rarely spoke more than necessary to them. This was the most Riand had ever heard from Malzra, at least in words directed at him.

They stood in a low-domed laboratory, the skylight admitting the noontime sun. On all eight walls stood bookshelves loaded with scrolls and books, sketches and maps and blueprints. Floor space gave way to racks of chemicals and substances, storage bins of various mechanisms either complete or in parts, and much more. Dominating the room was the master's Eugenics Matrix, an alleged Thran artifact of which Riand had heard numerous rumors but few facts.

Just now, Malzra's attention centered on the dragon's egg.

Riand's clothes were not fully dry from his aquatic foray, and he nervously wrung out his sleeve. When not bow-shouldered from worry, Riand stood nearly as tall as Master Malzra, though he was nowhere near as powerful of limb. Riand was wiry and whip thin. He wore cloaks with padded shoulders and collars to disguise his lanky limbs. His only full and vigorous features were his short, curly bronze-blond hair and his mind. He'd been here at the Tolarian Academy for seven years now after leaving Benalia. He rose to prominence among the senior students, bested only by the arrogant Gatha and a few others. With age, he'd hoped to grow out of his gangliness but only became a scarecrowlike adult whose passions for magic and study filled what his body did not.

Master Malzra, on the other hand, hardly seemed human at all. Clad in flowing scholar's robes of eggshell blue, the master of Tolaria remained unchanged by the years. Power bristled off of him. While most eyes that met his were filled with curiosity if not wonder, Riand shuddered when meeting Malzra's gaze—nothing filled them but cold hard purpose.

Malzra silently wove a gigantic hand of glistening blue mana and directed it to pick up the four-foot-long egg. The hand took the egg across the chamber and placed it wholly into the Eugenics Matrix.

"Master, what are you doing?" Riand protested, trailing sodden footprints across the brown-tiled floor. "Surely we can't do anything to risk the wrath . . . what happens if she comes looking for me?"

"Thank you, Riand. You've done well today. Please be so kind as to go fetch Master Barrin from the western watchtower. I need him for these experiments." Malzra moved around the machine, activating levers and buttons and assuming that his student had gone to do his bidding. He didn't notice the surprise, anger, and shock that crossed Riand's face.

Fuming, Riand stalked out of the room. He heard a sound that could only be the cracking open of a massive shell. Disgusted, he made his way down the two flights to the ground floor. By the time he'd reached it, revulsion had given way to fear . . . the kind of fear that left his mouth dry and grew a cold knot in the pit of his stomach.

He looked up once more at the low tower, wondering why Malzra needed a dragon's egg. Could it be for that secret Metathran project the other senior students whispered about? Riand wondered if this project was for the ultimate good, or if they all dealt with a devil and willingly blinded themselves to his ruthlessness.

Despite all else, the young man remained bound to the academy and to his work. He had made honor vows to Barrin and Malzra both. No matter how he felt about it, Riand knew his duty and followed orders to the letter.

He set out for the watchtower, a fair walk across the island. While he was capable of moving more quickly, the young mage wanted time to steady himself and his emotions. Riand kept a nervous eye on the sea while he worked his way along the southern coast, wondering whether the paths he now trod were safe after all.

* * * * *

As she helped lay to rest those slain in defense of her lair, Maraavis held onto her tears, anger, and frustration. She fueled her fury to white-hot intensity. Rather than wishing to comfort her merfolk children, her heart yearned only for her true child, the one stolen from her. Instead of giving Atadon's protégé any attention during the last rites for the fallen, she retreated to her cave and planned her revenge. She knew she neglected her duties as Protector of the merfolk, and it shocked her how little it mattered.

It had been over a century since Maraavis had felt such hatred and longer still since she had plotted revenge. Dragon hate-fires burned slowly and steadily, and hers had banked a long time to flare up powerfully now.

All attempts to summon her child-egg back had failed, but if she found the thief, she would find the egg. In the moments after his disappearance, the dragon carefully had avoided disturbing the waters directly within the nest. She now circled the nest of sea moss and kelp, sloughed scales and skin, taking in the foreign scents. Human fear came through the strongest, which suited her fine. Fear carried a powerful scent marker easily tracked, were it not for the annoying difficulty of tracking a teleporter. She drank in the scents nonetheless.

"I have your marker, man, and I shall find you in the seas or beyond. No magics you weave nor miles you cross can protect you from my wrath. And should my child be beyond rescue, you shall only wish that your life could end swiftly."

She sensed the arrival of her new priestess, the young girl Roas. The mermaid had barely a score of years to her, and her inexperience showed. She could not even summon the courage to look up from the shattered coral floor of the cave. She stammered out a formal salutation.

"Gr-gr-greetings, my mistress Protector. Honored am I to be allowed to gaze upon your greatness and your—"

"Enough pleasantries, girl. This is hardly the time." Maraavis cut the formalities short, the mermaid halting with a choked and startled sob. "I shall find he who sinned against us all and dared to threaten the Protectors of Cosiman's faithful. Tender my condolences to the families of those guardians who fell defending your future Protector in her shell. Their sacrifice shall be avenged blood for blood." Maraavis then turned her attentions back to the nest, while a crestfallen Roas slipped away to bear her goddess's pronouncement to the tribe.

Marshaling her concentration, Maraavis opened her eyes wide, willing them to see the powers inherent in the water. There they were—glowing embers of a white mana trail left behind by the burglar. They led nowhere, though, ending where the portal had appeared.

She idly tapped her fore claws on the coral floor, concentrating on how best to find the fugitive. The drumming of her talons halted as the severed talon failed to click on the ground, yet that hush sparked an idea.

Maraavis reached out with her mind, heart, and limbs, despite the injuries to them all in past hours. She called upon the powers inherent in all seven of the reefs over which she ruled, and she linked into the blue mana permeating her home. Allowing herself to merge with the waters and the casting, Maraavis tidewalked on currents of power and intuition. She reached out. No longer did her wing bear a ragged, bloody wound, but one both transparent and insubstantial. Her gaze penetrated far beyond her domains. She sniffed, though she hardly used her physical senses to do so. She sought out the familiar and that of herself and surrendered to the pull of the tides that drew her toward the Etlan-Shiis, toward her errant talon, and the one who took it all from her.

When Roas returned to the cavern, praying that Maraavis would grant her a true audience and stave off her fears and those of the tribe's, she found only empty water with nary a ripple to betray her mistress's exit. Her scent filled the waters, yet nothing could be found of her, and Roas found her faith faltering again. She whispered a prayer that the Protector would return to them swiftly, her mantle of vengeance sloughed away in the currents to be kind to them once more.

* * * * *

Tidewalking was less a matter of willing a watery simulacrum of her normal form forward as it was expanding her body and mind to encompass the waters around her. She became the ocean for miles around, only pulling herself together when she found her quarry. When at one with the waves, Maraavis hardly knew peace. All manner of life and its struggles existed within her. Still, she cherished the experience, for it reminded her that life is a cycle, that one life touches so many others in unknown ways and that death is as much a part of life as birth.

Notwithstanding her wandering thoughts, the dragon found her fragmented claw adrift in coastal shallows. Threads of white mana clung to it. Its inadvertent entry through the portal brought it only partway along the conduit created by the fleeing mage. Still, by knowing where she came from and where the talon lay, she could find her prey. Maraavis dissolved the talon as she passed over and around it, lest some mage find it to use against her. She remained on the same heading, permeating the shallows with her presence. Her watery wings only slightly disturbing the silt as they propelled her forward.

The dragon soon found herself in waters awash with wounded mana of all colors and temporal fluxes beyond any she'd ever encountered. Still, as part of the waves that pounded the shore, she smelled the presence of the one who filled her with sheer hatred. It was time to show the bipedal stripling just how much trouble one courted when facing a dragon. His bloody surprises on her doorstep demanded payment in kind. Humanity may have gained a reputation for power and drive in recent centuries, but dragons and the seas could still teach them much about cold and ruthless vengeance.

Maraavis delayed her reincorporation, preferring to watch and wait in the waves. In this form, she could more easily manipulate wide swaths of blue mana. After setting numerous magics into play around the island's coast and herself, Maraavis turned her attentions to the human.

He walked a slender path along the cliff, his body bathed in sea spray. Therein lay his undoing.

Maraavis sent her eyes along the flows, allowing her sight to dance along with her spell. Her sight became sea foam and sea spray. She urged it close and laughed silently as the young mage inhaled her senses.

"Now," the Maraavis-sea thought, "we shall see why you dare risk the wrath of a dragon and a mother both."

The dragon moved silently, reading Riand's mind and memory without betraying any presence at all. She observed his orders and his masters, and tasted his confusion and fears. She watched his tragically bungled attempts at detaining her merfolk priests and relived his and her own shock at his actual abduction of the child-egg. She intently watched its arrival on the island and its fate within the laboratory.

Maraavis left Riand's consciousness before her emotions betrayed her presence but not before she had learned a name to hate—Malzra.

This boy can wait. His master shall pay for daring to presume against dragons!

Riand moved carefully along the slick path, he hardly noticed the sea parting behind his back.

Maraavis coalesced and took again to the skies. She flew, invisible to the eye, her rage searing the air and the sea.

* * * * *

The mourning dragon wasted no time, drawing on the powers she had set within the coastal shoals. Using what she had learned of Tolaria, she flew swiftly, avoiding all of the temporal bubbles and magical chaos surrounding the island and heading directly toward Malzra's workshop tower. She approached the skylight at the tower's apex. Looking within for any sign of her missing egg, she found what she had feared.

Fragments of shell lay scattered around an arcane device that pulsed with strange mana energies. Near the machine stood the architect of all of her suffering, upon whom no reprisals would ever be enough.

Maraavis began her spell carefully, drawing upon more

power than she had tapped in centuries. She reached out to the shoals and to befouled waters filled with shipwrecks and waterlogged undead. She wove a sorcery her mother once called drought blast. To add more power to the spell, she abandoned her invisibility.

The dragon's looming shadow gave Malzra brief warning.

She unleashed her power. From within her eyes and wings and mouth came a light that pierced and dissolved the skylight, save for its metal frame. Magic bathed the room and Malzra in an otherworldly glow.

He ignored it, weaving a conduit around his strange machine.

All through the room, glass flowed upward and dissolved. Any liquids within beakers or elsewhere became powders.

Malzra himself became desiccated. His eyes sank in their sockets. His skin cracked, parched as if mummified in a desert. Still, he moved, comically staring at his hands in fascination. He tried to speak, but his dry throat and tongue prevented any interruption of the dragon's work. Abruptly, the beams stopped, though a bright blue glow suffused the room.

Above it, Maraavis shone with added power. Completing her spell, she breathed with force and anger and spite into the chamber, and unto Master Malzra.

Superheated steam filled the room. Maraavis heard a satisfying scream from the human as he disappeared in the billowing clouds of vapor. The force of the blast blew out the doors and windows, which helped the dragon view her revenge. Numerous flashes and subsequent explosions rocked the room. Mana discharged from various protective magics and other experiments.

At last, the attack subsided. Maraavis looked to find the mage's corpse.

Malzra stood, hale and hearty, at the center of the chamber! He examined himself and the heat-scarred stone floor. While the entire chamber lay in scalded ruin, he stood without even a rent garment. His blue robes steamed from the blast but were none the worse for wear.

Maraavis felt a shudder of fear as the man looked up. He rose effortlessly from the floor, levitating to her eye level more than a dozen feet above the skylight. She smelled the scent of white healing mana around him, but she also sensed more power from him than from anything she had ever faced.

The man stood on empty air, aloft on a web of blue mana. He nodded his head in brief salute. His eyes were not mocking, but they hardly seeming fully engaged. It was as if his mind worked on issues other than the one before him.

At last he spoke, smugly. His deep voice carried only a hint of irritation.

"Greetings, Lady Wyrm. I realize we may have our grievances, but reducing the academy to ruin seems hardly necessary for our introduction. Please refrain from such again. Now, shall we make this a formal draconic challenge, or can we discuss this as civilized beings? I should love to learn more of that spell. You absorbed all nearby liquids no matter how viscous and converted them to steam, yes? Fascinating."

His disrespectful tone rattled her even more than his survival. Suddenly, she realized—she faced a planeswalker! Her fury sloughed away inside her, filling her gullet with fear. The man had survived a two-pronged attack for which there was no defense. Still, her outrage and maternal wrath demanded satisfaction, no matter the cost.

She kept her voice strong and clear, perhaps louder than it needed to be, but she spoke as if she faced an ancient wyrm. "I am Maraavis, Protector of the Cosiman Reefs and daughter of Nequeel of Many Leagues. I seek retribution and recompense in combat for your pawn's invasion of my home, the deaths of my adopted people, and the theft and loss of my unhatched daughter. Be that formal enough, mortal? Or shall I call you planeswalker?"

Malzra smirked but raised his hands in acquiescence. "I have a few names, but they need be protected. Call me planeswalker as you have surmised. And I refuse your challenge, honorable Maraavis, for I don't wish to destroy you nor my academy in senseless battle. If you need blood for blood due to murders on my student's part, so be it. My orders did not call for merfolk deaths, and for that he should pay."

"You both should pay for the blasphemy you have committed against my daughter! Or do you now deny the scent of her still on your hands from having pried open her living egg?" Maraavis came eye to glaring eye with Malzra, her nostrils flaring and making his hair fly back. "While we may be outmatched in power, Malzra Planeswalker, I shall gladly die in combat to teach you and any of your students what it means to trifle with dragons!"

"And all I wish to do, Maraavis, Protector of Cosiman Reefs, is to end this without further destruction, yours or mine. While I regret the loss of a prize pupil, you may have his life—innocent blood needs answer for the same when spilt." Malzra seemed almost bored, as if he negotiated trade rights rather than the life of his student. "It truly helps neither of us, but it is all I can do for a blood debt, for I cannot return your daughter to you. Resurrection is as far beyond my powers as it is out of your considerable reach. And this, friend dragon, is why."

Before she could weave any defense against his spell, Maraavis's eyes locked on his and Malzra spoke directly into her mind. *See what I have seen, dragon, and know why such dire measures balance in the end.* The planeswalker opened his mind to her and forced her into the whirlwind currents of his memory. She now knew him to be the fabled Urza Planeswalker, the human who in part changed Dominaria forever. She saw what made him into the man who stood before her now, and she understood the dangers the world faced from beyond this dimension. While she still mourned for her daughter, she mourned as well for Urza's hardships and what he had sacrificed.

Urza nodded as they both blinked, ending the mental onslaught seconds after it began. At least they understood each other now, though the dragon's hatred still hung in the air.

"Tell me of my daughter's fate, then, Planeswalker. What of her in your schemes and plans?"

"Your egg is now an integral part of my experiments to create a powerful servitor race called the Metathran. Their duty, not unlike your own, is to protect this world against a great future invasion from something more dangerous than you or I could ever be. I hope to adopt the strength and power and grace of dragon kind from that egg." His words were quick but flat, as if rehearsed but not totally believed. "She shall live on. I promise you that."

"As will my eternal hatred for you." Maraavis hissed. Snapping her wings out, she darted into the sky and barreled through a crowd of levitating wizard students as if they were not there. "I go to seek my vengeance," the dragon roared to all within earshot, "and let none disturb me, or you shall likewise taste my wrath!" She lashed her tail in punctuation, its whip crack stunning a few nearby students as she spun up and away.

None of them followed or disturbed her as she headed to Jhoira's Cove.

* * * * *

Riand slowed his pace to a slow walk as he followed the coastal path down along the cliff. He descended closer to the crashing waves. The path had been diverted along the cliff to avoid a fast-time zone that barricaded its former route. As he moved carefully along the steep slope, he snapped his cloak ahead of him, feeling around for magics and the edges of the errant time fields. Brushing against a telltale tingle of magic, Riand ducked and quickly sidestepped the fast-time rift. He resumed his course more carefully. The young Benalish mage kept his mind on his task.

The path took a bend along the cliff, tracing a small cove. As Riand made the turn, waves smashed against the lower rocks, their spray and foam loud and close. The waves refused to fall. They coalesced into a sapphire-blue dragon, its wings outstretched, trapping him against the cliff.

"You," the water-drenched dragon hissed, "have stolen from me! Return what is mine or barter a thousand lifetimes in its stead!" The dragon's wingtips slammed into the cliff, shattering the path on either side of Riand. The noise of the impacts nearly jarred him off his feet.

Riand's fear almost overwhelmed him, just like before. He'd entered the reef as directed by Master Malzra, only to find it guarded by zealous merfolk. While he'd tried to delay and bind them, his panic added edge and urgency to his spells. The awry magics killed them. He didn't want to repeat that mistake again, even though his life depended on it.

Still, he didn't have to be a sitting duck.

Drawing upon the salt spray and his familiarity with Tolaria, Riand summoned wings and an updraft to rise toward firmer ground. He vaulted upward only to find himself battling the wind and spray of crashing waves. All of it was the dragon.

Regaining his bearings, Riand recognized the dragon's opening feint for what it was—an illusion! Tapping his knowledge of Benalish plains, Riand reached out and dispelled each of the dragon's illusions, hoping to uncover his true tormentor. He learned too late.

A pair of wings snapped at him from above. The first wingtip stunned him, shredding one of his newly conjured wings. Though his mind numbly registered the dragon's location, the second wing knocked him clear of the cliff. His magics failed to slow his fall. He managed only to turn over in time to see the jagged rocks of the shoals that heralded his death.

Riand's last thought, as his bones shattered against the rocks, was simply, "I should have been a baker, as Mother wanted. . . ."

Even in death, magic swirled around Riand. His body dissolved into a mass of glistening blue mana. The shimmering magic reformed on the cliff side once again.

With no recollection of his erstwhile death, the young mage made yet another attempt to pass Jhoira's Cove.

*   *   *   *   *

Maraavis glared coldly as her enchantments took firm hold of the young man on the cliff edge. He stood entranced, enclosed in an auric egg of shimmering blue mana. His eyes were seeing and yet blind. His limbs were feeling and yet numb.

Maraavis sat back on her haunches on a hillock above

him, manipulating the final strands of mana into a cocoon around the murderer. The sun beat strongly on her wings and back, but she felt no warmth.

She grew colder still as Urza stepped out of thin air next to her, unwanted but not unexpected.

"I let you have him solely in restitution for the lives he took from your merfolk. While I hope he survives your punishment, his usefulness may be at an end, save as a cautionary tale. I confess surprise again at another skillful and new enchantment. I've not seen its like before . . . and so little surprises me. What does he see? His horror, fear, and desperation are palpable." Urza stared down at her work. His face betrayed no emotion other than curiosity, a visage nearly as impassive as the dragon's own.

"Damn you, Urza Planeswalker! Had I the power, I would strike you—the truer villain—down with far greater cruelty than what I do to this stripling!" Maraavis hissed, harsh on her briny breath. "He exists in death's riptide for the next thousand of your days. He may likely survive this ordeal physically, though his soul could shatter before long. He endures countless deaths in his mind, no less than a hundred deaths for each merman and a thousand for the life of my child. To his credit, he recognizes some of the tactics within the feint to be illusions, but he suspects not at all that he entered an illusory world as soon as he stepped onto the path within that cove. And that is how he shall live and die until my punishment releases him."

Maraavis drew herself up to full height, spreading her now-whole wings before Urza. "You've a soul more callous than the worst of dragons, Urza. You obviously care very little for others' lives, whether my kin or your own. You are the one truly responsible for the death of my child and those of my merfolk children as well. The Cosiman Merfolk need—nay, demand—a Protector. You must swear to provide them defenders numbered seven seven's worth—the number of human life spans a dragon's life covers—to equal the protection of a dragon born to be a goddess." Her honor and that of her forever-unborn child demanded this stance, one of great risk against the powerful planeswalker.

The robed human nodded in assent. "Granted, noble Maraavis of the Cosiman." Urza replied almost curtly, as if this whole incident were wasting his time. While his face remained impassive, his eyes shone with sincere resolve. "In addition, give me a mark in your script—one that would have been your daughter's name. It is a simple matter to manipulate the genetic matrices to set a recurrent tattoo onto the skin of my Metathran creations, and I wish them to pay tribute to her. I vow the warriors we create from your child's sacrifice shall always bear her name with honor. I thank you for prudence and understanding, and I beg forgiveness for your sorrow."

The dragon glared and ground her teeth in an attempt to avoid screaming at her tormentor. Sorrow? He knew nothing of her sorrow. Still, through Riand's and Urza's minds, she had seen that their work was necessary. She resigned herself to making her child a part of that new legacy. Forgiveness would be long in coming.

A wingtip glowed bright blue, and Maraavis drew a twisting sigil in midair. "Her name should be Toraix, and this was to be her mark of power. Make sure none who bear it ever dishonor her or dragon kind, or you shall understand the true vengeance of a flight of dragons. That, Planeswalker, is power not even you can shrug off. Heed my words, for I and others shall be watching."

Urza nodded, tracing the illusion of the sigil onto his forehead, as if to show her how prominent her daughter's memory would be worn. Then he bowed deeply, as a measure of trust and respect despite all that had passed between them.

Maraavis took immediately to the air, flying high overhead and roaring loudly in a last mournful tribute to her child. The sound drew the eyes of all the wizards of Tolaria—reminding them they toiled with powers they could little understand or control. The dragon cast an eye ground-ward again, bidding good riddance to Tolaria and its ruthless wizards.

The master, Urza, had already turned his back and walked on open air up an unseen stair to his tower.

The boy Riand remained frozen, as was his fate for now. His paralyzed form reacted not at all as Maraavis clove the waters of Jhoira's Cove and swam sadly home.

* * * * *

That is the Mourning One's tale, the Last Protector whose daughter became the progenitor of the Guardians. Roas, the young mermaid, became an old crone and mentor before their arrival, but her granddaughter received the seven times seven, tall, blue-skinned Creatures from Above. Foreign to our waters and our race, they all bore the mark of Toraix. Seven Tall Ones served each of the seven Cosiman Reefs from that time forward. They serve us still, though they have not been seen—other than in answer to invasions and great dangers—in scores of years. Still, we know they are there. Like the dragons, they remain unchanging across the ages, their faces inscrutable but their hearts linked with ours as our Protectors.

Familiar

Denise R. Graham

The crone sang the song loudly and often.

OH! Helbi was a lusty wench,
And thirsty she was, too.
She'd get up on a pub house bench,
And, OH! the things she'd do!

She thought of it fondly as *her* song. After all, she had made it up, and she was the only living creature who could bear to hear it. The dead didn't much care for it either.

The young dragon had found only one sure way to make her stop. "Tell me the story again, Mother."

Moragh glanced up from her darning. Jarod lay on a

hand-braided rug in the little cottage's main room. With firelight dancing from his pearly scales and diaphanous wings, he seemed to be made of flame, a phoenix not yet risen. "Already? But I just told it again last night!"

"Please?" Her young charge gave a soulful blink of catlike eyes. Between his powerful yet graceful claws sat a pot of hideously twisted meadowsweet. He'd been trying to coax it into a likeness of his mother, but as usual his power had eclipsed his control.

She eyed the ruined herb and teased, "Ah, so you've finished torturing that poor thing then? Good." A casual wave of her fingers brought the little plant back to its natural shape. She shook her head ruefully. "Sometimes I swear you're all spell and no craft."

His tail twitched like a damp cat's. "Maybe, but you still can't do this," he challenged, blowing twin smoke rings from his nostrils.

The old woman sighed and smiled. "All right, Jarod. Fair enough. Off to bed with you, and I'll tell the story." Her ancient rocker creaked in protest as she rose to stir the cauldron of oils and extracts over the fire. The dragon padded over to his nest and settled in. Though he curled into a tight ball, his tail and claws jutted out at awkward angles. They'd have to build him a bigger nest, and soon. Probably not in here, though. If she widened the door again, she'd have no wall left at all.

The snap of a twig outside stopped the crone in her tracks. She strained her ears in the stillness and sniffed the summer air, but found no danger. She considered casting a small spell to enhance her senses, but didn't want to waste any of her precious elfwort.

Jarod raised his head. Their steady gazes met as they waited, alert but unalarmed. After a brief pause, the night creatures resumed their quiet symphony. It was probably just the old she-wolf out for a prowl.

"There was a great crash," Moragh began, tucking a light blanket up around his serpentine neck, "and the ground shook so hard a shelf fell off the wall. Crockery and herbs smashed all across the floor. So I ran outside to see what was happening."

"And there I was," Jarod chimed in.

"And there you were, right in the middle of my garden."

"Squashing the squashes!" he beamed.

"Squashing my squashes!" she agreed.

"But I was only an egg," he continued solemnly.

"Are you telling this story, or am I?" Moragh asked with mock sternness.

Jarod grinned sheepishly and drew a silky wing over his eyes. She smiled and smoothed it back into place.

"But you were only an egg," she went on. "Lucky for you it was such a muddy spring and my garden was so thick with plants, or you'd have been scrambled when you fell from the sky. There were so many cracks in your shell, I didn't think my strongest magic could hold it together."

"Do you really think my dragon-mother was trying to protect me from a bad dragon, like you said?" Lustrous scales rippled as he tilted his head. "Do you really think she had to drop me to save me and herself?"

"It makes sense, doesn't it? If you'd been dropped from a very high place, I couldn't have rescued you. Someone must have swooped down to give you a softer landing."

"I know it *could* have happened that way, but do you really believe it did?"

"I like to believe that, yes," the crone answered gently. "Humans don't know much about the behavior of white dragons. We see them migrate every fourteenth spring from their homelands in the north to their hatching grounds in the south, and that's about all we know for sure. They're quite a sight as they fly over the forest, I can tell you that." Across the roof's low, rough beams, her eyes traced the path of remembered dragons.

She shrugged. "Some people claim the white dragons compete for the best nests on the way to the hatching grounds. Perhaps your mother dropped you during such a battle. Or maybe she sensed you were going to hatch before the flight's end. She couldn't let you hatch in midair, could she? Or it could be that all the rain we had that season simply made your egg too slippery to hold. You could have been dropped for any number of reasons. And since we'll never know for sure, we should believe what we like."

He pondered this a moment and apparently decided this was probably the best answer he would ever get. Brightening again, he prompted, "So then what happened?"

"Well, the cracks kept getting bigger. Then I heard tapping from inside the shell. You rocked back and forth for a while, tapping away. Then you stopped. Then you started again. It seemed to take forever, but finally you did it. A chip of your shell broke away—"

"And here it is," Jarod interrupted. "My first chip." His clever claw snaked out to lift it from its place on a nearby table. Moragh had coated it with a thin, transparent lacquer to preserve it. The dragon held it to his head and grinned. It looked like a tiny hat carved of finest ivory. "I can't believe I pushed my head through a hole this small!"

"Well, your head was much smaller then, as was the rest of you." She took the chip off his head and put it back in its place. "You pushed your snout right through that little hole and hissed at me, you wicked little wyrm."

Mischief gleamed in his eyes, and he laughed. "So what did you do?" he prodded.

"I hissed right back at you, to show you who was in charge. You looked at me with those big, gold snake eyes, and you thought I was your mother. You followed me everywhere, tried to do everything I did. Just like a duckling, you were. I could hardly get my gardening done with you underfoot. When I pulled a grape from a vine, you pulled the vine from the ground. When I planted a handful of seeds, you planted my vials of potions and herbs. Took me weeks to find them all." She shot him a playful scowl. "When I cast a spell to grow the seeds into plants, your spell turned them into a small jungle. Oh, you were quite the handful. I thought I'd run mad before I got you housetrained. And your appetite! You tried to take a bite of everything you met. Until you met that porcupine. You were a bit more careful after that." She chuckled at the memory.

Rousing from her reverie, she sighed. "Ah, but you've grown so fast. Who'd have thought an old hermit like me could ever get so attached? I know it's selfish of me, but I got used to having you here. Now we need to start watching for the white dragons, though. They'll be flying right over our heads soon, and that'll be your best chance to return to them."

Jarod shifted uncomfortably at the turn in conversation. "But you're my mother! I belong here with you."

"Now, don't get yourself all upset. I don't want you to leave either, but that's the natural order of things. The young grow up and leave the nest to make a new life of their own. Besides, you need to learn to live among your own kind. I was old when you found me, and now I'm older still. Even a druidess can't live forever. When I'm gone, you'll have to

Denise R. Graham

know how to fend for yourself. Only the white dragons can teach you that. They may not accept you at first, because you're different. But your place is with them. You must accept that yourself, or you'll never convince them."

"I'm not going," he grumbled. "You always said we had to stay here, stay together to protect each other."

"Yes, because you kept flying off and getting into trouble when you were little! You're not a baby anymore." Moragh smoothed his ruffled scales. "Hush now. This is no kind of talk for bedtime. When the time comes, you'll be ready. You'll see. Everything will work out fine. Would you like me to sing you to sleep?"

"No!" Jarod shuddered at her suggestion, then quickly made an excuse to spare her feelings. "No, thank you. I think I'll sleep better if it's quiet." He yawned. "See? I'm tired already."

"All right then. Sweet dreams."

"You, too, Mother."

Moragh put out the lamp. She felt guilty for upsetting her young one, but she felt equally guilty for not addressing these things with him sooner. She should have led up to it gradually, taught him to look forward to striking out on his own. The way she'd told it made it sound like some terrible ordeal he'd have to face. Maybe it wasn't too late. Tomorrow she would start teaching him about the sense of fulfillment that came only with independence. Hadn't she herself built her whole life around it? She'd have to give him these lessons in small doses, though. He could get very stubborn when he felt she was pushing him. Yet another sign that her little dragon was growing up.

She fell into a fitful slumber. Soon it gave way to a deep, vivid dream. In it, Jarod had a family of his own. He soared with his magnificent she-mate and their beautiful hatchlings high above a vast plain. Yet something seemed wrong with

128

this vision. A shadow lurked at the edge of it, but she could not look at it. Her mind's eye filled with the thrill of her young one, hunting and happy and free.

* * * * *

Jarod watched his mother's small, shadowy figure move nimbly through the dim glow from the fire and disappear into her room. She didn't seem so old to him.

He'd never mentioned it, but he did wonder about other dragons sometimes. What they were like, how they lived, how big they grew. What she-dragons looked like. But he was in no hurry to find out. At this point, his fear was still bigger than his curiosity. With some final rustling to fit as much of himself into his nest as possible, he closed his eyes and drifted off.

He didn't know how long he had slept when a slight draft woke him. The cottage usually stayed quite cozy through the night. One eye squinted into the darkness. A strange mist drifted across the room, a light film like the traces of a fire's last breath. It resembled the trail he sometimes left after breathing flame. He sniffed the air anxiously. No, it wasn't from a fire.

A twig snapped outside. In a flash of embers on scales, Jarod rushed to the window. He peered into the forest depths, where lonely flickers of moonlight played across the ancient, huddled trunks. The night was unnaturally still, but he could see nothing out of place.

Wait.

There. A movement in the underbrush. A glimmer of moonbeam on . . . what? Something white. Though the dragon could catch only glimpses, it seemed close to his own size. The thing remained still for a moment. Then a tawny flash revealed . . . an eye! Looking at him!

As quick and silent as a phantom, Jarod squeezed through the cottage door. The gloom beneath the trees seemed complete. There was no sign of the . . . of *it*. He dared not name it until he was sure. His great heart threatened to burst in his chest. He must know for sure. A chill breeze tickled his nose with an unfamiliar smell. Was this the scent of another dragon? He had to know.

From off in the forest came a loud rustling that could only indicate the passing of something large. Jarod set off toward the noise. Here and there among the trees hung the same strange mist he'd seen in the cottage. He followed this hazy trail when the woods fell silent. It occurred to him, as he surged through dense, sinister areas he'd only flown over by day, that perhaps he should have called for his mother. A small voice inside urged him to turn back, but the ghostly vision lured him deeper into the gloom. Hadn't Moragh just told him he needed to learn to fend for himself?

The unfamiliar scent grew stronger as he moved through the thick underbrush. Whatever it was, he must be closing in on it. Now a hint of something else mingled with that fragrance, something he couldn't quite place. He slowed his pace, moving more cautiously. Too late, he recognized the other element, not a scent but a sense. The sense of danger.

The silence exploded with a whirring rasp, followed by a harsh snap. A thin band of pain bit into Jarod's neck, pulling him up short. He thrashed, trying to break his captor's grasp, but succeeded only in tightening its hold. With a sizzling hum, a flash of light threw the black woods into stark relief. Searing agony tore through every shred of him. The only smell now was of his own burning flesh.

The dragon's bellow of anguish and rage shook the towering

trees to their very roots. In the instant before darkness descended again, he glimpsed a figure silhouetted against the forest. Not the vision that had lured him here, no. This form appeared human, and it pushed toward him instead of away. The jolt of pain released him almost as suddenly as it had taken hold, and he collapsed gratefully to the cool soil, momentarily blinded in the returning night.

"Get up," a deep voice barked.

Dazed, Jarod turned his sightless eyes toward the sound. He drew in air to breathe fire at his assailant.

"Obey!" the voice shouted, and a fresh blaze of pain shot through him. The flame died in his throat. His limbs twitched, and his body convulsed with the fury of the onslaught. When at last the torment stopped, the voice repeated, "Get up!"

Desperately he lurched to his feet. "What's happening? Who are you?"

"I'm your new master," boasted the voice. "You will do as I say or be punished."

Jarod focused on the dim outline of his attacker as his eyes recovered. "Punished?"

"Punished, you simple beast. Like this." Another burst of pain drove him to his knees. "Understand?"

This assault lasted only a moment, just long enough to get the point across.

"Yes!" the dragon hissed. "Wh-what do you want?"

The creature laughed. A lamp at its feet flared, and Jarod saw as it straightened that it was not a human after all. Other than his mother and himself, he had seen only the residents of the forest, but Moragh had told him stories of folk from other regions. This one, with its gills and powerful torso, must be one of the merfolk.

"Why, everything, of course." The merman untied the slender tether from the tree trunk where it was anchored and took up the slack as he walked warily toward his quarry. "And you will be my means to that end."

One razor-sharp claw slashed viciously at the merman. Before it connected, however, it spasmed wildly, pain surging through it.

"No-no," the creature taunted, giving his best impression of a nagging fishwife. "Bad dragon. You mustn't harm Vaerix." He continued in a more serious tone, "You see, I make my current magic flow through you when you displease me."

"Current magic? What is that?" Jarod asked, hoping to buy some time to plan his escape.

"It is much like any other magic, only it sings with the currents. The currents of the seas, the currents of the lightning, the currents of the winds, the currents of the flashing eels that light the sunless depths. They're all related. I find it superior to the old magic, although my dragon illusion worked well enough on you, didn't it? Not to mention the magic I used on the old woman to make sure she did not interfere." He chuckled.

"What have you done to my mother?" the dragon cried.

"I might tell you one day," he drawled, "if you're a good dragon."

Jarod resisted the urge to attack him again. For the moment, he was at the fiend's mercy. As soon as an opportunity presented itself, however, the mage would regret this moment.

"But what am I saying?" Vaerix continued. "Of course you'll be good. You'll be splendid! I came here hoping to capture any old dragon that happened to pass this way. I'd have settled for one that was sick or injured. But when I found you living with the druidess, I knew you would fit my needs perfectly. It's an omen, I tell you. This proves that my plans are destined to succeed, just as the lightning that struck me proved that I was chosen for greatness. And you, lucky dragon, have the honor of aiding me on this quest. Let us be on our way." He picked up the lamp.

"But it's nighttime!" the dragon protested. "I haven't had any sleep."

"You should have slept during the day, as I did. Failure to prepare results only in failure." The merman started off into the trees, heading farther from the cottage.

The line between them tightened as Jarod hung back. "But I had no way of knowing—"

The mage held out his hand toward Jarod, and another flash of pain wracked his body. His teeth clenched together in a horrible grimace that failed to contain his outcries. When the current magic released him at last, he lay gasping and helpless.

"I will explain it for you one last time. I give orders. You obey. No discussion. Is that clear?" The merman lifted a hand menacingly. "Or do you need another demonstration?"

"No!" the dragon panted. "Please, no more!"

"Then come."

Vaerix led him for what seemed like hours until they reached a narrow road cutting through the forest. A short distance ahead, a large, enclosed wagon waited at the edge of the path. A scruffy mare dozed beside it, moonlight picking out her protruding ribs.

Jarod wondered why a mage of Vaerix's power would travel by such modest means. Surely the profit the merman could make with his magic would more than pay for a fine carriage and a whole team of horses. Instead that poor little mare, which clearly wasn't getting enough to eat, had to pull that big, rickety load by herself. At the moment, he envied her the rest she was getting. He could hardly wait to join her.

Suddenly it occurred to him that this whole misadventure could end for him and the mare quite soon. They weren't the only ones who needed rest. Vaerix would have to sleep sometime. Without the accursed current magic to stop him, removing the tethers around their necks would be a small matter indeed. He would flee and take the horse back to the cottage, where his mother would take good care of them both.

"At last we can begin!" Vaerix exclaimed.

"Begin what?" Jarod asked. He flinched, realizing too late that this simple question could get him punished, but his so-called master seemed in a talkative mood again.

"My journey to greatness, you fool! Did you comprehend nothing I've told you?"

Any response seemed guaranteed to provoke his captor, whose quicksilver moods eluded Jarod. He decided merely to hang his head and hoped his silence would give no offense.

"With you pulling the wagon, we'll reach the cradle of my new empire in two days' time. Then I can begin my rise to power." He looked over his shoulder at the trailing dragon. His eyes gleamed with the reverence of a zealot's. "No more hiding. No more pretending to be a mere peasant. All my plans and preparations can finally unfold into glorious reality! Oh, it's been months in the making, but soon I will reap the rewards of all my efforts. Do you have any idea how long it took me just to create a cage that could hold you?"

"A cage?" Jarod's heart sank.

"A very special cage," the merman enthused. "Current magic flows through it and into anything that touches it. The beauty of it is that it not only keeps you in, it keeps others out, so no one can steal you. The current starts and stops at my bidding, so the cage can be hauled in the wagon when we travel. Now, let's get you hitched up and be on our way. No time to waste."

They had reached the wagon, and Vaerix hung the lamp next to the driver's seat. He looped the coiled tether like a sash over his shoulder to free his hands. Humming tunelessly, he set about adjusting the cart's traces to fit his new beast of burden.

"We're leaving tonight?" Panic rose in the pit of the dragon's stomach. If they traveled too far, his mother would not find them in the morning. He had remained calm until now, relying on her to rescue him if he couldn't escape on his own. She could easily follow their trail in the forest, but once they left it, how would she ever find him? Worse, what if Moragh needed *him* to rescue *her*? He still did not know what Vaerix had done to her, and the mage's mad plan was taking him ever farther from her.

Well, Jarod wouldn't go without a fight. Vaerix bent to his task, completely absorbed, his back to his prisoner. As silent as a stalking panther, Jarod turned ever so slightly. His tail lashed out with deadly force, hurling his enemy like a clump of dirt against the front of the wagon. The mare whinnied fearfully at the sudden uproar. With a desperate thrust of haunches and wings, the dragon shot into the night sky.

Before he had even cleared the treetops, pain filled his very being. The tether tied to his neck had not pulled free of Vaerix as he had expected. Instead it had gotten tangled around the merman, binding him to Jarod. They dropped like deadwood. The dragon received far worse injuries for his longer fall, and he sprawled on the roadside, momentarily stunned.

Vaerix struggled to his feet, swearing expansively. He sent a rapid succession of bolts searing through Jarod, each blast punctuated by a nastier expletive.

"Stop wasting valuable time! You *will* do as I command!"

His words disintegrated into meaningless shrieks as the intensity of Jarod's suffering seared all coherent thought from his mind. His eyes rolled back into his head, and the smell of sulfur filled his nostrils. He did not know how much time passed until at last his senses began to return. The first real sensation he registered was of a burning light in his eye.

Vaerix leaned over him with the lamp, forcing his eyelid open. He let it fall shut when the dragon flinched.

"So you're alive. Good. I'd have been very cross if you'd died. But make no mistake. I will kill you if necessary to keep you from escaping. There are other dragons, you know. You were just the most convenient. If you continue to cause difficulties, I will replace you."

Jarod decided then that he would rather die than let this madman use him in his monstrous quest. He did not know whether he could move, but he did not feel inclined to try just then.

The merman hurriedly finished his work on the wagon. As he tightened a final knot in the straps, he called over his shoulder, "On your feet, dragon. It is time to go."

Jarod plodded through the night, tired and weakened, hope fading with every step. The wagon bumped torturously behind him along the rutted road, miring often in the mud. Vaerix rode alongside on the mare, never relaxing his rein on his captive. He would not let his guard down again.

Moments before dawn, Vaerix called a halt. He ordered Jarod to pull the wagon a short way into the trees, where he unharnessed him. Again looping the tether over his shoulder, the mage pulled him to the back of the wagon. There he unloaded a collapsible framework of thread-thin wires. When unfolded, two sections leaned together to form the roof of a cage, and two smaller sections hinged to the ends to become the back and the door.

When Vaerix ordered the dragon into the cage, Jarod went with no fight. He was too beaten and desperately in need of sleep. Inside, there was barely room for him to turn around. When his body and mind had recovered a bit, he would look for a way to escape.

The merman secured the flimsy door and reached a hand toward the cage. The wires crackled and glowed briefly. When they stopped, they appeared no different than before.

"Remember the currents," Vaerix said. Picking up a twig, he tossed it at the cage. A loud sizzling sound cut the air as the twig struck the wires and hung there for an instant. Then it burst into flames and fell to the ground. "I've cast a small illusion over us. If anyone comes near, they'll see nothing but forest. I expect you know what will happen to you if you call for help or try to escape." Without waiting for a reply, the mage shut himself in the wagon to sleep.

By the time Jarod opened his bleary eyes, the Glimmer Moon was glowing low behind the thick canopy of leaves. The rattling from inside the wagon told him Vaerix had already risen. He wondered what the lunatic had in store for them next and immediately began searching for some means of escape.

He formed and rejected several ideas: too risky, too slow, too impossible. When his enemy emerged at last, he still had found no way out of his waking nightmare.

The merman held the lamp in one hand and raised the other. Jarod flinched. A smile touched Vaerix's lips.

"Just releasing the currents from your cage," he said, "but I'm pleased to see you haven't forgotten your lessons." From a pouch at his waist he produced a handful of dried apples, which he tossed at his prisoner's feet. "Eat quickly or travel hungry." Again he passed his hand before the cage.

The hum and faint trace of smoke told Jarod the currents had returned to the wires. He hurriedly devoured the apples. A nice, fat boar would have suited him better after his night of hard labor, but he counted himself lucky to get even this.

"We should reach the seat of my new empire by first light," Vaerix supplied cheerfully as he saddled the horse. "After a small demonstration of your power and my control over you, I shall lay claim to the town."

Jarod wanted to delay departure as long as possible, perhaps give his mother a chance to catch up with them. He thought he might distract the mage with some questions, maybe even get him to let down his vigilance a bit.

"Your magic seems ample for any task, Master. By capturing me, you have proved your powers exceed mine. Why do you need me at all?"

"Because even simple peasants will eventually realize that my magic extends only so far. Everyone knows I can be in just one place at a time, but when I tell those simple folk that I control not only you but all white dragons, their fear will be great indeed."

"But I would never dream of harming any—"

"Ah, but they don't know that," Vaerix cut in. "That's the beauty of my plan. The fools will beg me to spare them from dragons who have no intention of attacking them!"

"No. Not if I tell them the truth."

Vaerix held up a hand in warning. "You'll tell them nothing. When I announce my conquest to the town's inhabitants, I will need to give a demonstration of my powers. You will perform like a well-trained cur. If I command it—and since you continue to defy me, I believe I shall—you will sit up, roll over, play dead. You will even kill, if I require it. And you will never breathe a word. The instant they discover you can speak their language, your miserable life will end."

Jarod's eyes narrowed, but he held his tongue. The merman had made two critical mistakes. First, he had revealed an important weakness: his beloved current magic had a limited range. Once the dragon discovered the length of the mage's reach, he could figure out how to elude it. Second, he had divulged his plans. Now Jarod would be able to find a way to thwart them or, failing that, force Vaerix to start all over again, next time without him.

Satisfied at his captive's apparent submission, the mage turned back to the business at hand. He bustled about the camp, preparing for his "journey to greatness." The ever-hungry mare had grazed to the end of her rope, which she had then managed to wrap around a tree trunk. Vaerix slogged through weeds and nettles to untangle her. This drew him farther from camp than he usually ventured.

Jarod saw his chance. Steeling himself, he called to his jailer, "Your plan is flawed, you know. It will never succeed."

"Miscreant!" the merman shrieked. He reached out, but nothing happened. Arm outstretched, he stormed toward the cage. "Do not presume to criticize my glorious plans. Ignorant beast! I will teach you to show proper respect!"

Vaerix took several strides before a bolt leapt from his hand and struck the dragon. Jarod writhed in pain. The current went on and on, reducing him to a heap of spasming flesh. When at last it stopped, tears welled in his dull eyes but did not spill. The agony could not equal his elation. He had seen what he needed. He *knew*. And best of all, Vaerix had no idea that he knew.

The mage's reach was just a few paces longer than the tether around Jarod's neck.

It took a while for the dragon to recover from his latest

"lesson." The merman's impatience grew, and with it his cruelty. He accused Jarod of stalling. He went so far as to blast his prisoner again, trying to call his bluff. Unfortunately, the dragon was not bluffing, and the added punishment incapacitated him even longer. This only further infuriated Vaerix. His reason spiraled out of control along with his temper.

In the end, the mad mage distracted himself with striking camp until Jarod recovered enough to travel. A wave of the merman's hand cut off the currents in the cage. He opened the door, tied the end of the tether around his waist, and led Jarod out. Then he collapsed the cage and packed it back into the wagon. Finally, he harnessed the dragon, and the mismatched companions set off down the road once more.

Several hours later, they stopped to eat. Curiosity finally got the better of the would-be emperor. "The notion is absurd, of course," he began with feigned nonchalance, "but why did you say my plan is flawed?"

Jarod considered carefully before answering. The only logical excuse that came to mind put him in danger of further torture. "Well, you're planning to tell the townsfolk you control all white dragons. But I've been separated from them since before I was hatched. I'm not really one of them."

To the dragon's relief, Vaerix laughed and shook his head. "Stupid animal! I know that, but the simple humanfolk do not. As long as they *believe* I have that power, they will not risk any action that might provoke its use. I won't need to prove anything. They will believe it, because I will convince them it is so." He shook his head again, chuckling and muttering under his breath about the ignorance of others.

Late that night, they reached the town, a humble cluster of buildings huddled together at the edge of a small lake.

"Behold, dragon! This is where my empire begins!"

"Here?" Dubiously, Jarod looked around. Judging from Moragh's stories, the dark collection of human trappings hardly qualified as more than a village. "This is your empire?"

"Bah!" the merman spat. "You're as blind as the rest. I'd hoped for more from a dragon. Look around! See how many trees have been damaged by lightning? How the houses are built to withstand storms? The currents flow strong here, and my power with them. I will turn this backwater burg into a seat of wondrous might and grandeur. My followers shall build my palace there." He pointed toward the lake's edge. "You see, I too have been cut off from my own kind, just as you were. My people feared my current magic. They said it was abnormal and dangerous. So they made me an outlaw. Such is the way of the world—the ordinary seek to thwart the extraordinary. But I will teach them the folly of their ways. Since they will not have me in their world, I am creating a world of my own. Once word of my wondrous new empire spreads, the merfolk will flock to me, clamoring to become my subjects. We can be reunited at last!"

"But what if they do not want to be your subjects?" Jarod asked.

"Oh, I expect to encounter some resistance at first, naturally. But those who won't come willingly shall be easy enough to compel. Eventually they will learn to accept my supremacy, just as you are learning."

The dragon averted his eyes. The choice between joining freely or being compelled to join was no choice. He did not dare suggest this to his jailer, though.

"So you see," the madman continued, "we are really just two of a kind, you and I. We have both been separated from our societies. We have both learned to transcend our native ways, and we both want to be reunited with our own kind. How fitting that we misfits should struggle together to put things right."

Jarod railed at these disturbing notions. There was another similarity: Both used magic that was unnatural for their kind. Jarod feared his green magic might one day drive him insane, as the current magic had the merman.

"Come," said the mage, interrupting Jarod's thoughts. "Let us take a closer look."

Vaerix directed the dragon down to the shore, where the woods met the water. "We'll rest here until sunrise. I want my new subjects to witness my arrival in all its splendor." Repeating the morning's procedures, he set up camp and retired to the wagon. The sounds of the merman shifting around soon stopped as he settled down to sleep.

Jarod already had his work well underway. The area was rich with weeds of all types, including the wild raspberry he wanted. He had selected a healthy little vine near one side of the cage. This runner had grown far from its original plant, and showed promise of flourishing still more.

Forming a picture in his mind, he whispered soundlessly, "Grow, my thorny green friend. Grow!"

And grow it did. It sent fresh, strong roots into the moist soil beneath one wire. As the roots took hold and spread deep into the dirt, the vine wound out along the forest floor. It stretched, growing ever stronger and longer. Its thorns thickened and hardened into living daggers. Each leaf became a verdant headsman's axe. As the plant grew, it coiled low to the ground, sprawling and spiraling, at last surrounding the wagon's door.

A fainter shade of darkness seeped slowly into the clouds in the east. The time had come.

A second vine sprouted from the main plant. This one surged upward, straight and tall, heedless of the flimsy wire structure it bore on its upper leaves. Higher it climbed, tipping the cage until the structure collapsed, hissing and spitting, on the ground beside Jarod. With a wordless roar of defiance, he burst into the predawn sky. He hung there, wings unfurled and claws outspread, etched against the heavens like doom incarnate.

From within the wagon came an answering roar, a thud, and another roar. The door flew open, and out stormed Vaerix, rubbing his head.

"What is the meaning of—" His outburst died in his throat at the sight of the terrifying form raging against the sky, the end of its tether dangling a mere stone's throw away.

The dragon's will became the vine's action. With blinding speed, it whipped around the merman's ankles, legs, and arms, ensnaring him like a hungry serpent. Its thorns pierced his skin, and its leaves drew thin lines of blood. The bonds allowed him to lift his hand only slightly, but he turned it toward his escaped prisoner. His lips curled back as he strained to blast the fugitive, but the dragon remained just beyond the range of the dread current magic.

With a thought, Jarod pulled the vine tighter. Thorns and blades bit deeper into the struggling villain.

"What did you do to Moragh?" he thundered.

"Nothing!" the mage sputtered, wild eyed.

"Liar!" the dragon bellowed. His jaw clenched, and green barbs raked Vaerix's flesh.

The merman shrieked. "Release me, infidel! I am your master! I command it!"

"You command nothing!" the dragon snarled. Luxuriant knives tore into muscle and sinew. "Tell me what you did to Moragh!"

Vaerix's screams rose to a feral crescendo. "N-nothing! I

swear it! I merely sent her a dream to keep her asleep. Go see for yourself! Ah!" His cry of agony caught in his throat as a length of vine cinched itself around his neck.

Jarod paused, torn between the need to ensure his mother's safety and the hunger to make Vaerix suffer. Moragh was more important to him than any revenge. The vines would hold his tormentor long enough for him to guarantee his mother's welfare. And, if the mage had lied, if he had harmed her in any way, he would pay with his life. The vines would keep the mage's bloodied form here to die a slow, terrible death of starvation or exposure, assuming wild beasts didn't devour him alive.

In the distance, a rumble had been building unnoticed. At last it grew too loud to ignore. It rose from among the human dwellings and sounded like a cave full of angry hornets.

Jarod's angry and triumphant bellows had alerted the townsfolk. Seeing a rampant dragon attack an unknown traveler, Vaerix's intended subjects had sounded the alarm. Now, mustering their meager defenses, they swarmed toward the beast.

Jarod was mesmerized. More humans than he had ever seen pressed toward him, brandishing axes, pitchforks, a few bows, and smaller items that appeared to be crockery. Their angry murmurs grew louder as they drew near.

"Hurry! Before it eats him!" shouted someone in the crowd.

"Put down your arms," Jarod called to reassure them. "The villain is in my grasp."

These simple folk had no experience with dragons. In their tumult, they heard only what they expected to hear: horrible roars and menacing growls. The few with bows fired at the dragon, while those with axes set to freeing the merman.

"That's right, my people!" Vaerix exulted. "Kill the monster!"

"No!" Jarod shouted. "You don't—" His explanation turned into a sharp gasp as an arrow nicked his wing. The jubilant cries this brought of the townsfolk infuriated him. They would not rob him of his revenge! Wheeling away from the mage, he swooped to take a slash at the nearest archers.

A small pot struck his flank and burst into flame.

He reared up into the air with an angry howl. Roaring his defiance and frustration, he fell on the mob again, but there were too many of them. His chest heaved as he drew a deep breath and unleashed a wall of flame upon them all.

He banked and retreated. The sun rose with him. He sailed off into the sky, never turning to glance at the battlefield. Let the fools have Vaerix, he decided. They deserved each other.

The narrow forest road fell swiftly away beneath him. He tore the tether from his neck and cast it away. His bright eyes scanned the trees for the familiar garden that marked his home. His only thoughts now were of Moragh. His thoughts, however, were soon interrupted.

The inhabitants of the town had not been the only ones to hear his war cries. A pair of white dragons, the first of this migration, soared toward him, eager to confront this strange intruder. When they caught sight of the young dragon, injured and alone and ahead of them on the flight to the hatching grounds, they let out twin roars of challenge.

Jarod hesitated, awestruck by the magnificent creatures. Their opalescent scales gleamed brilliantly in the early morning sun. Even from a distance, they were clearly much larger than he. Were these adults? Their golden eyes glinted, wild and fierce. One was male. The other, a female, held a large egg tucked tightly to her chest. As swift as the wind, they bore down on him.

Jarod's wide-eyed wonder evaporated at last as he realized they meant to attack him.

"Wait!" he called. "I'm not your enemy."

The other dragons showed no sign of comprehension.

They called to each other in a language Jarod felt he could almost understand. In moments they would be upon him.

What could he do? In his weakened condition, he'd never outpace them, and even at his best he could never hope to fight them. There was no place to hide. A thin trail of smoke told him the cottage was near, but neither Moragh's wisdom nor her magic could defend against this threat. Besides, this was not her fight.

Jarod answered their challenge with a roar of his own. It had sounded so fearsome to him once, but now, after hearing theirs, it fell thin and weak. No matter. They might have greater strength and numbers, but this was his territory. He would find a way to make his knowledge, his magic, and even his size work to his advantage. Pushing his doubts aside, he hovered, waiting.

When his rivals drew near, he plunged into the forest. The male snapped in his wake, and the female hovered above. His mind spoke to the treetops, which generously made way for him. As he passed, branches whipped together, battering the pursuing dragon and keeping him at bay. On they raced through the woods, wide avenues opening before Jarod and sturdy gates slamming on his adversary.

Darting and dodging, he led the other deeper into the forest. Fear and anger drove him, flogged him to near-madness. Yet beneath these emotions lurked an odd undercurrent of response. His recent adventures had changed him, for deep in his heart, he found this battle . . . *exhilarating*. This devilish rush of energy and emotion, this surge of exertion and sensation, this clash of wills and wits, it all felt right somehow. As if he'd been born to it.

Dappled sunlight fell on the place where he had chosen to make his stand. Carefully he settled on a rocky hillock on the far side of a small glen. Branches closed in to force the other dragon to ground. The larger male crashed through the underbrush, charging.

The path Jarod created led straight into a broad patch of poison ivy, which writhed with magical growth. The spell also accelerated and intensified the plants' toxic effects. Wicked irritant seeped between the lunging dragon's scales and into his skin. Before he could reach his quarry, his claws and tail were covered in a stinging rash. He tried to fly up out of the ivy's grasp, but the trees bowed together to block his escape. The crazed dragon dropped to his side to lick and gnaw at the merciless welts, but only succeeded in getting more of the same on his haunches. He howled and rolled in misery, spreading the affliction still further. He was thrashing helplessly, victim of his own burning, swelling pelt.

Jarod watched him a moment, repulsed. What was he doing? This was not his way; this was Vaerix's way. This was wrong.

Moragh had told him the time had come for him to join his own kind, but these dragons clearly did not want him. He could force his way among them, as Vaerix would, but that would never win their acceptance. How could he make them see he was one of them, when he didn't speak their language and they couldn't understand his?

Something Vaerix had said came back to him then. "They will believe it, because I will convince them it is so." Then Moragh's voice rang in his mind. "Your place is with them. You must accept that yourself, or you'll never convince them." Suddenly, Jarod knew what he must do.

The trees parted, allowing him to rise, and he bellowed to command the berserk dragon's attention. Jarod inhaled deeply as if to douse him in flames.

The grimace his captive turned up at him was wild with

anguish. The helpless rage in the larger dragon's eyes said it all: he was at Jarod's mercy, and he knew it.

Jarod let his breath out harmlessly. Then he reached out with his mind, and the forest released his prisoner. The large male snarled as he shrugged off the last of the ivy. Just as he prepared to launch himself at Jarod, angry screams from above snapped both their gazes upward.

Another battle unfolded in the sky, between the lead female and a second egg-bearing serpent. The larger one flapped her wings and hissed, maneuvering to block the other's path to the hatching grounds. The smaller one showed no interest in a confrontation, her entire focus bent on making her way to the hatching grounds.

Jarod realized he had inadvertently disrupted the order of the migration. That would explain why the pair had attacked him. They thought he'd stolen their rightful place at the head of the flight.

The two females faced off. The smaller dragon dived abruptly to one side, attempting to duck around the other. The lead female whirled and struck out like an adder. Her sharp teeth nipped her adversary's neck but did not penetrate the scales.

The second female spun away, feinted left, and plunged under her attacker.

The lead dragon was momentarily thrown off guard but recovered quickly. She lashed downward with her tail, swatting her opponent back. Their battle dance continued, thrust and block, feint and counter. The lead dragon relied on her superior strength, but it proved of little use against the agile newcomer. The larger female let out a shriek of fury.

Her mate sprang to her aid. Streaking into the air, he folded his wings and rammed the unsuspecting challenger. His head drove into her flank like a shot from a catapult.

The force of the blow sent her spiraling sideways, free-falling toward the ground. She thrashed frantically to right herself, her claws splayed for balance. The egg she had been carrying fell. As her precious cargo dropped toward oblivion, she cried out, a piteous keen that rent the sky.

Far below, the treetops wove themselves into a lush, green mesh. The egg hit this net at high speed, but the branches bowed gently on impact, softening the blow. Jarod plucked the egg from the makeshift cradle he'd created and soared to where the smaller female hovered, frozen in shock and disbelief.

As Jarod returned the egg to its mother, the lead female released a short roar of warning. Her rival backed away and made an odd ducking motion with her head, like a deer sipping from a pool. The larger female appeared mollified.

Her mate gazed at the net of branches below, at the rescued egg, and at the young dragon mage. He let out a low snarl.

Jarod didn't understand exactly what that snarl meant, but it seemed to indicate some sort of truce. Uncertainty fluttered over his heart like a moth over a candle's flame. He ducked his head in his best imitation of the small female's gesture.

The lead pair exchanged a brief glance. Silently they turned and resumed their flight to the hatching grounds.

A distant roar brought Jarod around with a start. More white dragons were coming their way, some alone, some in groups. His eyes met the small female's. She made a soft trilling sound in the back of her throat. He had no idea what *that* meant.

"I'll join you as soon as I can," he said. "There's something I have to do." She couldn't understand any of this, of course, but he felt he had to say something. He motioned for her to follow the lead dragons. She looked at him quizzically. Then she set out once more toward the hatching grounds.

Jarod wheeled away from her and flew faster than he'd

ever flown before. He reached the cottage in a matter of moments. Moragh, working in her garden, straightened at his approach. Her wise old eyes seemed to absorb everything at once: the battle scars, the newfound strength, the profound ache of parting. She smiled sadly and nodded.

Words formed on his lips and died. He circled the clearing once in farewell. Then he sailed off in the direction the white dragons had gone. The *other* white dragons, he corrected himself silently.

He was leaving home, and he was going home.

Part III:

Wild Dragons

Many dragons have ruled the mortal races, and many others have been ruled by them, but the most fortunate serpents live forever free.

We cannot know of most wild dragons. They dwell in remote desolation, removed from mortal eyes. Contact comes only when a mortal is truly lost, or when a dragon is.

The first two stories tell of lost mortals, adrift upon savage seas. Read of a modern mariner who lands upon a volcanic isle where dragons flock as thick as swallows. Read of an ancient mariner who wrecks upon a dragon isle growing cold with the coming Ice Age. Battling in sky and sea, the castaways seek to escape the lands of wild dragons.

The third story tells what happens when the wild dragon is the castaway, lost in a strange forest. Hurled from his home by an invasion before the invasion, the dragon is soon surrounded by wilder creatures than he—the Steel Leaf elves. . . .

Deathwings
Paul B. Thompson

Before the storm, his was an ordinary life. Born in sight of the Voda Sea, he first shipped out at ten. He learned barbering while still a boy, cutting his shipmates' tough, matted hair with a fish-spine comb and straight razor. With his barbering lessons, he learned to deal with the sailors' hurts too, sewing up cuts with red thread and a sail-maker's needle, and lancing boils with the same razor he shaved them with. When age gave him his first gray hairs, young sailors he tended came to call him "Phys," short for "physician." From that time on, he had no other name

Phys revived with sand in his mouth and water in his ears. The sun was well up, and the turbulent night had given way to a clear, hot day. He stood up, water streaming from his sodden clothes, and gazed at the placid ocean. It bore no trace of the tempest that had raged across these latitudes for three whole days. The sea had no memory. Yesterday's storm was as unknown as tomorrow's.

Of Phys's ship, Magin, there was no sign. There wasn't any jetsam on the beach or flotsam in the water. Phys had no idea where he'd washed ashore. It was a strange beach. The sand was as black as charcoal, fine and sharp. Above the high tide line there was the usual bridle of broken shells and drying seaweed. Beyond that, a steep hillside of glistening black rock rose to meet the steep, stark cone of a flat-topped mountain, the highest point on this island, if island it was. Phys knew the shape. He'd sailed enough on the Voda Sea to recognize a volcano when he saw one. This one was sleeping. A few plumes of gray smoke rose from the crater, drifting northeast with the onshore wind.

He took stock: he was alive, with no broken bones or serious wounds. His canvas shirt hung in rags, but his leather trews were intact, if thoroughly soaked. Amazingly, both rope sandals remained on his feet, and his surgeon's kit was securely lashed to his waist. Other than these few items, Phys had nothing—no food, no water, no weapons. Still, with land under his feet, he had hope. Whether island or coast unknown, where there was land there was life.

Wading out in the surf, he stripped his clothes and rinsed off the abrasive sand. The black grit would cut like ground glass, and he wouldn't have gone a mile before it ate holes in his clothes and skin. He slogged ashore, wringing out his clothing. He tied his hair back with a strip torn from his already shredded shirt and started up the beach.

It was hot. Gulls and sandpipers stalked the black strand, seeking unwary crabs and sand fleas. Phys reached the thin line of palm trees growing between high tide line and the dark fingers of hardened lava creeping down from the mountain. Scrub around the trees was tough and thorny, but he did find stonenuts on the ground. Stonenuts were large, hairy things, the size of a child's head. Inside was sweet white meat and a thin milk that was good to drink. Phys had eaten stonenut meat before; they were common trade goods in the tropical seas.

He pounded a nut open with a heavy lump of lava and greedily drank the juice. Head back and eyes shut, he heard a distant sound—a sort of trumpeting. He dropped the half-drained nut and listened hard. Nothing. Then he heard it again, three distinct notes—ta, ta, ta. It came from above. Shading his eyes, he quartered the broad blue sky.

Nothing. Nothing. There! To the north, above the rim of the smoldering crater, something circled, black against the bright sky. If a bird, it was an enormous one, with short, angular wings. Even as Phys spotted the thing, it gave voice again, ta, ta, ta. After a few more turns, the giant bird dipped below the edge of the mountain and did not reappear.

Phys cinched his rope belt a little tighter. If there were birds that size here, he'd have to watch his step. Animals didn't get that big without eating big meals—like an occasional shipwrecked mariner.

Having found food, his next task was to ascertain just where he was. By night he could sight the stars and fix his position, but by day all he could do was walk the beach and see if he was on an island or not. In thirty-two years at sea, Phys had never heard of a island of black sand, capped by a smoking volcano. Magin had been on a southeastern tack when the storm struck, and the three day ordeal drove the ship south by west, far off the usual trade route. Phys's landfall might be an island, or the tip of an unknown continent. Avoiding the thorn scrub and sharp lava beds of the upper beach, Phys kept to the high tide line and put the sun at his back. He walked for hours, and the terrain became monotonous—black sand, battered shells, stinking seaweed. The beach unrolled before him, innocent of footprints or debris.

In time the sun passed behind the frowning crater. Smoke from the volcano, cooled by the shade, drifted down the mountain. Phys got a whiff. He expected brimstone or the hard stench of molten rock. Instead, the gray plume smelled of burnt palm.

That stopped him in his tracks. Why should a volcano smell of burning wood?

Before he could solve the puzzle, a black shape flashed overhead. Close by, he heard the call of a giant bird, ta-ta! ta-ta! Instinctively ducking, he felt a rush of wind and saw two creatures sweep over him, feathered feet dangling. Phys threw himself to the ground. The birds shrieked at each other. A third appeared, and Phys scrambled to the foot of a horse palm to keep the monsters from flying up behind him.

The first two birds alighted, running down the beach until their momentum was lost. Try as he might, Phys could not see any heads on the creatures. They seemed to be all wings and feet. Wings still spread, they perched at an angle on the sand and stood still. To his surprise, from under the dark wings two humans appeared.

They were short, lithe men, scantily clad in loincloths. Their feet were shrouded in bulky feathered boots, and their heads were encased in round, brightly colored helmets. They approached Phys on either side, weapons leveled. These were strangely shaped too: long, bamboo poles topped with a flat, yellow metal disk, set edgewise in the shaft. Phys needed no demonstration to know the disks were honed sharp. On closer inspection, he saw the two men were daubed all over with light blue pigment, which rendered them nearly invisible against the daytime sky. Their boots and helmets were also stained in shades of pale blue.

Flanking him, the strangers halted. The one on his right said something in a language Phys did not recognize. From his tone, Phys well understood he was being told to make no sudden moves.

He showed his open hands. "I'm unarmed, see? My ship went down in the storm last night. I am alone," he said, keeping his voice and movements calm.

The stranger on his right answered in his own language. Phys had no idea what he said.

They stood apart for some time, uttering incomprehensible phrases at each other. The feathered men grew increasingly impatient. At last one put a wooden tube to his lips and blew on it sharply. It made the piercing ta-ta call Phys had heard before. With the flat side of their weapons, they herded him to the open beach.

They stopped a few paces away from the "birds," which Phys could see clearly for the first time. They were devices made of wood, to which were attached triangular panels of a flexible blue-gray material, like leather. A harness under this sail-like apparatus allowed the men to hang beneath the frame as they flew through the air. They were extraordinary devices, though far more primitive than the fabled airships of Tolaria.

The stranger sounded his whistle again and was answered from on high. Phys turned toward the sound and saw a large flying sail swooping at him. His escorts stood back, sharply ordering him to stand still. He watched, amazed, as the device bore down on him. Was this some weird form of execution? He steeled himself for the coming blow.

Instead of a lance in the guts, a tangle of lines enveloped him. Phys was snatched off his feet. In seconds, he was racing over the black beach, hanging from a net below the rider of the third glider. The rider shifted his controls (a pair of tillerlike levers, one in either hand), and the device shot upward, throwing Phys deeper into the net. He held on with all his strength, worried about being carried aloft. After a few moments he relaxed. He'd always been an adept mast climber, so he was not afraid of heights.

The glider spiraled upward, carried by the warm breeze off the ocean. From this height, Phys could see far out to sea. Whitecaps harrowed the green waters, and clouds piled thickly on the southern horizon, but there were no sails in sight. The craft canted to port, sweeping over the island. They were at half the height of the volcanic cone, yet the rider flew on, straight at the black mountain. Phys wondered if he intended to dash him against the stark, jagged surface, but as they neared the volcano another updraft caught the glider and lofted it over the crater rim.

Amazed before, Phys was now stricken with complete astonishment. Spread out below his dangling feet was a city, built into the rugged walls of the crater. Gardens of flowering plants and shade trees lined the crater floor, interspersed with tall, blocky structures made of black volcanic rock. Some were as tall as four stories, and hearth smoke rose from chimney holes—the same smoke he'd smelled from the beach.

Around the perimeter of the crater city were scores of flat-topped stone towers, buttressed into the wall of the volcano. These towers swarmed with activity. Thousands of people labored on some kind of construction atop the towers. Phys couldn't imagine what they were doing. The crater city hardly needed artificial defenses; the outer slopes of the mountain were a far more formidable obstacle to attackers than any man-made wall. Yet the high platforms bristled with a large number of spindly structures, apparently of timber and hides, which resembled nothing so much as temporary siege hoardings.

The glider, which had been peacefully circling, put its nose into a steep dive. Phys let out a yell as they plunged downward. The rider aimed his machine at the green sward bisecting the crater floor from east to west. He hurtled in, oblivious of his passenger's anxious cries. Just as Phys's toes started skimming the grass, the rider cut him loose. Net and all, he hit the ground and rolled. The glider zoomed upward and away.

Phys threw off the net and got to his feet. Immediately he was surrounded by more armed men, this time without feathered helmets. Though small of stature, they were well made, handsome people, with flat noses, olive skin, and hair ranging from black to chestnut. They ringed Phys with leveled spears. Towering above them, he felt like a bulky, sunburned giant.

Over the crowd of warriors, Phys spotted a party of well—dressed older men and women approaching. Unlike the guards in their skimpy loincloths, the nobles wore long robes of white or yellow cloth, as thin as gauze, belted at the waist with golden chains. Most wore fan-shaped headdresses of dyed feathers, and some carried long staffs.

Here comes the local gentry, Phys thought.

A very old man, stooped and as bald as an egg, stood out in front of the others. In simple garb with no headdress, he leaned on a tall, plain staff. He looked Phys in the eye and spoke a few interrogative sentences.

"I do not understand your tongue," Phys said. "Does anyone here speak mine?" The nobles and soldiers just stared. The old man repeated his questions word for word, more slowly. Phys shrugged and shook his head. The well-dressed folk muttered and clucked their tongues. It was obvious they considered the stranger feeble-minded, unable to understand a few simple questions.

The old man rapped his staff on the ground, silencing his garrulous colleagues. In a quavering voice replete with authority, he ordered forward a bearer burdened with an ornately carved box of green-veined alabaster. The youth held the box for the old man, arms outstretched. The leader said a few words more, and the guards drew up in a square, shoulder to shoulder—not around Phys, but around the carved stone box. Solemnly, the elderly man bowed to the box, crossing his arms until his wrists touched below his chin. Everyone else present, save the guards, imitated his genuflection.

The old man raised the heavy lid. Within the box, which was about a foot square and eight inches deep, Phys saw the gleam of bright metal. Curious, he pushed up on his toes to see over the guards and instantly found a hedge of sharp disks thrust in his face. He smiled disarmingly and resumed his former stance.

Reverently, the aged islander lowered his hands to the box. When they rose again, he held a collar of white metal, studded with dark red stones. Hinged at the back, it was closed by a heavy metal hasp. The base curved to fit the wearer's shoulders. Rings were riveted to the front and back. Except for the smooth-cut jewels, it plainly resembled a prisoner's restraint.

The old man turned and walked slowly toward Phys. The

guards parted for him. Standing before the castaway, the old man said a single syllable word.

"You're not shackling me," Phys said flatly.

The old man's brow furrowed, and he barked the same word again.

"No!"

At his nod, the guards grabbed Phys and forced him to his knees. He struggled until one of the warriors struck him across the shoulders with the shaft of his weapon. Phys grunted from the blow, and while he was distracted, the heavy metal collar slipped around his throat. The old man closed the hasp and stepped back. So did the guards.

Suddenly released, Phys hesitated, unsure what to do. He could shuck the collar off with one hand—so why hadn't the old man locked it on him?

"Arise, stranger," said his aged captor.

Phys complied before realizing he understood the old man. "You do speak my language!" he exclaimed.

"No," he said. "You now speak ours."

Phys raised a hand to the strange collar. The old man stopped him from touching it.

"How is this done?" Phys asked.

"You wear the torc of Xenporo, a sacred relic of our ancestors. It imparts knowledge of our noble tongue to those it touches."

He carefully removed the weighty collar. When Phys protested, the old man said, "Fear not. The effect lingers after the torc is taken away. So long as you remain in its sphere of influence, our language will be all you speak or understand."

He returned the strange relic to its case. The guards remained, wary of the strapping stranger.

"Who are you people?" Phys said.

"It is for us to ask the questions," said the elder. Wrinkles spread over his face as he frowned. "Time is short, and we've none to waste on idle talk. Who are you, stranger, and how did you come to our sacred shores?"

Phys saluted after the fashion of Benalish mariners and replied, "I am a mariner, called Phys, a cutter of hair and healer of wounds. Until yesterday I was on the Magin, now lost. The great storm tore our ship asunder, and all perished but myself." The assembled islanders were visibly relieved at his explanation.

"It was a mighty storm, Mariner Phys. You must be favored by your ancestors to have survived." The old man interlaced his fingers and bowed his head slightly. "This is the island of Ru-nora, and we are the people of Ru-nor. I am Zulakan, first magistrate of the people. These are the elders of the five tribes—Shinka, Kezel, Xentala, Muhish . . . " he named each elder in turn, all fifteen of them. "It is rare for a stranger to trod the shores of Ru-nora. Perhaps your coming at such a time is an omen . . . you are welcome, mariner, but I fear you will not savor your time with us."

Phys, wary but pleased by the friendly reception, said, "Why is that, my lord?"

"Every soul on this island faces imminent annihilation. Chance has placed you in our hands, and therefore you must share our fate. Come. Let us return to the temple of Xenporo the Wise. I will tell you of our plight along the way."

Zulakan led the tribal chiefs away. Startled, Phys hastened to follow. Imminent annihilation? What could the old man mean?

They crossed the wide, grass-covered avenue to a paved square, surrounded on three sides by hulking edifices of basalt. Zulakan led them to the center building, a squat spire covered in weathered bas-reliefs. Once within, as promised, he began the tale of Ru-nora, and the curse about to fall upon them all.

"In ages past," Zulakan explained, "there was a mighty land called Ithra-nan. It was ruled by a race of omnipotent wizards, whose powers were so great they rivaled the gods. After untold centuries of glory, one wizard grew restless and greedy, eager for new worlds to conquer. This ambitious sorcerer-prince, Ya-magoth, resolved to seize sole power and spread his rule into the heavens. Other wizards united against Ya-magoth and foiled his plans, but they were unable to destroy him. A truce was arranged, and Ya-magoth and his followers chose to leave Ithra-nan rather than submit to the will of his brother wizards. Ya-magoth chose a dark star in the sky as his new home and departed, leaving this curse on his foes—the elements themselves would rebel against the rule of Ithra-nan. The earth would split open and swallow them, and storms would ever after ravage the place where Ya-magoth last stood on this world.

"And so it happened. Ithra-nan was split asunder by earthquakes. Volcanoes erupted in the city streets, and the sea rolled over the verdant land, submerging it forever. Five tribes took flight in five ships—Ru-nor means 'five ships' in the language of Ithra-nan—looking for a place to settle. They sailed many days without sighting any land, till at last they came upon this solitary island. At first our ancestors feared the vast crater. They'd seen the devastation wrought in their homeland by volcanoes vomiting fiery lava. But land was land, so the colonists went ashore. They discovered the volcano was long dead, and the empty crater was ideal as a ready-made fortress.

"They named the island Ru-nora, the Land of Five Ships, and began rebuilding their lives. It was a hard, unforgiving sanctuary. The island has little fresh water, and the wind-blown sand is so erosive it cut down their early crops before they could bear fruit. Over time they adapted to life on Ru-nora, and their numbers grew.

"Then, in the eighty-eighth year of the colony, Ya-magoth's curse asserted itself. A terrible tempest arose from the southwest and lashed the island for three days. After it passed, the southern sky remained dark and heavy, and the true storm arrived three days later."

"What 'true storm'?" asked Phys. Ensconced in the dark, incensed-ridden hall of the temple of Xenporo, Phys raptly listened to Zulakan while he ate his fill of fresh fruit and smoked fish.

"The coming of the Deathwings," Zulakan said. "Terrible creatures, in untold thousands. At Ya-magoth's bidding, they threw themselves on Ru-nora, seeking to destroy the last colony of Ithra-nan. They nearly succeeded. Most of our ancestors died in the first attack. Only the wisdom of Xenporo saved them from total destruction. His torc, preserved in its case all the way from Ithra-nan, inspired the magistrate Tochicha to build kites to protect Ru-nora, next time the Deathwings came. And return they have, every century and a half since the founding of Ru-nora."

Phys had trouble with the word, "kites." Though he knew the Ru-noran language as well as any native, he had no reference for comprehending a completely new word. He was about to inquire about the mysterious kites when a runner entered the antechamber and burst past the waiting priests. In defiance of protocol, the young islander threw himself at Zulakan's feet.

"Your Wisdom," he said. "Urgent news of Tilan!"

He thrust a small green scroll at the old magistrate. It was made from a single large leaf marked with daubs of colored paint. Zulakan read it and leapt to his feet. Phys put aside his tray of food and likewise stood.

"Grave news," Zulakan said. "Our chief flyer has fallen from Teezlan tower. Death is near." He slipped the message leaf into his robe. "You pardon, Mariner Phys. I must go."

"Good sir, may I help? I am a barber-surgeon of some experience."

Zulakan hesitated only a moment. "Yes. Come."

At the door of the sanctuary a conveyance awaited. It resembled a large wheelbarrow in reverse, with long handles projecting forward. Three sturdy men stood between the poles. Zulakan climbed in the box-shaped barrow part and bade Phys sit by him. When they were seated, the bearers took hold of the poles and jogged away.

"Teezlan. Hurry," Zulakan said. The three men bobbed their heads in unison to indicate their understanding.

They rolled swiftly through the almost barren streets of the city. Phys saw gardens overgrown with neglect, rubbish piled up beneath windows, and flagstone walks drifted over with windblown sand. The Ru-nor were such diligent people Phys deduced some other task was taking all their time. He said as much to Zulakan.

"Everyone on the island labors on the kites," he said. "Nothing else matters but finishing them. If we cannot repel the Deathwings, gardens and garbage will matter little."

As they neared the crater wall, Phys saw the high stone towers rose well above all other buildings in the city. Lashed scaffolds of bamboo climbed the sides of every tower, and gangs of islanders swarmed over them, working furiously.

The flat tops of the towers were thick with the odd structures Phys had seen from the air—square structures fifty feet high, lightly framed, with bottom and top ends enclosed in some sort of dark fabric.

The runners took them to the foot of one platform where half a hundred islanders milled about in uncharacteristic idleness. Zulakan climbed out of the barrow with evident discomfort. Rheumatism, Phys thought, watching the old man's labored movements.

The crowd parted for the high magistrate, revealing a crumpled figure lying on the ground. No one had even dared to straighten the fallen flyer's limbs. When Zulakan saw Tilan lying thus, he stopped short and drew his breath in with hiss.

Anxious to help the injured man, Phys stepped around Zulakan. There was much muttering in the crowd at the sight of an outlander, but no one interfered when Phys knelt by the fallen Tilan. He loosened the surgeon's kit from his belt and unrolled it. Steel instruments gleamed.

The first thing Phys noticed about his patient was she was a woman of less than twenty-five summers. He touched her forehead and throat. Her skin was clammy, and her pulse steady but faint. Gently, he slipped his fingers around both sides of her neck and felt to see if her neck was broken. It wasn't, so he carefully lifted her head. The back of her scalp was sticky with blood. Phys let her head down and peeled back one eyelid, then the other. Both shrank when sunlight hit them, and both were the same size.

"How far did she fall?" he said, to no one in particular. No one answered, so he repeated the question more sharply.

"From the top of the scaffold," said a muscular fellow in a grimy loincloth.

Phys squinted upward. The platform was as high as the

tower, which meant Tilan had fallen a hundred feet at least. By rights the woman should be dead after a fall like that.

As if reading his mind, a teenage boy added, "She fell through the scaffold, like this." He flopped his hand from side to side. "She didn't fall straight from the top."

Phys nodded. He probed Tilan's chest and sides, finding two broken ribs and a large bruise across her abdomen.

"I need a bucket of clean water, some rolled cloth, and a brazier of hot coals," he announced. No one reacted until Zulakan ordered the items found.

"Will she live?" he asked anxiously.

"I'll do my best," Phys said. "After I tend her, she'll need to be carried to a cool, dark place and kept there for at least twenty days."

That provoked more comments from the crowd. Zulakan said, "Are you sure, Mariner Phys? She'll be needed in two days' time."

"This woman has cracked ribs and a concussion," he replied.

"Put her to work too soon, and she'll fall again. Next time she may not be so lucky."

The supplies Phys asked for arrived in the arms of three brown-skinned boys. The water and coals were fine, but the Ru-noran idea of cloth was not. They brought a length of dry woven grass, fairly pliant but far too stiff to serve as a bandage. Phys shucked off his tattered shirt and tore it into strips.

Her head wound cleaned and dressed, Tilan was placed in the man-drawn cart and whisked away. In silence, the crowd watched her go.

Zulakan clapped his hands. "Work must resume," he said. "There's no time to mourn!"

The islanders filed back to the scaffolding. Young boys and girls clambered up the outside poles like squirrels, hanks of rope and bolts of fabric on their backs. Older men and women stood in line to climb the ladders provided. Given the primitive state of their dress, Phys was struck by the large rolls of heavy cloth the Ru-nor used for their kite building. He mentioned this to Zulakan.

"It's not cloth," the old man said. He called over a girl bearing some of the material. The bolt was as tall as she was, yet she carried it with ease. "See," said Zulakan.

Phys felt the material. It was smooth and fibrous, like leather, with a distinct grain. It stretched when he pulled it between his hands and snapped back when he stopped. It wasn't cloth but some sort of animal product.

"What is it?"

"A remnant of the Deathwings," said Zulakan. "There are caverns in the crater filled with it—an ancient nest site. Some say Deathwings shed their skin, as snakes do, and this is the result. Others believe these are the cauls of their newborn." Zulakan let the girl go on her way. "No one truly knows."

Phys offered to join the effort, and Zulakan agreed.

For the rest of the day he labored hard, carrying building materials from the crater floor to the top of the high platforms. It was hot, tiring work, and Phys's mind never stopped turning all through the sweltering afternoon. He didn't really believe Zulakan's story of lost empires, Deathwings, and the curse of Ya-magoth. Yet the people of Ru-nora were plainly terrified and worked like slaves to finish their defenses in the time they had left.

The defenses made no sense to Phys. He understood from Zulakan's description that kites were meant to fly, but these things were so large and heavy, Phys couldn't imagine them skimming through the air like the Ru-noran gliders.

The raw materials Phys handled were strange, too. Besides the tough, elastic fabric, painstakingly collected from caves and sewed into long rolls, there were silver-white tubes of various lengths and diameters. The Ru-nor used them for the framing of the kites. These were hollow and very strong. At first Phys took them for metal, but they more resembled porcelain. The tubes were incredibly hard and inflexible, and Phys wondered where the islanders got them.

There were twenty-two kites on Teezlan tower, where Phys worked. Though each kite was fifty feet high and twenty feet on each of its four sides, the completed devices weighed only a few hundredweight. Phys saw eight Ru-nor pick up a finished kite and shift it to one side. Once in place, they anchored it to the tower top with heavy ropes tied to ancient bronze rings set in the stone.

His fellow workers labored on relentlessly, seldom pausing or resting. By sunset Phys was staggering with fatigue. The islanders stopped working when it became too dark to see. Everyone dropped where they stood, and teams of children appeared with supper—fish stew served in stonenut bowls.

Torches flickered in the dark streets of the city below. Phys sat, aching back against a bamboo post, and watched the blazing brands come closer and closer. Aged Ru-nor, too old or too crooked of limb to work on the kites, came bearing a torch in either hand. They formed rings around each platform and stood as human sconces, looking on silently as supper was dispatched. Children gathered the bowls, and work resumed.

After his forty-ninth trip to the ground, Phys rebelled. He threw off his back-sack and made for the city. Islanders stared, branding him a shirker with their eyes, but he didn't care. His hands and feet were blistered from climbing all day, and his back protested eloquently with every jarring step. Maybe these fanatical islanders could work without respite, but he needed a few hours' sleep.

He also wanted to inquire after the woman Tilan. He got directions to her home from one of the elderly torchbearers, who refused to lend him a light. It was intensely dark at the bottom of the crater at night, and he stumbled along, trying to distinguish one set of black shadows from another. A few stubbed toes later, he found himself at her modest house. Soft yellow light filtered through the screened windows. The door was a simple hanging mat of woven grass.

Phys said loudly, "Hello? Hello? It's Phys, the mariner. May I come in?"

"Enter," said a muffled voice.

He parted the hanging curtain and stepped through. The house was a single room, simply furnished with stools of soft palm wood, wicker baskets, and a stone table. A small, smoky flame burned in a bowl of volcanic rock. The lamp sat on the table, highlighting the face of Zulakan. Beyond him was a low bed made of rope strung across a driftwood frame. Someone was lying on the bed.

"Welcome, Mariner Phys," said the magistrate.

"Greetings to you, Zulakan." Wearily, Phys sat. "I did not expect to find you here."

"I should not be. There is so much to do." He turned to the figure in the bed. "I had to see how young Tilan was faring."

Phys sat by her bedside. He felt for the pulse in her throat.

Tilan opened her eyes.

"Who're you?" she said thickly.

"A healer," Zulakan said. "He treated you after your fall."

"You're not of the Ru-nor."

"I come from across the sea," Phys said gently. He probed the gash on her skull. Wincing, Tilan tried to evade his touch. Phys pulled her hands away. "My ship was lost in the tempest, and I washed up on the shore of your island."

She bade the magistrate bring the lamp closer. Tilan took the heavy stone bowl in both hands and held it near Phys's face.

"You're very ugly. Your nose is big. Are all your people so oddly colored?"

Phys burst out laughing. "Among my own, I'm considered very ordinary." Phys asked the old man, "Does she always speak so bluntly?" Zulakan nodded ruefully. "Then her candor is not a symptom of an injured brain."

He performed a few more tests to see if Tilan was mending, and found no problems other than deep soreness and a headache.

Zulakan offered him accommodation at his own house, situated behind the temple of Xenporo. Phys accepted, and after giving Tilan's face an affectionate pat, Zulakan led him out.

In the dark street Phys said, "She is your granddaughter?"

The old man's footfalls were light, almost nonexistent. "No."

"I'm right in thinking she's some kin of yours?"

"She is."

They walked on unspeaking. Phys's sandals crunched loudly in the cinder gravel.

"I am very old," Zulakan said, breaking the silence. "Access to the relics of Ithra-nan has prolonged my life well past a natural span." Phys listened closely. "I've forgotten how many generations exist between us, but Tilan is the last of my line. I hoped to see her married by now, but she's very outspoken and scares off her suitors."

They arrived at the rear of the dark mound of the temple. Zulakan's house was a modest structure grafted on the back of the sanctuary. Each man drank a cup of fresh water and retired to rope beds on either side of the room.

Gazing into the shadows, Phys said, "I have no children, no wife. Serving at sea, I was never on land long enough to accomplish those things." He let out a breath, composed his thoughts, and added, "As I may be here a long time, perhaps I can find a way 'round Tilan's sharp tongue. With your permission, of course, wise Zulakan."

He could feel the old man's eyes on him. "If we live, you may try," was the stark answer.

* * * * *

Day dawned cool and gray, a fact that troubled Zulakan deeply. The sky was the color of slate, and the southern horizon was tinged as blue as lapis lazuli. A chill breeze circled the crater, stirring dust into tiny whirlwinds. Seeing them bothered Phys. Sailors regarded dust devils as bad omens.

"They're coming," the old man said. "Their numbers are blotting out the sun! Tomorrow they will be here!"

The sky was certainly in an unnatural state. Phys, naked to the waist like most Ru-nor, shivered slightly. "How do you know their coming so closely? By magic?"

"I have seen it twice before," Zulakan said distantly.

Phys blinked. The Deathwings swarm came once every hundred fifty years. If Zulakan remembered two attacks, it meant he was over three hundred years old. . . .

Paul B. Thompson

Fear was abroad in the city. Elderly Ru-nor, last night's torchbearers, congregated in the streets, speaking in terror-drenched whispers. They thronged around Zulakan, begging him for reassurance. He offered such words, but Phys could tell he was mouthing platitudes he did not really believe.

Near the crater wall they found further signs of panic. In the dirt lay lines of islanders with bloodied heads and fractured limbs. Working through the night without respite, exhausted men and women had fallen prey to accidents. Local healers moved among them, administering palliative potions. Phys was shocked by the lack of splints and clean bandages. He remonstrated the venerable magistrate about his people's care, and the old man agreed.

"We have forgotten many of the healing arts of our ancestors," Zulakan said, surveying the pain-filled scene.

Phys set about organizing a field hospital. Islanders were not eager to take orders from an outsider, but due to Zulakan's authority, they grudgingly did as they were told. Under lowering skies and occasional showers of icy rain, Phys splinted a hundred limbs before noon. He had to use rope and palm wood, but it was better than nothing. Once bandaged, the islanders hobbled back to work. Phys protested, saying the injured should be allowed to rest.

"All must work," Zulakan said gravely. "Today even I will climb a scaffold and lash frames." And he did, despite his great age and infirm limbs.

Newly injured (or reinjured) workers kept coming in all day. At times the press was so great Phys was standing in a sea of bleeding, broken humanity, reaching out to him with anguished hands. There was no art, no skill to deal with pain on this scale. Phys coped by focusing on the next broken arm, the next gashed leg.

The wind increased. Leaves and dust swirled about; palm-frond sheds collapsed; door and window mats tore loose and sailed away. Light streaming down from breaks in the rolling clouds was oddly tinged in unnatural shades of blue.

Phys lost track of time. Daylight did not change as on a normal day, and the endless parade of injured people filled his every moment. He had no idea how long Tilan had been watching him until she hobbled over and spoke to him.

"You're the outlander who came to my house last night," she said.

"Yes. Will you stand aside? I'm very busy—"

"I can see that. A lot of busted heads, yes?"

"Heads and everything else. Stand back, please, I need to get to the next person."

Tilan shifted, one hand clutching her side. "My ribs hurt," she said.

"Two of them are broken," he replied tersely.

"Can you heal them? It's important."

"So is every wound and fracture here!" Tilan and Phys were both taken aback by the vehemence of his response. He softened his tone and added, "I can wrap your ribs if they're bothering you."

She insisted, so he got a roll of gauze and told her to sit. Gauze was the closest thing the Ru-nor had to real cloth. Normally reserved for elders and priests, it was made by soaking the leaves of certain local trees in seawater for many days. The green matter of the leaves dissolved, leaving a soft, fibrous membrane behind.

Tilan sat patiently, her back straight. Long black hair hung down in two locks on either side of her face. Her skin was smooth and uniformly brown everywhere he could see. When Phys asked her to hold her bodice out of the way so he could get to her ribs, she took it off completely. Phys bit his lip. Tilan was a fine looking woman. Remembering his training, he tried not to notice too much.

"Inhale," he said. Tilan drew in a breath, paling from the effort. Phys wrapped the gauze tightly around her ribcage several times and tied the ends. "That's it."

"It is? I could have done that!"

"Perhaps, but I've done all I can," he said.

Tilan stood up and worked her arms back and forth. "Ai, it still hurts," she complained.

"And so it will. I've strengthened your ribs to resist movement, but there's nothing else I can do. If the pain is bad, one of your local healers may have a potion—"

Tilan put on her woven grass top. "I want none of their putrid draughts! My head must be clear. Tomorrow I do battle with the Deathwings."

Phys said, "You're in no shape to fight!"

"I must," she said. "I am the chief flyer. My kite will rise first and guide the others into the air." He started to argue, but she silenced him with an upraised hand. "Save your words. Nothing short of death will keep my from flying tomorrow."

The groans of the injured grew too loud to ignore. Phys resumed his splinting and bandaging, but kept glancing at Tilan as she limped away.

* * * * *

Thunder rolled, echoing through the vast crater. Phys awoke with a start. He was alone. Last night he'd fallen asleep surrounded by a thousand injured islanders. Not one remained. The scaffolds were empty too. Dazed, he ran to the foot of Teezlan tower. The clouds were ripping by at astonishing speed, illuminated now and again by fresh bolts of lightning. The pallid light in the crater might be dawn or the continuing aurora of the Deathwings' storm.

People were moving atop the platform. Phys saw similar movement on the other towers. There were islanders on each platform, clad in feather cloaks like the one hanging around his shoulders. He hurriedly climbed the bamboo framework.

When he reached the top, he saw two score Ru-nor marshaled and waiting. They wore feathered helmets and capes, and each stood at attention with a brace of long spears in each hand. The weapons were made of the same hard tubing as the kite frames, tipped with wickedly serrated heads of similar material.

He spotted Zulakan and Tilan in the crowd. The old man was girded for battle like the others, but the weapons and gear weighed him down. He leaned heavily on his spears, his brown face pale. Injured or not, Tilan looked splendid in her flying gear. Seeing the aged man beside her, Phys made a decision he'd been wrestling with since last night.

"Mariner, why are you here?" asked Zulakan.

"To take your place," he said. "Let me fight with Tilan."

"This is not your battle!" she shouted above the surging wind.

"I'm in the same danger as everyone else. Let me go in your place, Zulakan. You're too old for war and too valuable to the people of Ru-nora to risk your life fighting."

"Mind your own business, outlander. Zulakan has pledged to fight beside me," Tilan said.

"Tilan, wait." Zulakan removed his feathered helmet. "He's right," he said. He gave the soft, round headgear to Phys. "I am too old to ride the wind. I would gladly die fighting for Ru-nora or for you, Tilan, but our cause and your life needs a stronger partner."

"He is not one of us!" Tilan protested.

"He's a strong and brave man," Zulakan countered. "Alone among all his crew, he survived the tempest and gained our shore. I believe he was destined to do so. He may go. It is my order."

The wind shifted, striking the creaking kites from a different angle. All twenty-two lifted, pulling against the straps holding them down.

Zulakan stared at the tormented sky. "The time is right, good child. May the ancestors bless you!"

Tilan threw her arms around the old man's neck. In deference to her ribs he did not embrace her but caressed her face with a dry, spotted hand.

"Farewell, Wisdom! I shall return with blood on my spears!" she said.

She strode to the kite at the center of the platform. It was more elaborate than the others, with birdlike appendages attached to the four corners of the frame.

Phys clasped Zulakan's hands. "Take care of her," the old man said.

"I will."

"Come on, outlander! Move those long legs!"

Phys ran to the kite. Tilan was standing in a kind of bamboo cage in the center of the kite, suspended by struts and ropes. She shoved her spears into a wicker sleeve and began working with the complicated lines inside the kite. Phys climbed in. The wind was kicking up, and all the kites were hopping and tugging at their anchors.

"What do I do?" he said.

"Stand back and try not fall out!" Tilan replied.

Tilan shouted something and yanked a thick cord. It whipped free, and with a neck snapping jerk, the kite lifted off straight up, leaving Phys's stomach behind on Teezlan tower. Despite himself, Phys yelled and gripped the walls of the cage. Tilan unfastened more lines. The kite soared on, rope paying out of a compartment beneath the floor of the cage.

Up and up they went. When there was no more line, the kite snapped to a stop. Phys looked down. They were just above the rim of the crater, hundreds of feet above the platform. Here was where the wind was strongest, the very teeth of the gale.

Tilan danced back and forth, working various lines. One large cord, the thickest Phys had seen, protruded through the floor of the wicker box, making a loop. A polished stone pin as thick as Phys's forearm kept the loop in place.

The kite twisted a little but was remarkably stable in the tearing wind. Phys looked beyond the crater and saw palm trees outside the volcano bending and thrashing. Waves were piling up on the south beach, surging well above the high tide line. Out to sea, a silver-sided waterspout churned past the island. Such storms were the terror of seamen, but compared to the struggle now unfolding, it seemed like a minor diversion. Tilan did not even spare it a glance.

"Make ready," she warned.

"For what?"

Without any explanation, she kicked the stone pin through the rope loop. The thick line snapped out, leaving a sizable hole in the floor. Up shot the kite again. When the rope ran out, they were at the end of a seven-thousand-foot tether. A single strand of woven vine rope, two inches thick, held them to the ground.

Around them, other kites were soaring majestically into the tempest, starting on their right and proceeding around the rim of the crater. Tilan hastily explained a pilot kite had to be launched first, to gauge the wind. Once it was clear the first kite could stay aloft, a common anchor line was released, allowing all the other kites to rise. They were released in sequential fashion so none collided as they rose.

Before Phys's astonished eyes, several hundred kites reached the end of their lines, forming a fence completely around the volcano. In each kite, two armed riders were posted, ready for battle.

Tilan jerked a spear from the socket and attached a line from the kite frame to her waist. She ordered Phys to do likewise, and when they were secure, she opened the top of the cage and climbed out.

"Where are you going?" he called, squinting into the blasting air.

"To fight! Come! This is what you asked for!"

He chose a weapon. Before climbing out, he noticed the butt of the spear was divided into two spherical knobs. It wasn't carved that way; it was all one piece, smooth and seamless. He stared at the spear shaft. As a surgeon, he knew what it was, and by extension, what the kite frames were made of.

Bone. Very large, very hard bone.

"What are you waiting for?" Tilan said.

Cold fingers of fear closed around Phys's heart as he mounted the spindly kite frame. It wasn't the storm or the dizzying height that frightened him. It was the new knowledge burning inside his head. Only one creature could have bones this strong, this large. What Zulakan and the Ru-nor called Deathwings, the rest of the world knew by another name. Dragons. He was going to fight dragons in midair, armed with a few spears.

Tilan has taken up a position midway between the upper and lower cells of the kite, where the frame was open and she could see best. She leaned against one of the main frame members, one leg tucked under her. Her cape was tied to her wrists and ankles so as not to blow away. Phys's feather cloak whipped hard in the wind. He undid the frog and let it blow away.

"Can you see anything?" he said.

She peered directly into the stream of air. "You'll know when they come," she said. "The sky will burn when they are near."

To underscore her words, a flat arc of lightning flashed across the sky, south to north. All the hair on Phys's body prickled. A blast of hot air washed over him. The kite bucked, and he clutched at the frame instinctively. He was secretly pleased to see Tilan do likewise.

The sky darkened. Patches of wind-driven rain lashed them and then quickly passed. Lightning began to crackle from clouds to earth. The air was so charged, it made Phys's muscles twitch.

Tilan stood up, bracing one foot against the frame. She shifted her spear to an overhand grip.

"It begins."

Phys followed the line of her nose and saw only a darker than usual cloud speeding toward the island. Seconds passed, and the blue-gray mass closed rapidly. All the storm clouds boiled and churned, but this newcomer actually writhed through the air. He soon saw why. It wasn't a cloud at all, but a mass of flying creatures. Deathwings. Dragons.

Four bolts of lightning exploded in quick succession. Blinded, Phys lost his balance and fell back on the roof of the cage. His spear dropped free and snagged in the floor of the wicker box. By the time his vision cleared, the dragon swarm was upon them.

He sat up and saw Tilan jab at a sleek blue flank as it flashed by. The dragons were all shades of blue, ranging from the largest, who were deep royal blue, to the smallest, who were the color of a clear summer sky. They weren't enormous dragons. The biggest one Phys glimpsed was fifty feet from nose to tail. Most were far smaller, around twenty feet. They darted and wheeled about, narrowly avoiding kites, lines, and each other.

Tilan was fighting furiously, stabbing and raking at the iridescent blue hides. Sometimes she scored. The ivory tip of her weapon would cut a red streak down a dragon's back or belly. Phys wondered what substance could slice a dragon's hide like that. Then the answer came—dragon teeth. The Ru-nor had a wealth of dragon artifacts in the crater—skin, bones, teeth. The blue dragons must have been coming here for millennia, long before humans settled the island. But why? And why did they periodically return in such numbers? "Mariner, get up here!" Tilan screamed. "I need you!"

Shocked out of his ruminations, Phys recovered his spear and climbed the rigging. Dragons darted by in all directions. He thrust his spear at any that came near, but they always dodged before he could connect. It took a while for Phys to realize the dragons weren't actually attacking the kites or their human riders; they were milling about in a state of confused excitement.

One beast, a thirty-footer, bore down on them. Tilan saw

it coming and poised to strike. Alongside her, Phys raised his spear to his shoulder and waited. The broad reptilian head, horned with golden spikes and trailing bright blue barbels, came straight at them. At twenty yards, Phys drew back to cast. Tilan shouted, "No!" so he held his stroke. At ten yards he glanced at her for confirmation. She gazed steadily at the massive creature, unblinking.

Eight yards . . . six yards . . .

"Now!"

The blue dragon opened its mouth, showing rakish yellow teeth. It bellowed, and in the next moment, a pair of spears pierced its throat from the inside. The dragon's jaws snapped shut, splintering the spears. It rolled to its right, folding its long wings back. Blood gushed from its lips and nostrils. Down it went, to be lost among the swirling mob of its fellows.

"Hurrah!" Phys cried. "We did it!"

Grinning, Tilan clapped a hand to the back of his neck and shook him.

A stream of fire flashed through the open section of the kite. Phys and Tilan broke apart. He thought it was lightning, but when he found his feet again he saw a smallish dragon hovering off their starboard side, wings pumping. Its pupils were slitted, and its lower jaw hung down. The air stank of sulfur.

"Watch out!" Tilan cried.

The dragon extended its neck and fire gushed forth again. Phys threw an arm over his face to protect his eyes. His arm was singed, but he held on. When he lowered it again he saw the main frame and fabric of the kite was intact. Dragon breath did not burn dragon skin and bone, but the wicker cage was smoldering.

Tilan had caught the fire full on, and her feather cape was blazing. Phys tore it off her with his bare hands and let it fall. The helmet saved her face, but she was seriously burned.

Nearby, a trio of dragons directed their fiery breath in unison at a kite. Again the basic structure survived, but both Ru-nor fell from their craft, clothes aflame. Phys heard them scream all the way down.

More flames erupted in the sky as the dragons at last noticed the humans and their flimsy devices. Phys helped Tilan to the wicker cage and left her there. He got a second spear from the sleeve and returned to the rigging.

Only a few dragons were attacking. The vast majority were far too busy doing something else. Phys looked on in wonder at the spectacle unfolding before him. Had any living man ever seen such a sight?

The blue dragons were a mating swarm. They coupled on the wing, clasping each other belly to belly with their powerful legs. While some mated, others dodged and flapped in seemingly pointless maneuvers. Phys had seen seabirds' courtship, and knew they performed ritual dances to attract a partner. The blue dragons had their own ritual of flying prowess. When a male and female came together, it was because they knew their chosen mate was a strong and agile flyer.

A mating pair, locked together in aerial passion, slammed into the kite. Framing tubes flexed, and one snapped loudly. Phys was thrown from his perch. He would've died without his safety line. As it was, he ended up dangling facedown a dozen feet below the bucking kite.

He let the spear fall and tried to reach up and back to the line around his waist but couldn't bend his arm backward enough to grasp it. All around him dragons raced to and fro, hundred and hundreds of them. Had any cared, they could have snapped him off his line like a trout taking a fly. Fortunately for Phys, they were too busy with their amorous displays.

The safety line shook. For a heart-wrenching second Phys thought it was breaking. Then he felt himself being hauled slowly up. Twisting, he saw Tilan, scorched and battered, pulling him up hand over hand. With her broken ribs, the effort must have been agonizing.

"Stop," he said. "You'll puncture a lung!"

She paid him no heed. Phys weighed too much for her to lift, even if she'd been healthy. Only by using part of the frame as a fulcrum was she able to move him at all. In time, she got Phys close enough to grab a strut. He heaved himself into the cage. Tilan, gripping her side, slumped against the wicker wall. Her lips were spotted with blood.

"You fool," he said. "Can you breathe at all?"

"A little. How goes the fight?" Tilan said weakly. Phys had to put his ear near her lips to hear her.

He looked past her. Somehow the battle didn't seem as important right now. A third of the kites were down. Some were blazing wrecks on the outer slope of the volcano. Others, weakened by collisions, had been torn apart by the storm. The ground was covered with blue dragon bodies too.

"It goes well," he said, smiling. "I see lots of dragons on the ground."

"Good." She coughed, and bright blood flecked Phys's cheek.

"Listen, Tilan—how does it end? When is the battle over?"

"The sun . . . the sun will break through and drive the

dragons away. When the dragons disperse, the wind will fade."

He checked the tormented sky. The clouds were as thick as ever.

"Rest," he said. He didn't have to say it. Tilan had passed out. He gripped her wrist. Her heartbeat was rapid, fluttering. He didn't like it, but there wasn't much he could do seven thousand feet up.

A mighty blow snapped the kite up and down like a toy. There were no dragons near, but when Phys looked down, he saw a fifteen footer snarled in their anchor rope. The small dragon was bleeding badly from head, shoulders, and wings, showing far more damage than Ru-noran weapons could cause. In the rough and tumble mating flight, the small dragon no doubt met with many violent rebuffs from competitors. Unable to fly with badly damaged wings, it clung to the stout cable.

Phys flung a spear at it, piquing it on the right shoulder. Outraged, the little dragon snapped its jaws at its frail antagonist. Blood was in its eyes, and its third snap cut the rope. The small dragon plunged to earth, and the kite bearing Phys and Tilan soared away, free.

Terrified, Phys flung himself to the floor of the wicker cage. Without its anchor line, the kite bounced and spun, climbing ever higher with the full storm behind it. Other kites crashed when their lines were severed, but Tilan's pilot kite, with its winged appendages, flew like a bird. The kite ripped through the clouds, rotating madly, then popped out into bright sunshine.

The crazed twisting motion ceased. Phys opened his eyes. Below was a solid, unbroken mantle of white cloud, from horizon to horizon. For the first time since going aloft, Phys felt no wind on his cheek. The sun was gloriously bright and warm. If Tilan's lore was true, they were safe from the dragons above the clouds, as they could not bear direct sunshine. But how could they get down? There were many lines and knots in the rigging, but Phys knew nothing about them. He realized he could do nothing but ride it out and see what happened.

He stretched Tilan out and examined her. She was breathing better. A broken rib may have cut her lung, but it had not punctured it. He adjusted the bandage around her ribs and made her as comfortable as he could.

The kite sailed on. It was sensitive to his every movement, so he had to be careful not to change position too suddenly. Gradually his terror faded, and exhaustion claimed him. Phys dimly remembered seeing the sun settle in the west, ushered to sleep by a wreath of glittering stars.

Next thing he knew, warm rain was spattering his face. He looked down and saw they were only a few hundred feet above the sea. A single gray cloud floated above them, sprinkling the kite.

Tilan slept on. Phys tried to get his bearings, but the sun was the only beacon he had. The sea below was rough, and rollers appeared as the kite sank lower and lower. He stood up—carefully—and saw a coastline ahead.

"Tilan! Tilan, wake up!" She groaned and turned her face away. "Tilan, land!"

The breeze dropped, and so did the kite. It bounced up a few feet, and then sank toward the surf. An onshore gust caught them just before the trailing edge of the frame touched the water. Turning sideways, the great kite hit the sand, and rolled up and over the dunes.

Holding Tilan close to protect her, Phys tumbled around

the cage like a die in a cup. When the kite came to rest, he immediately kicked open the cage door and dropped to the sand. He left Tilan there, groggily holding her head in her hands.

Phys walked up the dune to its highest point and looked around. He knew that range of hills above the beach! This was a few miles east of Benalia City. He'd shipped out of there many times. A civilized land at last!

He ran back to Tilan. "Good news!" he shouted. "We've come down in a good place! We can get help here!"

She raised her head, brow wrinkled. Her reply meant nothing to him.

"Tilan?"

She nodded, knowing her own name. The words that followed were Ru-noran, which he no longer understood. They'd come too far from the influence of the torc of Xenporo.

Phys took her hand, and surprisingly, she let him hold it. "Hush," he said gently. "I'll learn your language, or you can learn mine. It doesn't matter. We have all the time we need."

The Fog
Tim Ryan

Someone jabbed him in the shoulder, shouting for help. When he sat up, a vulture leapt screeching into the air. He cried out, but his throat was dry and swollen, so the best he could manage was a soft hiss. Blinking salt and sand from his eyes, Agrippa the Wayfinder climbed to his feet.

As a pack of wolves will circle a lone lion, menacing the noble beast, so the dense fog undulated about Agrippa, enveloping him completely. He turned slowly but could see only a small diameter of blood-spattered sand at his feet. Blood snaked down the inside of his left arm and ran off his fingertips. Quickly he found the shoulder wound and applied pressure. Looking up, he saw no vulture, no sky. Only the pounding of the ocean's surf came from beyond, and that too surrounded him. All else was consumed by the fog.

Where are my men? My ship? he thought. He could not shout or even croak their names. He tried clapping out a battle cadence to rally them, but the only response was the roar of the waves.

Did we run aground or break apart in a storm? Why don't I know this? What has happened here? Desperately he searched his mind, but the memories remained clouded. Unable to recall the immediate past, he focused on the present. He desperately needed water, food, and protection, and knew his men would need the same. He must work inland to find these things, but which direction should he go? The fog pressed closer. He was weak, and somewhere above a vulture circled. His men would be weak, too; wandering the wrong way could cost their lives.

Agrippa looked down again and studied the imprint his body had made in the wet sand. He must have swum ashore, so his head had been pointing toward land. Dragging his feet to leave a clear trail, the Wayfinder began walking that direction, his good arm out before him.

Quickly the sand became drier. Soon afterward it ended in a rocky cliff wall. He studied what little he could see of the rock. Climbing it blindly in this fog would be suicide, even if he were well rested. Walking along its base was his only option. He turned right, keeping his wounded shoulder to the wall and freeing his good arm to protect himself. He walked slowly, climbing over anything in his path to stay within view of the cliff.

After a time, he came to a place where fresh water rolled down the cliff. Cupping his hands, he caught some and splashed it into his mouth, crying in pain as the salt there burned anew. He spat out the water and chunks of caked brine, carefully rinsed out his mouth, and wiped the crusted salt from his eyes and face. Finally able to drink small handfuls of water, he began to feel alive again.

As he cleaned his shoulder wound, Agrippa examined the cliff. The water had carved a narrow but gently sloping path into the rock. If he was careful, he could climb it and perhaps find a better water supply and some small game at its source. Agrippa finished binding his wound and started to climb. He scrambled stiffly, grabbing weeds and wedging his feet into small fissures to propel himself upward.

As he climbed, the fog gradually thinned. He glimpsed longer stretches of the slope he was on, though the beach below remained shrouded.

Agrippa began to remember. All had been well on the ship. As night fell, a shimmer of land appeared on the horizon. The winds had died at about the same time, and the sea was calm. Rather than rowing in and navigating a strange coast during the black of an ocean night, he ordered the helmsman to hold the ship's position and wake him just before dawn. Instead he had awoken on a beach.

When he reached the top of the cliff, the fog had thinned enough that Agrippa could see a long stretch of the rocky coastline. The empty beach he had stumbled blindly across was nothing more than a small shelf of sand tucked among perilous rocks. He doubted his ship would even fit on it. Somehow he had reached the only place in view where he could swim ashore safely. The magnitude of his fortune struck him, along with a wave of realization. The beach was empty. His comrades had not been so lucky.

Agrippa's knees buckled, and his forehead touched the ground.

Their names and faces, their voices and deeds passed

before his eyes on a current of anguish and sorrow. His fellow soldiers, his men, had been lost to him on a calm night as he lay sleeping. He had been afforded no chance to fight or protect them. It was not right that these brave men should die senselessly and forgotten. He must find his way home to sing of their courage and honor.

Smearing his face with mud and whispering a prayer for the fallen, Agrippa rose and marched on.

The tan rocky soil at the cliff tops was covered with wild scrub grass and dotted with shrubs. The creek flowed from a small wood, wrapped in fine tendrils of mist, at the top of a hill farther inland. If there was good hunting nearby, it would be there.

He had no bow or sword. His only weapon was a hunting knife sheathed at his belt. He drew the blade and examined it with satisfaction. It had been a gift from King Lyssius of the Isles of Argive for a service well done. It was neither ornate nor fashioned into an exotic shape. It had no velvet-lined scabbard encrusted with precious gems. Still, the knife was extremely well crafted—the metal was light yet strong and held an edge—and it was superbly balanced for throwing. The handle was wrapped tightly with good leather that had not become too worn over years of steady use. In short, it was a practical gift from one practical man to another—a sign of understanding and respect. It was everything that knife stood for that had kept Agrippa the Wayfinder in service to the king.

Agrippa had been a bold seafarer when his reputation earned him a summons to the king's court. Over the years Agrippa had become first a captain in the king's fleet and then one of his most trusted negotiators. Those early years of honor seemed somehow brighter, etched in fire. Now the days grew colder, and the wise men predicted famine. Agrippa had been sent out across the sea paths to search for fortune and to return with food.

The thought of food brought him back to the present. He sheathed the knife and strode toward the trees. The rest of the day he spent carving two fallen saplings into spears and fashioning two crude stone spearheads. Exhausted, he sat down in the shade and fell asleep.

He awoke at dusk to see the vulture drinking at the creek. As he grabbed a spear and stood, it saw him and leapt straight up, lighting on a high branch above him.

Agrippa wavered, disgusted at the thought of eating a vulture. Hunger taking over again, he drew back his arm and hurled the spear, piercing the creature's breast and knocking it to the ground.

Hastily he built a fire to cook the bird, and then ate ravenously. Afterward, he climbed the tree and passed the night in its branches.

Dawn rose weakly on a chilled breeze. Agrippa shivered but noted with satisfaction that the fog was gone and the sky was clear. Hefting his two spears and using them as walking sticks, he departed camp. Behind him the breeze stirred two long black feathers that still stuck to the carcass, half buried in the ashes of the night before.

The Wayfinder returned to the cliff and continued along its edge, eyes cast down toward the coastline. From the curve of the coast and the fact that his maps had shown no land here, he guessed that the island was fairly small. He would walk its perimeter in hopes of finding a less treacherous beach where he could build and launch a raft.

As the sun climbed the sky, the breeze was no longer cold, but the air remained cool and sharp in the manner of an autumn day. The walk loosened his muscles. He began to feel stronger and in control, but the island's coast was unyielding. It was all sheer cliffs and foam-spewed waves.

Just before the peak of day, the cliff doubled back on itself, revealing a bay protected by a broad reef. The water here shone so brightly that Agrippa had to squint and shade his eyes. Inside the bay the water was serene, and looking out toward the open sea he could see a narrow passage cut into the reef, making this an ideal place to launch a raft.

Encouraged by the site, Agrippa plunged ahead through the tangle of thorn and berry bushes that crowded the cliff edge. He mounted a rise, and the beach was revealed in one blinding golden spike of light.

Dropping his spears, he turned his head and cupped his face. Rings of red and yellow fire played behind his eyelids. Holding hands to his eyes, he waited until he could clearly see his palms before spreading his fingers slightly and looking again.

The beach shimmered and vibrated and seemed to float above the water. It was not sand but seemed to be grains of pure gold.

"By Urza's wrack!" he cried aloud. "Pari's Golden Beach is real! It's real!" With one sack of that gold sand he could honor his men with a year of funeral games and feasts. Their names would echo down the halls of time.

Agrippa had crossed the seaways to seek gold and purchase grain—purchase life itself—for his people. To have found *this* gold, though, this beach that had ruined his great-grandfather Pari's name, was a double boon.

Pari claimed to have glimpsed a beach of gold on the horizon just before a storm carried his ship away. He was an old man when it happened, and the kindest people called him senile. Others used harsher names. They had forgotten how, after the world-splitting blast, their coastal waters were thick with desperate raiders. They had forgotten how, in his prime, Pari had set out with twenty men and one ship and made safe again the Isles of Argive. When Pari died, there was a banquet, but more guests smiled secretly than mourned. Only a few of his family remained afterward to dampen the old sailor's shift with tears.

Now, bathed in the golden light of the beach, Agrippa vowed to restore his great-grandfather's name.

Suddenly Agrippa saw movement at the water's edge. He crouched in the bushes and watched as a brown seal rolled sideways in the surf. The very water seemed to transform itself into a long arm pushing the seal up onto the beach. When the arm grew front legs, though, Agrippa could see it was a dragon the color of the deep blue sea. It separated itself from the water, lifted the seal in its powerful jaws, and slithered slowly up onto the beach.

Instinctively Agrippa gripped his knife with one hand while studying the beast, trying to find a weakness. Its body was wide and muscular, ending in a long, thick tail. Two fins, vestiges of wings long gone, rose from its shoulder blades. Its legs were very short, so that it seemed to slide more than walk. Agrippa thought it probably could not rise up on its rear legs, so if he had to fight it he could not count on delivering a good jab to its heart. He would have to take a spear in each hand, blind the beast, and then kill it with multiple wounds to the head. He wasn't looking forward to a fight, but he knew he would never be able to launch a raft safely with a sea dragon nearby.

The dragon stretched out fully on the beach and snapped its jaws, swallowing half the seal and leaving half on the sand. A few moments later the rest disappeared into its mouth. The dragon had moved slowly coming out of the water. Having just eaten, it would probably be even more lethargic. As Agrippa watched, it stopped moving altogether and seemed to be sleeping in the sun. This was a good time to move closer and locate the dragon's lair.

Agrippa looked farther along the coastline and saw that the cliff he was on sloped gently downward to meet the far side of the beach. It would take him an hour to get there, but it was the only safe path in sight. Silently Agrippa crawled back from the cliff edge and walked through the woods for a few minutes, so that he would not be seen from the beach. He then turned and started down the hill.

The ground was uneven and full of loose rock, so it took him longer than he had expected to reach the bottom of the hill. He rested for a moment, checking his knife and spears. Satisfied, he moved quietly toward the spot he calculated would offer a good view of the beach and a chance to make sure the dragon was still sleeping. Crouching low, he rounded the corner of the hill and saw Pari's Golden Beach crawling with sea dragons.

Agrippa ducked back behind the hill, cursing softly, "By Mishra's blazing ruin! What have I done to deserve this?" There were perhaps fifty dragons on the beach. His mind raced, looking for a way out. He sat for a moment and then peered around the corner again, setting aside his panic to think like a captain.

He studied the writhing pack of sea dragons. Some were still, but others moved with fluid speed, much faster than he had seen the lone dragon move an hour before. As they wove in and out of each other, they snapped and pushed and clawed like feral beasts fighting over a carcass. They crowded around the section of beach directly across from the channel that cut through the coral reef.

Peering more closely, Agrippa saw that the sand was not gold, but instead was littered with gold: coins, jewelry, drinking cups, ceremonial masks, armor, and even statues. The air above the gold rippled with heat. It was here that the dragons fought. The rest of the beach was simply sand.

As the day wore on, the sea dragons settled into a motionless mass. Evening began to spread its dark cape across the sky. As if by some invisible signal, the dragons stirred and together slid farther up the beach. Agrippa cautiously rounded the corner he had been hiding behind and saw that one by one they slithered into a cave in the cliff behind the beach. The cave's mouth was wide enough to allow only one dragon through at a time and, Agrippa estimated, was tall enough to allow them to rear up if in fact they could.

"I'll not be sneaking up on them as they sleep," Agrippa said to himself, amused at the thought of stealthily working his way into the cave, stone-headed spear and knife in-hand, only to find himself amidst fifty sea dragons. His smile hardened. He hoped it would not come to that.

* * * * *

Four days later, it had come to that. Agrippa had spent the time walking the remainder of the island's coast, and he could not believe it had taken so long. Finally he arrived back at the cliffs above the beach where he had washed ashore. He spent the next day studying the surf on that beach, waiting for a low tide that never came. The waves pounded mercilessly against the jagged rocks at the beach's edge, shooting geysers of foamy green water into the air and onto the sand, as if the sea were trying to drown the island. There was only one path off the island, and it led through the dragons.

At dawn of the next day, Agrippa Wayfinder stood atop the cliffs of the golden beach. The dragons had not stirred from their cave, so he watched the sunrise. At the first touch of the sun, the beach began to glow a reddish gold, forcing Agrippa to squint. It was then that he marked the shape of a tall-masted ship, sails full of wind. His pulse quickened as he realized the ship was coming about and making speed toward the island. No doubt the crew had seen the light and realized they had found Pari's Golden Beach.

Agrippa ran down the path he had taken days before to reach the beach. A powerful swimmer, he was confident he could swim out past the reef to meet the ship if only he could reach the water before the sea dragons awoke. As he rounded the bottom of the hill, though, he saw he was too late.

The dragons were crawling out of their cave in tight formation. Above them and before them rolled a dense bank of fog. As they fanned out in the water, the fog spread with them, assuming the shape of the pack. When the last dragon touched the ocean, the fog grew heavier, completely hiding them from view.

Agrippa shuddered, realizing what had happened to his own ship and crew. He watched helplessly as the broadening fog bank rolled swiftly toward the ship. The wind no longer filled the ship's sails, leaving it to float motionless on the calm water. He imagined the crew was confused by the sudden turn in the weather: How could a fog bank move toward them so rapidly when there was no breeze?

Burning with impotent rage, Agrippa cursed the unknown captain, willing him to turn his ship about and make way. Finally, oars bristled out along the entire length of the ship and began thrashing the water. The ship strove to turn and flee the fog, but the captain's decision came too late.

The ship was swallowed in fog. Everything was still. The rowers seemed to have ceased their labor. The fog hovered for some time. Agrippa watched as the fog then drifted back toward the beach, gradually rolling faster and faster. As it passed the reef there was a booming thud and the ringing crack of splintered wood. He heard no screams from the crew or sounds of battle, only a single shout of surprise as if a merchant had offered the man far less for his corn harvest than he expected. The ocean seethed at the edges of the fog, the turquoise blue becoming a deep cloudy purple.

The first dragon surfaced on the beach, trailing wisps of fog. Clutched in its mouth was something round and shiny that it tossed up onto the sand with a flick of its neck. It quickly swam back into the fog. Another dragon surfaced, flinging what looked like a small statue and something dull and limp onto the beach. The dragon slithered up on the shore to retrieve the last item. Agrippa was horrified to see it was a human leg.

For hours the sea dragons salvaged any bits of gold that they could from the wreck, though they came out of the fog less and less frequently.

Agrippa crouched on his haunches and leaned back against the hill. He would be patient and learn everything he could about the serpents. He had started his seafaring career as a lookout and could sit calmly for longer periods of time than any man he knew. During one voyage, he had taken an eight-hour night watch in the bitter cold, while his crewmates slept below, their shivering snores tempting him to close his eyes for just a moment. . . .

An enormous mouth burst through the fog and was closing about his head when Agrippa thrust the spear upward with his entire body, splitting the bottom of its jaw. He pushed the spear point up through the roof of its mouth, splintering the spear's shaft with a loud crack.

Bellowing in pain, the dragon whipped its head back and forth.

Agrippa struggled to hold fast with one hand to the remnants of the spear shaft. In an instant, the knife was in his other hand carving open the dragon's throat. Its life fled in steaming gouts of blood that darkened the sand at his feet.

As the monster sagged to the ground, Agrippa found himself backed against the hill and surrounded by fog. His second spear was gone, and somewhere beyond the twitching head in front of him were another fifty sea dragons.

Agrippa turned and made a mad scramble up the hill, trying to remember the lay of the land and struggling to get above the shroud of fog.

As in a nightmare, dark and primitive, a man will suddenly find himself on hand and knee, pursued by a shadowy thing, grasping at clumps of grass, tearing handfuls of soil in an attempt to escape, so Agrippa struggled blindly up the hill. Each stone his hand fell upon became a hard talon, each eddy in the fog the precursor to an attack. After hours that were minutes, he clawed his way out of the fog into the clear air of the cliff top.

Looking back, he could see dragons swimming in from the reef, but the beach was hidden from view. Agrippa turned and ran inland as hard as he could.

Only when he reached his camp, heaving from exertion,

did he stop to consider what had happened. Somehow the fog had crept over the beach and surrounded him, and he hadn't even noticed. It had dimmed his senses and clouded his mind.

Shaken, Agrippa spent the day fashioning two more spears and keeping a watchful eye on the horizon for fog and serpents. The day wore on, and he hoped he was safe, for it was past the time when the dragons returned to their cave.

As Agrippa turned a third sapling in the fire to harden it, they came. Four blurry blue shapes, low on the horizon, converged on his camp from several directions.

He glanced down at his feet: two ready spears and one shaft in the fire. It wouldn't be enough. Briefly he considered climbing a tree to get out of their reach, but the dragons could simply wait him out. So he grasped one spear in each hand, laid the third shaft at his feet, and put his back to a large tree.

The dragons approached, wisps of fog hanging about them. As they drew nearer him and nearer each other, the fog thickened but not enough to obscure his view. They moved slowly now, even stiffly. When they reached the circle of firelight, he could tell something was amiss. They were not attacking. Instead only one crawled forward. It stopped short to lie down in front of the fire, curling as much of its body around it as possible. The others watched Agrippa with small blue eyes but came no closer.

Fire reflected in rainbows off the blue scaly serpent, and it moved more smoothly and quickly, becoming almost liquid. The dragon snaked its snout into the fire, as if to snatch a burning log, but recoiled with a grating hiss. It tried again, whipping back in pain and frustration.

Seeing this, Agrippa knew he had found his way out.

The dragons needed intense heat probably as much as they needed food. The golden beach flashed through his mind: That's why the dragons fought over the choice spots on the beach—the gold became hot in the sun and reflected the suns rays, doubling, tripling their strength. Just as cold turned seas to ice, it would do the same to sea dragons.

If these monsters need heat, Agrippa thought to himself, I will give them fires to warm their nights. It will keep me near the gold my people need and the beach I need for escape.

Moving slowly, Agrippa bent down and set his spears on the ground. Then, arms open, he approached the fire and grabbed two logs by their unburned ends, holding them aloft like torches. The blue eyes bore through him. Looking steadily into the eyes of the dragon nearest him, Agrippa upended both the logs and dashed them to the ground, grinding out the last living embers.

The dragons bellowed angrily and closed around him.

Agrippa reached into the fire and pulled out the last two burning logs and held them aloft. The dragons responded quickly by forming a tight circle around him, cutting off any chance he might have to dash out the flames. They circled him tighter and tighter until their smooth scales were brushing his legs and waist. Then they shifted their movement, and Agrippa allowed them to push and prod him toward their cave.

The sea serpents followed his every motion. They seemed to be straining against their instinct to gather warmth from him by simply tearing his body apart and eating it.

His estimation of the cave's mouth had been close. Its height was twice his own, and its width a little less so. Stepping inside, he waved the torches and saw the cave immediately grew taller and wider as it sank into the ground. He could not see the back wall. The interior dripped with the dank stench of animal refuse. The rotted remains of trees and animals, compressed for years by the soil, dripped from the cave's ceiling in yellow and green clumps.

As Agrippa stepped farther in, the dragons shifted, leaving a bare expanse of cave floor. Here, he set down the two logs, one propped against the other, and fanned the embers to flames. As he withdrew, the dragons surged slightly forward. He retreated toward the cave door, knowing he would need more wood to really impress them with the fire.

He stepped back again, and a loud hiss exploded across the back of his neck. He turned to see a dragon blocking his path, jaw unhinged, a mouth full of daggers thrust before him. He stood still a moment and then slowly circled around the beast, eyes cast down at the floor to hide any aggression. As he withdrew from the cave, four dragons detached themselves from the pack and surrounded him, though not as tightly as before. In this way he was able to walk where he needed to— back up the hill to the trees for wood—yet the dragon escort made it clear he was not running away.

His first days were like that, constantly surrounded by the beasts. By day, they brought him fish to eat. By night, he built eight separate fires in the cave, letting them die out by morning lest the dragons think they no longer needed him. As the days grew into weeks and he proved an able firebringer, the dragons returned to their activities, allowing him to gather wood on his own and build the fires by night that kept them warm.

The weeks grew into months, but Agrippa had not wasted the time. While the dragons swam the bay feeding, he built a small sturdy boat with two oars, which he hid beneath the great supply of wood he piled on both sides of the cave mouth.

He stacked the wood in two loose, precarious piles held in place by dried vines. At night he tended the fires and sometimes slept on his feet. So it was an endless cycle of night and day, pain and labor, planning and waiting.

Then one night as he sat before the cave, unsleeping, eyes on the horizon, he saw a star low in the sky go dark and moments later shine again. It was the mast of a ship passing by. Straining, he could see the blur of its hull against the sky.

"Now, my men, you shall have your revenge, and you Pari, your name. Give me your strength, and your names shall live!"

Looking into the cave, he saw the fires had died down; the dragons would be lethargic. Creeping now, he went first to one side of the cave mouth and then the other, lighting the main stacks of wood. Dried for months, the wood caught quickly, and the fire spread, twin torches blazing high into the night. When the fires burned through the vines, the great pyres fell into the cave mouth, forming a vast burning blockade.

Agrippa dragged his boat from its hiding place and across the beach, throwing choice gold statues and armor in as he went and pocketing a few coins to buy his passage. Pushing off from the shore, he could hear the dragons roaring in pain as they tried to push through the flames. He smiled grimly as the barricade held. Agrippa rowed out onto the bay.

Once he passed the reef, the beach did not seem to be covered with gold; instead, the very sand seemed to burn in the same inferno that engulfed the cave. Agrippa looked over his shoulder at the ship. It was raising sail and starting to tack away from the island. He rowed faster, hailing the ship.

"Twenty pieces of gold to save me from the fiery dragons!"

As he neared the ship, there came a tumbling crash of logs. A few dragons came hobbling forth, a thin mist rising up from them that must have been part fog, part smoke. They moved crookedly, and as they touched the water their skin hissed, salt burning their charred flesh, ending their pursuit. Bellowing in rage, they prowled the shore. Their bodies, silhouetted by the flames, cast fearsome shadows on the water.

Turning around in his boat, he saw now that the ship was angling toward him. Not taking any chances, he stowed the beach gold in a box he had built under the boat seat. These sailors could have the gold in his pockets, but he, Agrippa the Wayfinder, would be the first to tell his people of the deaths of their men and bring home the treasure of Pari's Golden Beach.

Dreamwings

Tom Dupree

The bush rustled softly in the warm, gentle breeze and joined the sweet sighing chorus of the forest. Luscious green leaves and inquisitive new tendrils waved the tiny wind through, and shiny dewdrops shuddered and fell to the leaf-carpeted ground, still glistening from last night's rain.

Then the bush raised itself up, looked this way and that, and started to walk.

It took a few tentative steps toward the base of a tree and curled up at its side, shivering slightly. Now the bush looked a little less like a bush than it had only instants before. A sharp set of eyes staring into the bush would have noticed another set of eyes staring right back. A branch might shimmer and morph into a green reptilian snout, and the root that dragged behind the ambulatory shrub could resolve into a tail. The beautiful leaves might all of a sudden look less like leaves and rather more like small shingles for a roof. Green shingles.

But the bush was fighting against all that, just as hard as it could.

Changing its shape was not something that this bush enjoyed; it took entirely too much concentration. It was hard enough simply to assume a counterfeit color—that could frequently be sufficient for protection—but to add or subtract height and weight, to make other beings believe you were something you weren't, was an all-consuming proposition. Absolutely exhausting. Yet the primal emotion of terror will make industrious workers out of even the most frivolous of us. And this bush had the most effective motivation that exists. It was frightened beyond measure.

These trees—so small of stature, so thin in the trunk. They were not like the mighty behemoths of the bush's home. There, the towering, ages-old plants formed a base floor with their prodigious interconnected roots, protecting the jungle from the black sea that roiled beneath. The bush sniffed at this foreign place and smelled a sweet perfume of sap that hung in the forest air, a cloying scent that made it blink. Not the familiar woody musk of the bush's home.

With a resigned exhalation, the bush gave up the pretense and returned to its natural self. It grew into a great reptile whose scales glistened with the nurturing color of the leaf and the blade of grass, the emerald hue that was its—*his* heritage and his heart.

The color he remembered was red—the fiery rage of a

spitting, roaring beast many times his size. How had that horrible creature found its way to his home above the woods? It had no business there. It had simply appeared, in the wink of an eye. All was pandemonium from that instant on. He only remembered running, jumping, flying in panic away from the inferno. Taking himself anywhere, everywhere but here. Then came a crackle of bright power . . . and blackness . . . and finally this forest. Reflexes kicked in, and he had imitated the first thing he saw when he awoke, groggy and stunned.

I am not a bush, he thought.

I am Strnak.

The trees were straight, slim, tall, not like the giant hulking shapes of home. Patches of sunlight dotted the leafy floor. A profound weariness shook Strnak's frame, and he plodded away from the tree base. He looked around for the shrieking red thing, but it had vanished. Or maybe it was he himself who had vanished and been sent to this strange place.

Then he stopped still.

There was a noise. Coming from the tops of the trees.

Strnak froze and thought he heard light laughter, a fragile tinkling sound that frightened him only because it was unexpected. He started to shift forms again but decided against it. He was still jittery after his headlong flight, tired and slow. *Time to stop being frightened of my own shadow*, he told himself. He looked up to discover the source of the sound.

Just there . . . up in the trees, almost beyond his field of vision . . . was a house. But it was the strangest and most wonderful house Strnak had ever seen.

At least it looked like a house at first glance. It was hard to tell where the tree ended and the adjunct began. The bark from the massive brown trunk had actually grown into the dwelling itself, pouring into the rooms and windows as if it had been made of liquid. There was no difference now between house and tree; they were the same. Strnak had never seen the like.

Another high-pitched musical laugh cut the forest air, and Strnak cocked his head to hear it better. He ducked against the foliage as a figure appeared against a railing, high up in the tree. It was a tall, bony fellow, perhaps half Strnak's height. He had bushy brown hair, baggy lived-in clothes, and a large grin on his face as he stuck his head out to drink in the early morning air. A moment later, Strnak knew where that grin had come from.

Stepping out beside the wiry man was a smaller creature, a female. Her long blonde hair and perfect white teeth gleamed against her tan skin, that ruddy color that comes from spending a great deal of time out of doors. She put her arm around the man, and Strnak could see that both of their sets of ears had a decided point. Elves—they were elves. They went back inside, and Strnak smelled the lighting of a wick.

A tiny jobber wurm slinked under Strnak's paw. He recoiled, ramming his head against the tree.

The jolt made the door swing open again. The elf reappeared and began to climb down expertly and carefully. His oversized bare feet found footholds Strnak couldn't even see. Halfway down, the climber paused abruptly and listened.

Strnak was frozen with fright and confusion. He still needed to gather his wits, but there was no time. With a sudden effort that gave him a sharp pain in the head, Strnak strained his mind to remember the special countenance of an elf. He cast his thoughts back to the few elfkind he had spied upon in the forests of his home, and pushed harder. His efforts were rewarded.

His scales seemed to fall away, to be replaced by a green

leather vest over a brown shirt and leggings. He pulled back from all fours and rested on his haunches, and his powerful legs shrank and rounded. The wings that had carried him to this dismal forest retracted, folded, and grew hairy hands and dexterous fingers. The tuft of skin atop his head receded and closed in from left to right, with an unkempt patch of hair in the middle sprouting like so much grass.

Strnak was now, to all intents and purposes, an elf. He hoped the look would be sufficient for his new best friend, who had resumed his downward journey and now arrived on the forest floor with a satisfied thump.

"My sweet mother! Steel Leaf order, is it, huh? Where's your uniform? Oh my, you're incognito! A spy? I knew it. I knew it. Hey, what's wrong with you?" The elf padded up to Strnak and moved in a little too close for personal comfort, inspecting him with boundless naïve curiosity.

Strnak nearly shook with the strain of keeping each fiber of his body elflike. Finally he started and moved back a pace.

The elf still studied him intently. His happy, open face was tinged with concern, but he was unable to repress an occasional smile that showed off a dazzling set of pointed teeth. They didn't look fierce, only functional.

"You look as pale as a ghost, friend. What happened?"

Strnak coughed and indicated his throat.

"Someone slit your throat? Wow, Steel Leaf, that's a tough outfit. Don't see many of you lads out here in the middle of nowhere, but hey, nobody else ever comes out here either. Don't tell me, I should see what the *other* guy looks like. A Steel Leafer. How about that? Hey, can you show me your spear?"

Strnak opened and closed his mouth silently several

times. He imagined he must have looked rather like a fish, but the pantomime had the desired effect.

"Oh, my goodness. You can't speak at all, can you?"

Strnak clapped his hands together repeatedly and hoped the elf understood. It was true. He couldn't speak. Understanding another being's thoughts was child's play for his kind. Usually Strnak knew what was going to be said before the first words ever came out. His species could even visit telepathic communication on others, most easily when they were asleep. Dream time was always an excellent opportunity, and many a vivid dream down through the ages had actually been the invention of a dragon. But expressing his own thoughts in a spoken language was beyond him, and melding minds would invite more risk than Strnak was prepared to take.

"Mute, are you?"

More flapping—no, Strnak reminded himself, clapping. He had to force himself to wait for the other's sound to come out before reacting.

"You *must* be a tough guy, lad, getting in the order without talking. I'm Frankle. I've never seen a Leafer out this far. Lost, are you?"

Strnak shook himself, trying to reply affirmatively.

"Well, it's breakfast time, and Timorae never minds if there's one more face at the table. Come on." He bounded up the tree, once again reaching handholds and footholds that Strnak couldn't see at all.

Strnak hugged the tree with both hands and took a tentative step up. To his delight, his foot found a tiny indentation, and he was able to slither upward slightly. As he released his hand, though, the foot slipped out again, and he found himself on the ground, back where he had started.

Frankle looked down. He was almost to the entrance

already. "Not injured, no? Come on, then!"

Strnak sighed, paused, and strained with a monstrous effort. His feet—and *only* his feet—reverted to their natural state. Sweat poured from Strnak's forehead as the sharp talons bit into the bark, giving him the confidence to step upward gingerly, still holding the tree for dear life. It was all he could do to maintain the deception, to possess two shapes at once. A tense few minutes later, he was pulling himself up on the landing outside the entrance and grunting as he willed hair and toes back on his feet just in time.

"You must really be hurt, lad. That's the clumsiest climbing I've ever seen." Frankle grinned again.

Oddly, Strnak felt warm and welcome. A fire was already cutting the morning damp. He smelled the delicious scent of roasting vegetables wafting from a large metal crock, and it made him salivate. The house was deceptively large. It looked much bigger on the inside than it had while climbing up the tree. Or maybe that was the nature of a dwelling that could exist in a grand old tree—bigger than an outsider would suspect.

"Well, what have we here?" The beautiful blonde elf strode in with a tray—fresh hot bread, steaming green and yellow vegetables, and a bowl of whipped eggs—and smiled at her visitor.

Strnak instinctively backed away.

"What's wrong?" asked the petite elf woman.

Strnak stared at her blouse. Bloody crimson, it was, the color of war and violence. The architect of whatever had conspired against him.

"Sshhh. I'm not going to hurt you." Timorae followed his gaze and tried to understand. "Red? You don't like the color?"

"He can't speak, Timmie." Frankle's brow furrowed, and

he turned to the stranger. "Last night, there was a terrible storm—the worst I can remember. And we heard a horrible thrashing coming from outside. Lightning, falling branches, a real row. It woke us up in the middle of the night—"

"Oh my dear, were you out in all of that? Did something red hurt you last night?" Strnak could tell she was a woman of empathy and kindness. "You poor thing. Well, you're in a decent home now, safe and sound. Sit down and get your strength back." She served a plate for Strnak, and he sniffed at it gratefully.

In all the excitement, he hadn't thought about food at all. The wholesome scent was all it took to remind him just how famished he'd become. With a long sigh of anticipation, Strnak lowered his head into the plate and began lapping up his breakfast. He'd never eaten eggs before—or warmed-up food of any kind, truth be told—and something about them was faintly repulsive at first, but they weren't from his own species, and they felt wonderful as they reached his belly. The crackly green beans tasted quite different after being heated over a fire. Strnak frankly preferred the taste of those he ate in the wild, but these provided a burst of energy. Strnak moaned with pleasure as he ate. He was just reaching out with his tongue to snag an errant bean when he noticed the two elves staring at him with wide, horrified eyes.

"Great Freyalise!" shouted Frankle as Strnak looked up.

"My word!" said Timorae as Strnak retracted a reptilian tongue that had extended a full foot's length atop the plate.

"Steel Leaf order, my granny's garter!" Frankle sprang up from the table and fetched a very ugly looking knife, advancing slowly on his guest. "I don't know who or what you are, friend, but I'm pretty handy with this."

Strnak, who had sensed the elf's intention before he had given voice to it, had already stood up and moved back

213

from the table. Strnak whimpered and panted. The game was up. The two elves gasped as his face began to shimmer and elongate. Ears and snout pushed out of his head, leathery wings uncoiled and spread, and he tipped over on all fours. His head nearly reached the ceiling; he could not have sat upright had he tried. He filled up fully half of the main room by himself.

"A d-d-d-d . . ." Timorae shuddered.

Frankle summoned his courage and kept coming forward, waving the knife heroically but carefully.

Timorae reached out and stopped him as Strnak cowered away, moving as far into the corner of the room as his bulk would allow.

"Look, he's frightened too. Look at him." She took one step forward. "You wouldn't hurt us, now?" She raised a brave smile. "Would you?"

Sorry hungry

They looked at each other. Timorae touched her husband's shoulders. "Did you hear that?"

"I didn't hear anything. I *felt* it."

I tell thinks and see your thinks

Frankle blurted, "He can read our minds."

Yes read minds have better words when you sleep

"A green dragon," Timorae said. "All the way out here in nothingland." She turned to Frankle. "What do we do now?"

Go home

"What? Home? Where?"

I show you

Suddenly the room faded away, and the elves seemed to be floating in air over a vast forest that looked very much like their own. Then they felt themselves swooping down, so steeply that Timorae's stomach actually lurched.

Their flight path flattened out and cut through the tree-tops, and they glided at such a low altitude that they could see animals moving on the floor, each raising their heads at their passage. The air was hot and muggy, fit perfectly for the health of plant life. The sounds of jungle beasts made a steady background that felt safe and familiar. They slowed, and now they could see the ancient roots that covered the entire jungle floor; they realized how monstrous the trees actually were. They rose once again, sharply but gracefully, and burst through the tree line, rising higher until they could see a root-bound coast with waves pounding against huge black monoliths. It was beautiful, especially from way up here. They felt a sense of longing and anticipation that disoriented them for a moment. Then they seemed to regain their bearings. Toward one particular cliff side they flew, slowed, and softly perched at the tip of a cave. Inside, they could see a smaller green dragon raise its head in greeting. Four tiny emerald chicks flapped joyously and hopped toward them.

In a wink the image faded, and they were back in the room again.

Home

Timorae's balance failed her, and she collapsed into her chair. She had been unconsciously leaning forward while the dragon's mind-song played, and now she felt like she weighed a thousand pounds and was nailed to the ground. How wonderful it had been to fly. It was the most vivid dream she had ever had in her life. She was quite sorry it was over.

"Yavimaya." Frankle set the knife on the table slowly and deliberately, since he was fairly wobbly himself, and looked at the dragon with new respect. "We call your home Yavimaya."

"Frankle, that's impossible."

"It's just what the elder described. Face it, that was Yavimaya."

"Yes, okay, but think how far away it must be! Even if this beast can fly, how long would—"

Strnak

"What?"

Name Strnak

Frankle stifled a giggle as his wife blushed. Sometimes she could forget her manners in the middle of an oration.

"I'm so sorry, Strnak. Even though Strnak can fly, how long would it take? Not even a dragon has such strength. And did you see that ocean? How could he survive the trip? I don't believe it."

Frankle turned to the dragon. "Strnak, you're in our land, Llanowar. Far, far away from your home. Impossibly far. This is the very edge of Elfhame Basiphim."

"The very, *very* edge." Timorae put two of her fingers together and almost touched them.

The dragon shifted position slightly and snorted. The popping, shooing, and hissing sounds the elves made were nonsense to him, but he understood their meaning implicitly, just as it was being formed in their minds. Yet he was as confused as they—not over what they said, but over how this could possibly have happened. They were telling him his cherished home was far, far away.

"We're here to guard the borders of Hedressel. The druids' land." Frankle picked up the knife from the table and brandished it like a swordsman.

"Actually, that's not exactly right, dear. We're here to guard the guards." Timorae walked up to the huge dragon without fear, instantly warming his heart, and began to whisper. "I like it that way."

"Timorae, don't tell him."

She turned to face her husband. "Why not? I'm proud of it!" She touched Strnak's muzzle and drew him toward her conspiratorially. "The famous order of the Steel Leaf couldn't bestir themselves to offer young Frankle a commission. He tried—oh, he tried. But they said he hadn't the killer way. He was too gentle, too kind, too soft, cared too much for others. And you know what, Strnak? I agree wholeheartedly. These are precisely the qualities that made me fall in love with him."

"Timmie!"

"So my Frankle has not had the honor of joining his beloved band of painted, marching ruffians. He cannot spend his day pushing others about and devising ways to rule the sky and the forest. He cannot scour the countryside for 'half-breeds' and order an execution with the pointing of a finger. He is here with me, in this beautiful house far away from those preening idiots, which is as close as I care to come to paradise. So weep for him, poor thing. He will live a long and fruitful life and will remain the sweet man I met. And the Steel Leaf order can all become a pile of zombie snacks, for all I care!"

The dragon lifted its head and coughed, a sound that qualified as laughter. He thought about how much he had in common with an elf who wasn't fierce enough for his own people's army. He himself had never known friendship among dragonkind, except for the smaller green dragon who waited for him in the cave. That quiet life, away from others, was what he craved too, just like this elf maiden. Perhaps it made him a freak, a throwback, but that was his way.

Frankle walked up beside his wife. "Her problem is that she never lets her feelings out. Don't you think she should just go ahead and say what's on her mind?" Despite herself, Timorae couldn't hold back a smile. "Hey, don't pay any attention to her. The Steel Leafers are a fantastic group. They keep order and protect the weak, and I think I could have made a contribution. But I'm never going to win this argument, so I've just quit trying. Well, I signed up for auxiliary duty anyhow, and that got us this posting. Now we are the farthest outpost in the elfhame. It's our job to be the first sighters of anything unusual. And Strnak, today that's you."

"No! You're not going to report Strnak to those power-mad fools, are you?" Timorae's eyes blazed.

"Timmie, that is our *job*. Besides, you're forgetting something. How did he get here? However it was, couldn't something else follow?"

How

They were rocked back as they saw again through Strnak's eyes. They experienced the confused, panicked flight that had brought him here. Crimson roaring, jets of flame, flashing light, and then pitch blackness and the pounding of raindrops deep in the forest. They were breathing hard when the mind-song stopped.

"We've got to report this, Timmie. It's what we've been sent here to do."

"Fine, but we're not bringing a perfectly harmless creature in to the Leafers. We'll *tell* them about Strnak. At least as much as we want to tell. But let's get him down and away before they show up."

"And just how would you propose doing that? Look at the size of him. Besides, they'll search the whole area."

"You can change again, can't you?" Timorae rubbed the dragon's chin in friendship. "You'd better be able to, dear

Strnak, because I don't think you can get out of here otherwise."

It was true. The massive winged creature could barely turn around in the cramped room. He concentrated again, and the elves watched in wonder as his frame shrank and contorted back into a form resembling their own.

"Now let me think," Timorae rested her chin in her hand, "where we'll keep you when we greet the gallant order."

"Be careful." Frankle put his arm around the newly elf-sized shoulders. "Now I understand why you can't climb. But it doesn't take any talent to go down, you know. The trick is making sure you don't go splat."

* * * * *

It took Frankle until midmorning to navigate the treetops and arrive at the next outpost, which had to pass his news on to the next and so on. By late afternoon, a small contingent representing the order of the Steel Leaf had tromped its way out to their tree.

Frankle couldn't help himself; he still found the order impressive. Five snappy, curt, focused military elves, they were, the best and the brightest, their weapons spit-polished to a shine, their clothing and goggles impeccably clean, their faces painted with sigils of battle, heads shaved to yield the distinctive single row of hair that marked the Leafers.

A certain Commander Feemwlort was their leader, a veteran elf who had seen many campaigns, judging from the snow-white color of his tightly groomed ponytail. He and the soldiers thoroughly inspected the forest bed around the house and out as far as the eye could see, sniffing dirt, crumbling leaves, and annoying squirrels in every direction. The commander wasted no further time once the party had made its way up to the tree house. The other four Leafers were standing stiffly at parade rest upon the landing, fierce military snarls pasted on their faces.

"In the name of Fhedusil, I wish to commend you for your swift action," the commander began. "You have comported yourself well, young—er—"

"Sir, Frankle, sir," the first elf in line prompted.

"Yes, yes," he muttered, shuffling pieces of paper and finally coming to the one he needed. "Now, your report to this order mentions a disturbance yesterday. A fanciful creature that appeared during last night's thunderstorm."

"My money says the creature was made of ale," stage-whispered a Leafer to the next in line, and was rewarded with a derisive snort.

"Ooo, I'd have bad dreams too if I were stuck in this miserable hellhole."

"Silence!" The commander glared at his charges and turned back to Frankle. "Now, your report is in good order, and I suppose you've done the right thing by bringing it to our attention, but my lad, there's no evidence! Not a stitch of corroboration! It's a fantastic story you've spun, but there's one thing we all must know—where is your creature from another land?"

"Oh, it probably went back where it came from." All heads turned as Timorae came out on the landing, bringing with her a large tray full of teacups and sweet cakes and a big clay teapot with capacity enough to serve all.

"Precisely. And just where is that, milady?"

"Into the land of fairy tales!" snorted a soldier, and the rest spit and coughed.

"Elves!"

The noise ceased at once.

Timorae approached the line of Llanowar's finest and got close enough to the first Leafer to smell his sweat above the late afternoon breeze.

"Laugh it up, boys. But you might also want to thank Freyalise that you've got somebody all the way out here who has a sense of duty. If it had been up to me, you'd still be back in Staprion practicing how to walk in a straight line, and I'll bet you could use the practice, too. But your loyal associate here—and you should be so lucky to *keep* him on your squad—thought you needed to know what happened last night . . . and believe me, boys, it *did* happen."

Frankle looked at his wife with even more admiration than he'd already felt for her. Maybe she was right. These arrogant, closed-minded snobs weren't his kind of elves. Before, the sight of a Leafer in full uniform had seemed the height of ceremonial fashion, but just now, this bunch frankly looked foolish to him, almost buffoons. It was amazing he'd ever yearned to join their ranks. How blind he'd been. But then, some things just work out for the best. He would have looked ridiculous under all that paint.

Feemwlort moved toward the tea service and poured out a cup. "Please forgive the infantile outbursts of my elves, madam. No one is denying your story. At least no one *in command*. But surely you can appreciate my insistence on some physical evidence." He took a biscuit and broke it in two above the tray.

"Achoo!" said the tray.

The commander dropped his cup in shock, and the other Leafers sprang to his side, drawing their weapons but not really knowing why. They had been too far away to notice that the tea tray had a sniffle.

Cups clattered to the floor of the landing as the tray

shuddered, curved and grew, sprouting head, feet and wings before the astonished and sputtering members of the order.

"Bad luck, Strnak!" Timorae dashed in front of the dragon as the soldiers leveled spears. The giant beast tried to spread its wings, but only caused more damage at the table, sending a lovely batch of cookies crashing to the floor.

"Step aside, madam!" Feemwlort ordered, as one of the soldiers let fly a spear that missed Strnak completely and nicked Timorae's arm before it flew out into the forest.

This was too much for Frankle. He shrieked, jumped on top of the Leafer, and worried his head with blows until the soldier fell to his knees. Two others tried to pull him off while the fourth soldier flipped his bow to the front and clumsily tried to nock an arrow. Frankle was beside himself with rage. Feemwlort bellowed for attention. Frankle continued to pound on his poor victim until—

WWWRRROOOOOOOOWWWWWRRRRRRRR!

The noise stopped.

Everyone went as still as a painting.

It had been quite an impressive warning roar. Even Strnak was pleased with himself. He snorted in satisfaction. "Put those silly things away!" Timorae stood her ground. "Frankle—down, boy. It's only a scratch. Gentlemen, this creature is harmless."

"It's a *dragon*, milady!" shouted the bowman who had accused Frankle of imbibing too much.

"Stayed awake at Steel Leaf school for taxonomy lessons, did you, love?" sneered Timorae. Now it was Frankle's turn to stifle a giggle as he panted. "Of course it's a dragon, you blithering imbecile! And we are elves. Congratulations, commander, promotions are in order!" She looked at the shivering dragon. "I'm sorry, Strnak. I thought an inanimate object would be the easiest for you to do."

Feemwlort drew himself up to full height. "See here, madam—"

"No, *you* see *here!*" Frankle got up off the errant spearman and confronted the commander. "This . . . being . . . hasn't harmed a soul. Hasn't done a thing except startle you. Now you're ready to hurt it, maybe even kill it. And why? Not for its deeds—just for its appearance. But notice that it hasn't taken any action against you at all—even though it had plenty of chances."

"But dragons are—"

"And just what is it that they are? The world is rich and full, commander. There's a whole spectrum of possibility. He could have more in common with us than you suspect." The dumbfounded soldiers looked up at Strnak and back at Frankle. "I know it's true, sir. Because I . . . I've seen his mind."

"You've talked with this creature?" The commander frowned.

"No, but I've shared his thoughts. And I know what he wants. He just wants to go home."

"And just where—" Feemwlort stopped in midsentence. "What the—"

Of a sudden, something was extremely odd about the air. There was a strange sizzle and a smell of burnt matter. Frankle stared out beyond the landing and felt the hairs on the back of his neck rise. A high-pitched keening grew louder and louder until a titanic boom shook the forest.

Instantly, in midair beyond the landing, appeared a living crimson kite snarling with malevolence. Much larger yet slimmer than Strnak, the blood-red dragon barked, thrust its massive wings downward to keep itself afloat, and drew a breath with a deep, ominous gurgle.

"Take cover!" Feemwlort shouted.

The others, dumbfounded, ducked under chairs and tables—all except Frankle, who took a chair and held it in front of him, like a shield. The dragon stopped pulling in air and paused for a horrible second of utter silence. Then it expelled an inferno.

Superheated air rushed at Frankle and roared against the chair. The wood burst into flame and dropped in ashes. The fire ceased momentarily as the dragon slowly turned its head sideways to increase the effective range of its hellish fire. The smell of charred wood was everywhere. Flames were rising from parts of the landing. It wouldn't hold much longer.

The dragon's swath of flame moved across the landing and was headed for the main tree trunk when the behemoth suddenly caught its breath.

A smaller green form was coming straight for it, as fast as it could fly.

With a fierce roar, Strnak plowed into the larger creature, claws extended, and pushed it back to crash into a tree.

Stunned, the red dragon bit and clawed at Strnak, but he would not relinquish his hold. The fire breather lashed out at a green wing and drew blood as the two creatures crashed to the ground.

They snarled and wrestled, first one on top and then the other. Strnak wasn't able to spit fire, but he consoled himself with just plain old spitting, as frequently and as wetly as possible. Finally the irritated larger beast managed to push itself aside and faced Strnak as the green dragon backed away from the house. Once again, a basso gurgle sounded as air was drawn in to transform into an incinerating spray of destruction.

Strnak shuddered, closed his eyes, and braced for the conflagration.

Then the red dragon rose stock still and hiccuped. It twisted its head this way and that. Strnak opened one eye to look, and as the beast turned around to see what was behind it, he beheld its trouble.

Frankle.

Zipping down the tree faster than ever before, Frankle bore one of the soldiers' spears and plunged it into the red dragon's back. Feemwlort and two other Leafers were busily clambering down the tree trunk to join him, but Frankle hadn't waited for them. He'd leapt directly from the tree to join the fray.

Now the monster had the upper hand. Shaking Frankle off the back of its neck, it turned around to face him. It inhaled, initiating the fiery chemistry inside its lungs.

Now it was Frankle's turn to close his eyes and meet the inevitable. First, he looked up to the landing, and met Timorae's horrified gaze. So sweet, she was. It had been a nice life. He looked around him then, and everything seemed to be happening very slowly. The Leafers nocked arrows. Feemwlort lifted a spear. Strnak prepared one more pounce from behind. All of it would be too late. Frankle closed his eyes for the last time as he heard the terrible gurgle of dragon fuel being sucked into the monster's lungs.

A tremendous crash boomed through the forest.

Even with his eyes closed, Frankle saw bright light. He smelled a prickly, tannic odor. He opened his eyes.

The heavens split wide, and a deluge poured down on the forest. The dragon looked up and opened its mouth in amazement. It was as if a lake had suddenly appeared over their heads and decided to dump its entire contents at once. The rain came down so powerfully that soon Frankle could no longer see the beast, but he knew one thing: the torrent of water had doused its killing breath and the fires in his home.

The Leafers ran up to Frankle and pulled him, sputtering, out of the dragon's line of sight. The storm was so thick it obscured everything.

Strnak, in midleap when the rain came, completely missed the red dragon and plopped to the ground.

Lightning crackled again. Soon the rain softened, then stopped altogether.

The elves and Strnak looked at each other dumbly.

The red dragon had vanished, but something else had appeared.

The tree that was Frankle and Timorae's home began to shimmer and change. At ground level, the bark slowly resolved itself into a strangely elongated, wizened face. Nicks and burls formed a long, full beard, a craggy nose, and ancient eyes that shone with wisdom and purpose. As they watched in fascination, they realized that their home was a living, sentient creature—a creature that possessed powerful magic. *Greetings, children.*

They stared at the kind face in the tree and heard his emotion. A feeling of contentment and peace washed over them. Even the Leafers relaxed and took their hands off their weapons. *And winged child.*

Strnak knew the tree man was referring to him. He too felt a sense of rightness, of propriety. This was the embodiment of the spirit of the forest, of verdant growth and compassionate nurture.

You have been removed from a far place.

Strnak was suffused with warmth and love as he recalled his home.

It was evil sorcery whose kind does not belong here.

Strnak felt himself being lifted up, vaulted by a power he had never experienced before. He rose into the air on a magical current but felt safe and protected, as if floating in soothing water. He relaxed and gave himself up to the force that was propelling him. Whatever magic or misadventure had created the red monster and separated him from his lair, accidental or not, it was now over and done with. Strnak knew it.

I revoke the evil and return you.

Above the tree-man's head, a protrusion formed, pressing out from the tree—a green, glowing, organic sphere that pulsed and glistened. It separated from the tree and shot toward Strnak.

Live and love, brave one.

When it hit, it exploded in an emerald shower of heatless sparks. The dragon felt himself slowly being pulled somewhere far, far away. At the last instant, he turned to Frankle, and the elf sensed the laborious effort of mind-song. *Thank you, friend.*

And he was gone.

Frankle whirled back to face the tree, but its spirit had settled inside once again. Just knowing it was there made him even prouder of his home.

Timorae raced down the tree and gave her husband a huge hug. "What do you think of him now, Commander?"

Feemwlort extended his hand, and the Leafers shot into a formal salute. "That was quite a display, young elf. Quite a display. We may have been wrong about you. If you would care to join our order, it would be my honor to sponsor your commission."

"Sir, that's a great honor," Frankle said as Timorae tensed her grip on his arm. "But my place is here. And it always has been."

* * * * *

That night, the two elves drifted off into peaceful, exhausted sleep and had the same dream. They saw a set of graceful leathery wings gliding on air currents and slowing, descending, talons dropping as tenderly as snowflakes onto a cave entrance where others waited in blissful anticipation.

They never saw Strnak again in all their green days.

But that night, and on many other nights to follow, he was there.

Part IV:

Warrior Dragons

Dragons breed war. Whether defending their hoards against treasure hunters or extending their reigns to new lands, every dragon is a warrior. Why else have claws and fangs and fire?

When a lich lord seeks to turn a remote branch of the Vintara Forest into a festering mire, he must face down the ancient green dragon that rules the wood. Though he cannot destroy a venerable serpent, he can slay young dragons, raise them as undead warriors, and send them into battle. . . .

In the heart of sun-bleached Shiv, a small miracle survives—a hanging garden of green. Even small miracles need defenders. When a trio of ne'er-do-wells decide to claim the paradise for themselves, only one unlikely dragon can stop them. . . .

In the days before he fought in the invasion, Keldon Warlord Astor was sent to roust a wicked red dragon from its lair. But is Keldon fire any match for dragon fire?

The Blood of a Dragon

Edo van Belkom

The lich had spent most of the night preparing arrows for this moment.

In darkness blacker than pitch, he had unearthed the foulest smelling rot from the blackest part of the Nakaya Swamp. Then he'd coated the tips of his arrows with the decay, using the scale of a green dragon to apply the filth. All the while he'd mumbled incantations, again and again, until the arrows were enchanted with the darkest sort of magic. Now he had a quiver full of death-tipped black arrows, and they were ready to kill.

Lich Lord Deadalus had stepped out of the Nakaya Swamp an hour earlier, walking westward into the Vintara Forest. The forest was dense and made the going tough. It was just as well, since the spells cast over the arrows would lose more power the farther into the forest he traveled. Luckily he'd chanced upon what he'd been searching for early in the day.

They had been hard to find until he'd learned more about them and known where to look. The green dragons of Vintara spent most of their lives in the very top layer of the forest. They dwelt in trees the Garan Elves called "emergents" because they broke through the dense forest canopy. In those emergent trees, the dragons lived in sunlight and safety, high above the rest of the creatures in the forest. Even if the dragons could be found, how could they be reached atop the thick tangle of branches that made up the forest's canopy? It was an almost impossible task.

For some, but not for Lord Deadalus. While the dragons were safe from creatures of the forest, their habitat provided no such protection from a creature of the swamp.

The lich listened again for the sound of the dragon. It called out its song without a care in the world. Deadalus raised his bow in the direction of the dragon, pulled back as hard as he could without snapping the weapon in two . . . and fired.

The black-tipped arrow leapt from the lich's bow. With a whispered death cry, it sliced upward through the air. Normally, in the few seconds after the launch of an arrow in such a forest, there would have been the crash and echo of the arrowhead striking branches. It would quickly lose momentum and then slowly fall back to earth like an autumn leaf. The lich's arrow made no sound. Instead of striking branches and shredding leaves, it wove and turned like a fish swimming upstream. The arrow went around and through the tangle of branches and vegetation, not stopping until it found its target.

After the arrow's release, there was only silence, followed a few seconds later by the thud of the head piercing dragon scales. Silence resumed for a moment. Then came the cry of a dying dragon. Finally, leaves rattled and branches snapped. The heavy dragon fell from its perch and punched a hole through the canopy on its way to ground. There was a last profound thud as the dragon hit the soil, and silence returned once more.

"Ha!" cried Deadalus, slapping his hands together and stepping forward to examine his kill. "Right through the heart. . . . Death meets life. Death wins!"

The dragon was still alive, but not for long. The arrow had struck its heart with force enough to bury the shaft deep within its chest. The dragon lay there twitching and turning as the black tinge of death spread from the entry wound.

As the lich looked over his kill with pride, several of his minions—vermin mostly, both undead and alive, and several undead dwarfs, led by his number one, Mulago—swarmed around his legs. They gnawed at the dragon, trying to tear away its scales so they might taste the tender flesh beneath.

"Stop it!" shouted Deadalus. He kicked one of the vermin from the dragon's neck and sent it flying through the air, into a nearby tree trunk. "Idiots!" he shouted, stomping on the others and grabbing Mulago by the scruff of his neck.

All of the creatures took a step back from the dragon, wary of their master's wrath.

"I need it whole." He paused to glare at them all, making sure the message was clear. "If this one is damaged, you will all be punished."

The creatures shivered collectively at the thought of punishment by their master's hands.

"Understood?"

Mulago answered for all of them, "Yes, my master."

"Good," he said with a sigh. "Now, take this one back to the swamp and wait for me there."

Mulago nodded and then conscripted three vermin to help him drag the beast back to the swamp. As they began pulling and wrestling the creature through the forest, the lich could hear Mulago say, "Now I know why they call them *dragons*."

The lich smiled and turned back around to face the forest. "Three more should be enough." He marched forward, venturing deeper into the Vintara Forest.

* * * * *

"Does it please you, my master?" asked Mulago, smiling up at Deadalus with a mouthful of rot-eaten teeth.

"Yes it does," said Deadalus.

His minions had done an excellent job preparing the dragons for the transformation ceremony. They had laid out the four dead dragons in order from the smallest, which he'd killed first, to the largest, which he'd killed last, deep in the Vintara Forest. In fact, the last dragon was so much bigger than the others, and he'd been so deep into the forest, the lich had needed two arrows to bring it to the ground. Deadalus himself had had to help his remaining minions bring the creature's carcass back to the Nakaya Swamp. But it had been worth it. When this great green was turned black, it would be a powerful weapon in the fight to overtake the Vintara Forest.

"You've done well Mulago!"

The undead dwarf danced slightly, moving back and forth as if he could hardly contain himself.

Deadalus placed a hand on the dwarf's head to calm him. Mulago settled down but was still smiling with excitement. Mulago and the others had dug several deep graves in the muck. A foul stench—a sweet elixir to Deadalus's senses—rose from the holes as each one had tapped into the pool of decay that ran rich and deep beneath the swamp.

Several times the lich circled the dead dragons and their burial sites, whispering a string of words. Every once in a while he shouted something out for all to hear.

"Alive with the rot of the ages . . ." he would say aloud before continuing on with more words under his breath. "Festering with the death of generations . . ."

He used his foot to push the first of the dragons into its hole. The beast landed with a wet splash in the soft muck. Moments later, Mulago busily filled in the hole, covering the dragon with worm-infested blackness.

The lich continued the ceremony, giving each dragon the same ritual treatment before rolling it into the ground.

"Decay is your lifeblood . . . chaos your heartbeat." The second dragon was interred.

". . . to a black heart and evil mind." The third slithered into the filth.

"Darkness will be your light, death your way of life." The lich gave the last and largest dragon a push with his boot, but it would not move. He kicked again, harder this time, but the beast seemed to have ideas of its own, even in death. "Help me, Mulago!"

The dwarf scurried over to his master's side, and together they pushed at the dragon's carcass until it began to move ever so slightly. Deadalus gave one last hard push, and the dragon slid into the hole—taking Mulago with it. The dwarf's sleeve had become entangled with one of the dragon's tail spikes, and the dead creature's bulk had pulled him down into the hole.

The minions laughed and began to fill in the hole with

Mulago still in it. Even Deadalus gave a little chuckle.

"You'll pay for this!" said Mulago as the sludge was being pushed on top of him. He tried to utter the words again, but the muck covered his head, silencing him.

The minions continued to laugh, but Deadalus was no longer smiling. He needed a number one, and while he could probably do better than Mulago, the dwarf was all he had at the moment. Deadalus reached down into the earth, felt the hard nub of Mulago's head beneath his fingers, and clutched a handful of hair. In a single strong motion, Deadalus pulled the dwarf from the ground like a carrot.

The minions howled. Mulago, even covered with filth as he was, was keen on silencing each of them personally.

"Enough!" bellowed Deadalus. "We've no more time for fun and games. There is still much to be done before these dragons soar over Nakaya."

The minions grew silent.

"Mulago! Come with me!"

The dwarf reluctantly followed his master, but still managed to wave an admonishing finger at the minions around him.

That made them laugh even more.

* * * * *

The next day Deadalus, Mulago, and the rest of the lich's minions gathered around the burial site, waiting for the dragons to rise from their graves. After little more than an hour, Deadalus grew impatient and began digging up the dragons, starting with the first and smallest of the four.

He stopped digging when parts of the dragon's body came into view. Though a bright shade of green when it went into the ground, the dragon's body was now gray and black. The darkest shade appeared on its back, where the deepest green had once been. The dragon writhed in the muck, looking like a newborn bird making its way out of its egg.

Deadalus watched the dragon twitch and move, pleased that his sorceries had worked so well on the beasts. If all had gone well, the dragon would soon be under his control, an addition to his little group of minions. It would make him by far the most powerful lich in Nakaya Swamp.

Deadalus grew tired of watching the dragon flop around. He reached down, grabbed hold of one of its hind legs, and unceremoniously heaved the beast onto more solid ground.

The dragon chuffed and breathed a few gulps of fetid air. It shook itself like a dog who'd just swum across a river. Muck and filth flew through the air, falling upon Deadalus like rancid rain.

"Welcome," said Deadalus, extending a hand to the dragon.

The dragon, still groggy, reluctantly reached for the lich's hand.

"I am Deadalus," he said. "I am your master."

The dragon seemed confused over having a humanoid claim to be its master.

Deadalus could sense that it was trying to get away, but his grip on the beast's hand was firm. He pulled it closer. "I am your master," he said, making sure the dragon caught a sniff of his toxic breath. "You will answer only to me."

With those words, a calm came over the dragon, as if it understood its new role and had accepted it.

"I will name you, Rot."

"Rot!" said the black dragon.

"Yes."

Deadalus resurrected the other two dragons without any

problems, naming them Ruin and Death, which suited their foul demeanors well.

Then came the final and largest dragon of the four. As with the three before, Deadalus had dug down into the ground until the dragon's body parts were visible. The beast's legs and arms moved slowly, as if they had merely been asleep overnight, not radically transformed from green to black, life to undeath. Eager to see its magnificent black form rise over the swamp, Deadalus crawled down into the shallow pit and began pulling on its exposed leg. At the touch of his hands, the dragon's leg twitched, pitching Deadalus headlong into the swamp.

None of the minions dared laugh. Having fun at the expense of Mulago was one thing, but laughing at Lord Deadalus could only result in a slow and painful death.

"Well, come on you filthy rotten scoundrels, give me a hand!"

Instantly, the minions scrambled onto the large dragon's body. They dug more of it from the ground and pulled on its exposed limbs to wrest them loose. The dragon's legs and arms continued to twitch, sending smaller minions sailing over the swamp like dragonflies. There were a few chuckles, but any outright laughter would remind the lich of his flight. If that happened, heads would roll.

Finally the creature stirred in earnest, trying to right itself. It struggled for a short while, and then came a great wet sucking sound as it freed itself from the swamp. It crouched on its back legs, shaking muck from its scales.

"Welcome," said Deadalus, extending a hand as he'd done for the previous three.

The dragon, less groggy than the others, refused to offer Deadalus its hand.

The lich ignored the slight, knowing what the problem was. Because of its size—standing as tall as Deadalus and likely outweighing him by half—this last dragon had not spent enough time underground for its transformation to be complete. It was too late to put the dragon back into the muck, but there were other ways to finish the job.

"I am Deadalus," said the lich. "I am your master."

The dragon shook its head slowly from side to side, as if to fend off madness.

Without another word, Deadalus reared back and struck the side of the dragon's head with his mailed fist.

Dazed, the dragon struggled to remain upright. It finally gave up the battle and fell forward, chin first into the swamp.

Deadalus crouched down near the dragon's snout, reached for its upper lip, and lifted it. With the dragon's maw open, he took a handful of muck and forced it down the dragon's throat. This would finish the transformation from the inside, ensuring that the beast would fall under his spell as had the others.

Deadalus leaned forward so that his mouth was mere inches from the dragon's snout. "I am your master," he said, speaking almost directly into the dragon's nostrils. "You will answer only to me, and you will call me master."

The calm that had beset the previous three dragons overcame this one as well. It nodded its head slightly in agreement.

"Milord," it said.

"I will name you, Destruction."

"Destruction!" said the black dragon.

"Rot, Ruin, Death, and Destruction!"

The largest of the four black dragons rose up on its hind legs, completing the line up of dark beasts.

"Awesome!" cried Mulago.

The Dragons of Magic

It was indeed an awesome sight—four black dragons under his control.

* * * * *

They headed west, Deadalus and Mulago leading the way while the four dragons—Rot, Ruin, Death, and Destruction—circled overhead. Bringing up the rear were various minions, some of whom had been asked to come along, others who were simply following out of curiosity.

After some time, they reached the edge of the Nakaya Swamp, where it met and meshed with the Vintara Forest. Here the blackness of the swamp ran dry. The ground became hard, and the muck and decay that was the source of Deadalus's strength became a source of life. Things were changing, though. Deadalus had spent many years casting spells across the western edge of the swamp. At last his efforts were being rewarded. The swamp had been slowly moving westward these past few months. Nothing drastic—just a few feet each day. In a month, the swamp might have traveled a hundred feet westward, adding more than a half mile by the end of the year. That wasn't much considering the Vintara Forest was seven hundred miles wide, but a half-mile of new swamp across a front of four hundred miles meant two-hundred square miles of new swamp each year. As a result, Deadalus's power grew while that of the great green dragon Chloridon, who ruled over the Vintara Forest, would diminish.

Even with the swamp overtaking the forest, there was no guarantee Deadalus would be strong enough to battle Chloridon when the time came. That's where the new black dragons came into play.

Deadalus halted the procession and waited for the dragons to land. They came to rest in front of him, lining up from the smallest, Rot, to the largest, Destruction. Destruction was to be the leader of the dragons, as much for his size as for his spirit and determination. Despite being under Deadalus's control, the dragon had a sharp mind and would be a cunning leader for this type of mission.

"You will lead these three to the heart of the Vintara Forest, where the great dragon Chloridon has his lair," said Deadalus, walking back and forth in front of the dragons.

The dragons listened, stoic and unmoving.

"You will then enter his lair. Whether by brute force or cunning, you will wound Chloridon and return to me this vial filled with the great green dragon's blood." From inside his coat, Deadalus produced a tiny glass vial that hung from a leather thong. He handed it to Destruction.

"What madness is this?" whispered Mulago, hearing his master's plan for the very first time.

Without a word, Deadalus swung out and caught Mulago on the back of the head, sending the undead dwarf reeling. Unperturbed, he continued, speaking directly to Destruction.

"Do you understand what it is I want you to do?"

"Yes," said the big black dragon, hanging the vial around his neck.

"And you will do as I command?"

"Yes," the dragon said, pausing a moment before adding, "milord."

"Excellent," said Deadalus. He swirled his right hand before him and flicked it toward the sky. "Begone with you now, and return quickly!"

The four dragons leapt skyward. Deadalus could feel the air being pushed back by their wings as they climbed—four black specks against the blue.

When they were almost out of sight, Mulago turned to Deadalus and asked, "Why have you sent these valuable assets on—if I might be so bold—a suicide mission? They would have been invaluable to us under your command, good in a fight, keeping order or causing chaos. With four dragons, your dominance over Nakaya Swamp would have been assured for all times. I don't understand."

Deadalus looked at Mulago for several moments. His first instinct was to run him through with a dagger, but he had asked the question with respect and had at least waited until the dragons were on their way before speaking up. He deserved an answer, especially since his dim brain would likely never come up with an answer on its own.

"You've noticed that the swamp is expanding?" he said.

Mulago took a look around and nodded. "The last time I was here, that big spruce was dark green and surrounded by grassland. Now it's dead and in the middle of swamp."

"Precisely," said Deadalus. "The swamp is expanding, claiming more of the Vintara Forest every day. Eventually someone will notice the swamp creeping westward. When that happens, there will be a battle—green versus black."

"We'll be ready," said Mulago, gritting his teeth.

"Yes, of course, but I want to be more than ready."

Mulago was silent, looking curiously up at his master. "I'm afraid I don't understand."

Deadalus wasn't surprised. "If I can drink the blood of Chloridon from that vial—a vial enchanted with the blackest of my magic—I can bring Chloridon under my control and have him do my bidding."

Mulago sighed. "I had no idea such a thing was possible."

"It is—difficult, but possible," said Deadalus. "Even if I cannot gain total control, drinking the great green's blood will empower me, make me stronger, especially in the forest. After I claim the Vintara Forest, conquering the next piece of Dominaria will be that much easier."

Mulago was silent, looking up at his master with an expression that was a mix of wonder and terror.

* * * * *

In the heart of the Vintara Forest, two hundred miles north of the Jamuraan Sea, lay a huge, dense thicket. A squad of Garan Elves patrolled the outskirts of the thicket but were unable to penetrate it. The tangle of trees and vegetation were so rich that only the smallest forest creatures could travel through it. Accessible only from the air, the thicket proved an ideal lair for a great green dragon.

The large black dragon Destruction led the flight of four, with Rot on his left and Ruin and Death trailing slightly on his right. As they flew westward over the canopy of the Vintara Forest, Destruction recognized some of the vegetation below. He recalled areas of the forest where he had spent his youth, darting through branches and zooming high above the foliage, as free and as unbound as a dragon would ever want. It had seemed such fun then, but now just the sight of all that green leaf turned his stomach.

The others seemed to be having trouble as well, getting weaker and weaker with each mile of greenery that passed below their dark wings. Luckily, Chloridon's lair was only a few miles farther. Destruction was eager to reach it, do the deed, and return home to wallow in the swamp's invigorating filth.

The large black dragon took a look around to check that they weren't being shadowed by any greens—their former brothers in mana. With no other dragons in sight,

Destruction adjusted his wings, banked right, and slid from the sky, gaining speed with each passing second. In the thicket below, he glimpsed an opening that led down into Chloridon's lair. It would be best that they approach low over the treetops. Rot, Ruin, and Death followed Destruction down to the forest top. They skimmed over the trees like scythe blades, the wind rushing over their wings with a deadly roar. They reached the hole.

Destruction pulled up, using his wings like windsocks, and came to a gentle and silent landing on the tangled vines above the entrance. The others joined him. The shaft before them was huge. It had to be to allow Chloridon to move freely in and out of his lair. The sheer size of it was daunting, easily two or three times larger than Destruction. Nevertheless, the undead dragons had been given a task by their master, and they would complete it. Chloridon had size, but they had surprise, speed, and numbers.

Deadalus would have his blood.

They entered the hole in the thicket. The branches had grown in a tangle over the years, intertwining like the twigs in a bird's nest and making a tunnel that led into the lower levels of the forest. They followed the tunnel for several yards before stopping in their tracks. The main passage split here, with a second smaller one leading off to the right.

"Rot," said Destruction. "Go that way! See where it leads."

Rot nodded and headed off down the smaller tunnel.

Ruin and Death followed Destruction down the main tunnel, which was growing ever larger. They came upon another passageway, this one more scraggly and less used than the first.

"Ruin," said Destruction.

Ruin moved down the passageway.

Death and Destruction were watching Ruin depart when

something strange happened. One moment Ruin was moving away from them. The next, he was gone. A shriek cut daggerlike through the thicket, followed by a series of shorter screams—dragon screams. Then came the sound of tearing flesh and crunching bone.

Death turned and tried to run, but Destruction grabbed the smaller dragon by the tail and pulled him back. "We have a job to do," said Destruction. "You can die doing the job, or die trying to run from it. The choice is yours."

Death turned back around and joined Destruction. Together they pushed deeper into the thicket, following the tunnel until it opened into a large space, a nest made up of bushes and trees and grasses. Across the open space were several other openings, passageways leading through the thicket to different parts of the forest. In one of the openings, Rot appeared.

Obviously, Ruin had been the one to die. The small black dragon might have fallen prey to a trap or to one of the green's underlings, for Chloridon lay at rest in the middle of his murky lair, asleep by the looks of it.

Filling the vial with blood shouldn't be too difficult, thought Destruction, as long as the great green remains asleep . . . if he truly is asleep. . . .

"Death," Destruction whispered.

No response.

Destruction turned to find where the dragon had gone and caught sight of Death moving around the edge of the clearing. He climbed over brambles and bushes to remain partially hidden from view.

"Death," Destruction called again.

The dragon turned to answer, but as he tried to speak, an odd sound came from Death's mouth—like a claw slicing through flesh and bone. Death's head fell from his neck. His body slumped to the ground in a heap.

Only two black dragons remained.

Destruction looked across the clearing, trying desperately to catch sight of Rot, the smallest of the four, so they could coordinate an attack. It looked bad for them, but not hopeless. Rot was small but fast—

The bulk of the great green rose slightly, blocking Rot from Destruction's view. Chloridon settled quickly back to rest. Rot was gone. Gone, completely and without a trace.

The green had never been asleep. It had lured them all in, and now it would stalk down Destruction.

He pulled back into one of the tunnels and watched as Chloridon rose fully.

The dragon was huge. What Destruction had originally thought was his sleeping body turned out to be only his tail, curled round and covering him like a blanket. The rest of his form had been nestled in the bottom of the lair, which was more than a dozen feet deep.

Chloridon sniffed the air. He stalked forward. His arms stretched out, probing the tunnels. He jutted his head into them, seeking his prey.

Not wanting to be taken from behind and knowing he could not escape, Destruction rushed forward into Chloridon's lair.

With a movement quick enough for a dragon half its size, Chloridon sat up on its hind legs to face Destruction. The green's eyes were big and angry. Its maw opened in a sneer. Its back teeth had been ground flat from years of chewing leaves and flowers, but its front teeth were as sharp as any dragon's, meant to tear flesh and crunch bone.

Destruction's impulse was to flee, but he was too far into the lair to get away. Besides, he was still bound to his master's will. Curious, thought Destruction. Deadalus killed and resurrected me only to send me on a death mission.

"What brings you here?" hissed Chloridon.

"I was sent," answered Destruction, "by my master."

"For what purpose? Surely these three could have died just as easily in the swamps of Nakaya. . . . " Chloridon brought his right hand forward, and on each of his talons were the heads of Rot, Ruin, and Death, looking like ornamental rings.

Destruction wanted to lie, to claim they'd been sent to kill him, to set fire to the thicket, anything but the truth, but he found he could not. Chloridon's power was too strong. "I've come for some of your blood."

"Really?" Obviously Chloridon had not been expecting this. "And what's to be gained from my blood?"

Destruction took hold of the vial hanging from the thong around his neck and explained how Deadalus enchanted the glass so that the blood would empower him and grant him control over Chloridon.

When Destruction was done, Chloridon simply shook his great head. "Such grandiose plans. This lich of yours is obviously industrious and resourceful but perhaps not as clever as he'd like to think."

"How so?" asked Destruction.

"While drinking my blood from that vial quite possibly would empower the lich, or any other undead creature for that matter, no black sorcery could give him control over me—a living dragon. This lich, this Deadalus, must have spent too much time in the sun. His mind has been burnt by it, I think." Chloridon laughed, shaking the trees and bushes in the thicket with each deep bass chuckle.

Destruction watched darkly, still intent on the great green's blood.

"Easy, dark one," said Chloridon in a whisper. "I value my blood, especially when it's on the inside. For every drop, you should be prepared to give up a hundred drops of your own."

Destruction considered Chloridon's words. It would be utter madness to try for the great green's blood now. The black dragon's thought turned toward escape. Of course, even if by some miracle he succeeded, he would have to report back to Deadalus. The lich would likely punish him, but wouldn't kill him. If Destruction tried for the blood, he would surely die, but if he simply fled, there was a chance he might live.

"Yes," hissed Chloridon. "Escape. A wise choice." A soft laugh. "I might even let you go—"

Destruction took that as his cue, catching the great dragon in midsentence. He leapt for one of the openings in the tangle of branches overhead.

"—but not without a fight."

Chloridon lunged after the fleeing dragon.

The thicket erupted with sound of tearing talons and scraping scales.

* * * * *

It was difficult to fly.

The trailing edge of Destruction's right wing had been shredded, and there were all sorts of holes in his left. The air passed through the membrane as if it were netting, and several bones had been broken, making it difficult to keep his wings extended.

Luckily Destruction had only a few more miles to go. He could see the edge of the Nakaya Swamp off in the distance. Green turned to black where it was slowly being eaten away. It would be good to touch down on swampy soil, to feel its power course through his broken body and start rebuilding him.

Broken . . . that was hardly the word for it.

Destruction's body was gouged, torn, bitten, shredded, ripped, *and* broken. And for what? A few drops of blood.

Well, there was plenty of blood. Destruction was covered in it, both his own and that of the great green. He could even tell which was which. His blood was a dark crimson, and Chloridon's had a green tint.

Green-tinted blood. It was on the dragon's arms, legs, and wings. A long line of it ran down his tail, parts of it still fresh. There was more than enough to fill the vial.

Destruction stopped flapping his wings and just soared, not caring how much height he lost.

Enough to fill the vial . . .

Destruction spotted a clearing in the forest below, and he headed for it. Landing, he grabbed the vial hanging from his neck and tore it from the thong.

With a slightly shaky claw, Destruction began running the lip of the vial against his body, scraping up the green-hued blood. In no time at all the vial was full, brimming with Chloridon's strange and powerful blood.

Deadalus would be pleased.

What luck.

As Destruction replaced the cork in the top of the vial, he wondered, Had I truly been lucky?

I might even let you go—

There was no way he could have escaped the great green's lair without the dragon willing it. The dragon had said something else. . . .

. . . drinking my blood from that vial quite possibly would empower the lich, or any other undead creature for that matter . . .

Of course, thought Destruction, clenching the vial tightly in his fist and leaping into the air.

Strangely, flying didn't seem so difficult anymore.

* * * * *

"I think I hear something," said Mulago.

Deadalus strained to listen and then caught the faint sound of something odd. It didn't sound like dragon's wings at all, but the flapping of a main sail on a frigate. Then, as the sound grew slightly louder, a single black dragon appeared on the horizon.

A chittering cheer rose from the gathered vermin.

"One of the blacks returns," said Mulago.

"I can see that."

"Is it Destruction?"

Deadalus couldn't tell from this distance just how big the dragon was. The only thing he could determine was that it had been badly wounded and was having trouble staying aloft. No matter. It would be upon them in moments, and then the story would be known—and the blood of Chloridon would be his.

At last the dragon came to land, touching down softly on the moist black earth.

"Destruction!" Deadalus exclaimed. "You've returned."

The dragon nodded. "Yes, milord."

"And the rest?"

"All dead."

Deadalus paused a moment. He regretted the loss of the three other dragons. It had taken much time and energy to transform them. "And the blood?"

"Yes," said Destruction.

"You got it?" cried the lich.

Destruction nodded.

"Give it to me!"

Destruction extended his hand, the vial still clutched in his fingers.

"Give it!"

The dragon opened his hand, revealing the empty vial.

"What sort of trickery is this?" cried Deadalus. "Where is the blood of Chloridon?"

Destruction ran his tongue over his lips, cleaning away some, but not all, of the green-tinged blood that had spilled from the corners of his mouth.

"What have you done?" asked Deadalus, confused.

Instead of answering the question, Destruction lunged at the lich with bared talons.

The dragon was upon Deadalus before he had time to move. As his body was torn apart, all Deadalus could think was how such fire could fill the eyes of a dragon under his control. . . .

Because of a Twig . . .

Brian M. Thomsen

In the fire-hardened mountains of Shiv, a comet crashed.
Because of the comet, a crater was formed.
Because of the crater, the rains were caught.
Because of the rains, a lake was made.
Because of the lake, the plants could grow.
Because of the plants, a forest thrived.
Because of the forest, a paradise was born.
All because of a comet. . . .

According to druid chroniclers, the lush green paradise of Cometia wasn't always a sanctuary amid the wastes of Shiv. The forest's and lake's existence was the product of an outside force, the legendary comet from which the land took its name. It created a cool haven amid fire-scorched mountains of jagged rock. This deposit from the skies impacted the ground with such force that it carved out a new valley. The heat of the land was cooled by the icy comet, and its waters enriched the newly dug silt until the forest itself was born and thrived.

That was many years ago. The inhabitants of Cometia had since lived their lives in blissful seclusion from the fiery antagonists that surrounded them. Sheer, impassible cliff walls encircled their valley. But as an outside force once formed their paradise, a different outside force now threatened their survival.

Five ranges over, a volcano collapsed upon itself, sending a tremor for miles around. This tremor was felt and forgotten by the inhabitants of Cometia. Such things happened occasionally.

The tremor, however, cracked the wall of the secluded crater. It was not much of a crack, really, just large enough for a single individual to pass through. No one even noticed initially, from within or without.

Yet this crack had the potential of destroying their green paradise—if knowledge of the breach fell into deadly and competent hands. . . .

*   *   *   *   *

"You smell bad!"

"Look who's talking!"

"Quiet, you two! I'm trying to sleep!"

"What do you mean you're trying to sleep, you lazy son of an ill-formed Viashino?" Strother the Strange, a foul smelling dwarf even on the best of days, bellowed at the still-supine orc. He hit him upside the head with the flat of his axe.

"How dare you insult my parentage!" barked the rudely awakened orc. He quickly yet awkwardly stood to face his loutish tormentor. Their shouts echoed in the cave mouth where they camped. "Viashino blood has never tainted the lineage of the family Borg. As the ninth of my line, revered among all orcs of Shiv, I should know. You have no right to make such accusations!"

"I don't care who your mother is or where your father's been—even if you *could* pick him out of a lineup. It's your turn to go find work!" Strother insisted.

"Well, what's for breakfast?" Borg the Ninth retorted.

"Yeah," agreed the grouchy goblin. He went by the moniker Elam the Awful, and smelled appropriately. "I'm hungry, too. What's for breakfast?"

"I haven't found it yet," Strother replied.

"You mean I've been guarding our camp all night, and there's nothing to eat!"

"I'll get around to it," the dwarf shot back.

"Well, fine! Get to it!"

"Who died and appointed you goblin king?"

* * * * *

A lowly, would-be gardener by the name of Snap was the first to notice the breach.

Actually, Snap was a dragon, and as such would not usually have been allowed in Cometia's gardens, let alone permitted to tend them. A dragon ought to perform less pastoral duties. Snap's so-called "green claw" had, however, impressed the druid in charge of this patch. Thus he was unofficially allowed to help in daily duties.

Snap was tending his patch of cowslips when he noticed a thread of light reaching a corner that should have been in shadow until midday. Not wishing to ignore even the slightest disruption in nature's balance, he quickly brought the presence of the new ray of light to the attention of his druid supervisor.

Together, they found the crack in the valley wall. It was narrow and black, and full of foreboding.

The druid was left with a quandary. Snap was right to be concerned about any shifts in the nature's balance . . . but did he dare report the observation to the elven council, risking the question of what a dragon was doing tending cowslips?

The druid sighed.

Nature moves in mysterious ways, he thought to himself, and I must follow her lead.

Taking a moment to double-check that Snap was busy at some task that needed no supervision, the druid hurried off to the elven council with the news, which he would claim as his own.

* * * * *

As with most august bodies, the elven council was hard to impress. Still they decided to dispatch a fey scout to investigate.

The scout returned and reported that indeed a crack had formed in the protective crater wall.

Elf King Adamkin inquired, "And what lies beyond the crack?"

"A plateau surrounded by red rocks and infernal heat," the fey replied, wringing the sweat from the folds of its gossamer wings. "I would have explored farther but—"

The elf king held up his hand and shook his head. "There is no need," Adamkin replied. "We have lived in peaceful seclusion for many an eon. A crack in the crater won't change matters. I assure you of that."

* * * * *

None of the ugly triumvirate was in a particularly good mood. Going without breakfast is not the best way to start the day.

While Elam the Awful tried to nap (exhausted by his guard duty the night before), and Borg the orc scouted for food (driven out by his comrades' insults), Strother the Strange examined a cache of artifacts the three had found in the cave a few months before.

Since that time, they had survived off proceeds from the sale of the legendary Hannis Cauldron, a magical artifact that produced milk by the cupful. The goblin brigade had been eager to get their hands on the artifact, and had acquired it in exchange for three months' provisions and three draft waivers. (None of the triumvirate desired the duty and honor of protecting the goblin king, no matter what the price). Unfortunately, the provisions had run out a few days ago, as had the term of the waivers. The situation necessitated a certain amount of effort by the three to avoid going hungry or, even worse, getting drafted.

As usual, the heat of the day was prohibitively infernal, negating any chance of real rest for Elam. The grouchy goblin decided to take a walk, hoping to tire himself out enough that he could sleep, even in this dragon-be-damned heat.

Why do I have to do all the work? the goblin thought. The foul smelling orc and the dirty dwarf had even managed to sleep through last night's earthquake. It just wasn't fair!

Elam liked to climb, so he decided to scale a jagged rock

face in search of a mountain breeze to aid in sleep.

Instead of a breeze, he found a rocky plateau with a scant opening in the mountain wall. A short jaunt through the crack revealed an entire cool paradise just beyond.

Drinking water, food, and stuff, he thought. All mine! His mouth began to water in anticipation.

Then he noticed a contingent of elf archers and sentry craw wyrms that could devour him in half a mouthful.

It's not fair! he insisted to himself, and then brightened. Maybe Strother or Borg can help. Maybe they will know how we can claim this bounty without fuss or bother.

After all, they were much smarter than he.

* * * * *

Borg also wasn't having a good day, as usual.

Orcs were not known for pleasant dispositions. It was always too hot or too cold, there was never enough food, and what there was wasn't any good.

Worse, Borg was a coward, which made him of a similar disposition to the other two members of the ugly triumvirate, but set him quite at odds with the popular conception of his race. This fact made matters worse for the ornery orc.

"What have we here?" asked a snide voice from a nearby rock pile.

Borg looked up from the crevice where he had hunted bugs and saw a patrol party for the local goblin brigade, led by a big, ugly orc.

"A draft dodger," the commander said, answering his own question.

Borg shook his head mournfully. "No one in my noble lineage has ever—"

"Unless you and your cronies make another payment, you'll find yourselves on the front lines of some even more hellish place than this, to give your lives for the glory and honor of the great goblin king!"

Borg may not have been smart, but he could think on his feet. He quickly cut a deal whereby he would use his "black market" contacts to help provision the army for their next campaign.

"*You* have ties to the black market?" the orc commander asked incredulously.

"Of course," Borg replied. "Anything you need, and cheaper than wholesale."

"The price doesn't concern me," the orc answered. "That's your problem. We'll just say that our payment is *deferred*, if you know what I mean."

With a hearty, blood-curdling laugh, the brigade returned to their patrol.

His horned head hung low, Borg slogged back to his camp, only one thought on his mind . . . and it wasn't concern about pricing.

Where am I going to be able to drum up some black market contacts in this awful wasteland? Oh, well, he thought in resignation, *Strother and Elam are much smarter than I. Maybe they will know what to do.*

* * * * *

Despite his earlier proclamations, Elf King Adamkin decided certain defensive actions might be prudent. He mobilized a force from the abundant denizens of the paradisiacal valley.

The folk took comfort from their king's action; he knew how to protect his people.

The elf king himself was not quite sure. He alone seemed to realize that his standing army presaged an invasion that could well endanger their paradise.

Hoping for the best, Adamkin signed a draft edict that required the registry of all possible members of his warrior force . . . even a bucolic dragon by the name of Snap, who would soon find himself removed from his gardening duties.

* * * * *

Strother wiped the sweat from his dwarven brow and scratched himself, trying to alleviate the itches and irritations of uncleanness. Feeling little relief, he returned to his examination of the pile of junk.

Damned goblin brigade! he thought to himself. We should have held out for more for that Hannis Cauldron. Oh, well, maybe there's another one of those around here someplace.

The crusty old dwarf was quickly discouraged. The pile of junk seemed to yield little more than . . . well . . . junk.

"Blast it all," he bellowed and hurled a mace at a dented machine of some kind resting in the corner of the lair.

The mace hit the machine, sparked, and vanished as the crank on the machine began to turn. From its innards popped a venomous serpent, which quickly slithered toward the dwarf.

"Damned vermin!" he blasted. He hacked the serpent's head off with his trusty axe. "Just what I don't need! Well if worse comes to worst, we can always make serpent stew I reckon."

Strother took a few moments to examine the generator. A quick buff with sweat-dampened sleeve revealed a nameplate that read "Dirk the Dastardly."

"Well that explains it," he said to himself, recalling the legendary exploits of the crackpot artificer.

With the anticipation of a slightly fuller belly, he picked up the serpent's body and set about to cooking his comrades a meal.

* * * * *

"I have some good news, and I have some bad news," Borg reported, returning to camp. "I ran into the goblin forces who wanted to impress us, but I talked them out of it."

"Good," Elam replied with a swagger.

"I'm not finished," Borg continued.

"Why not?" Strother inquired looking up from the pot of serpent stew he was in the midst of preparing.

"That was just the good news."

"No," Elam insisted, "that was the bad news and the good news. Bad news—you ran into the goblins. Good news—you talked them out of impressing us."

"No," Borg corrected, " that was just the good news."

"What's the bad news then?"

"I told them we would outfit their regiment with provisions from our black market sources."

"What black market sources?" Strother asked with a squint.

"That's the bad news."

"You agreed to *provide* for them when we can't even provide for ourselves? They'll not accept a steady diet of serpent stew. Of that, I assure you," Strother retorted. He sampled his latest culinary creation and proclaimed. "Soup's on."

The three divvied up the stew and dug in with numerous slurps and gurgles until the bowls were as empty of sustenance as their souls were of virtue.

"Too bad," Elam said out loud, picking his teeth and preparing to belch.

"The stew wasn't that bad," Strother insisted defensively.

"Not the soup," Elam explained. "The situation. There's a bountiful valley dripping with proverbial milk and honey, right beyond that ridge."

"Sounds great," Borg inserted with anticipation. "What's to stop us from laying claim to it?"

"Somebody got their first," Elam countered, "and brought along an entire elf army. The last time I looked, none of us was inclined to take anything that involved actually putting up a fight."

"Maybe they'll leave, and we can clean up after them," Borg offered.

"Probably not in enough time to ward off the press gang," Elam said.

Strother stroked his beard and offered, "Maybe they will leave if we give them a little encouragement?"

With a smirk and a fiendish chortle, the smelly old dwarf proceeded to tell his comrades of the legendary serpent generator of Dirk the Dastardly.

"So, you see," Strother concluded, "as long as we keep the generator safe and fed with mana—magical items, and other sorts of fuel—we can produce an unlimited number of serpents. They'll infest the valley and drive those leafy vermin out. Then everything is free for our pickings."

"Yeah, but it'll be full of poison snakes," the goblin groused.

"Nope," Strother replied. "We just destroy the generator, and all of the serpents will also be destroyed. It was one of the quirks of Dirk's design. Of course, we have to keep it safe until then, but I'm pretty sure three such stout fellows as ourselves will have no such trouble protecting one little generator. Now let's move our camp to this plateau and get to work."

With that, the ugly triumvirate relocated their camp to the plateau. They transported their junk pile of artifacts along with the legendary serpent generator of Dirk the Dastardly to their new siege base.

Once everything was in place, they set in motion their invasion, one serpent after another until a continuous stream of vermin passed through the crack to bedevil the inhabitants within.

*　*　*　*　*

Down in the no-longer-peaceable paradise, the serpents were first seen as an inconvenience, more akin to a pest infestation than an actual invasion. Once the elf king realized that no end was in sight, his forces mobilized.

By that time, the serpents had already laid claim to the upper reaches of the crater. All too quickly and in great numbers, they descended the walls and entered the forests of the basin.

"What do you have to report?" Adamkin demanded of a recently returned fey scout. The elf king was the sort of leader who preferred to direct his forces from the rear and had sent a full contingent of fey scouts to determine the source of the serpents.

"They are coming from the crack at a continuous pace, almost as if they were one long serpent."

"It would appear we underestimated our vulnerability," Adamkin admitted. "Even so small a crack can be an unmanageable breach if the stream of invasion is relentless."

"Yes, sire."

"Still, how hard can it be to rid ourselves of these serpent pests? Let us convene a conference with the rest of your contingent."

"You just did, Your Highness," the fey replied sarcastically. "I am the sole survivor." With that, the fey stormed out of the king's chamber in disgust. On its way, it passed a contingent of druid chroniclers laden with pages upon pages of reports.

How quickly the casualties mount, the fey conceded, even from pesky serpents.

Something had to be done . . . if it wasn't already too late.

* * * * *

"Stop eating the serpents!" Strother bellowed.

"But I'm hungry," Borg groused.

"There will be plenty to eat soon enough," Elam assured. "The three of us'll go claim that which is rightfully ours, since we done stole it first with no one to say otherwise. And the best part is that the serpents' sting is much worse than its appetite, so they'll leave lots. Sweet brownie soup with fey dumplings, elven roast, and craw wyrm croissants. . . ."

"And we'll eat to our hearts' content," Strother concluded.

"And buy another deferment from impressment," Borg added. "I mean I gave them my word."

"What ever that's worth," Elam snorted.

"Whatever," Strother added. "There will be more than enough fodder to feed a goblin nation, let alone a goblin army."

"And we didn't have to do more than lift a finger," Elam chortled.

"I like this type of a war," Borg rejoined. "It's quick and painless."

"For us, at least," Strother concluded.

The ugly triumvirate continued to laugh as the generator, shielded from attack within the crack of the crater, continued to spew out venomous pests.

* * * * *

The first wave of defenders had already deployed, fought, and retreated with casualties in excess of fifty percent. Jungle cat warriors and elven riders alike nursed wounds—if they were lucky enough to return to the ever-retreating elven lines.

Druid healers and weird women ministered to the wounded as the second wave of defense moved against the venomous onslaught.

In the rear ranks of the second wave, the young dragon Snap tried to make idle conversation with his craw wyrm companion.

"Do you think we have a chance?" the dragon inquired.

"I used to," the wyrm replied, and then added with a chuckle, "until I saw the likes of you in this wave. We must really be getting desperate."

"I understand that the previous plans have been abandoned."

The wyrm nodded and said, "You can't out maneuver a stream of vipers. What it comes down to is nonstop one-on-one combat, with the hope that eventually you out number them."

"But they keep coming with more serpents. The more we lose, the more they seem to gain," said the young dragon.

"So you understand our problem," the wyrm conceded.

A cry of "For Adamkin and Cometia!" rose, signaling the launch of the second and final wave of defense.

"Whatever," the wyrm said in resignation. "One day is as good to die on as any other."

"Is it?" the scared young dragon inquired.

"Who knows?" the wyrm conceded and slithered off into melee against the serpent invaders.

The young dragon followed closely.

* * * * *

"I'm still hungry," Borg insisted.

"So am I," Elam agreed.

Strother stood up and looked over the generator, out into the green crater where the battle raged. "Everything is going according to plan. I guess grabbing every fourth serpent for food shouldn't get in the way of victory."

With that, the dwarf set about making his signature pot of serpent stew. Elam and Borg alternated grabbing up serpents fresh from the generator.

"O-o-o-m good, o-o-o-m good, just like mother used to make!" they all agreed and sang aloud.

* * * * *

The carnage was horrible.

Who would have thought snakes could overwhelm a craw wyrm or a battle beast? That was exactly what was happening.

Snap watched in horror as an emerald dragon stumbled slightly at the sting of a serpent. The stumble was more than enough to spell his death. As the flightless dragon tottered, more serpents took hold, stinging him higher and higher until even his neck and head were covered by the leeching wave.

"Oh, Cometia!" the emerald dragon exhorted with his dying breath.

The plague of serpents encircled his neck and constricted the creature's airway.

With an awe-inspiring thud, the dragon slammed to the ground, flattening a coterie of coyotes who had been frantically trying to ward off the onslaught. Both dragon and coyotes were now no more than serpent fodder.

Snap knew there was no turning back. Behind him lay only the wounded and helpless. The rest of the defenders fought ferociously ahead of him. He realized he was the last line of defense, a terrible burden.

He knew he could never live with himself if he fell and allowed defeat . . . but he also knew that if craw wyrms and battle beasts were overwhelmed, a dragon named Snap had as much of a chance as a fire elemental in the depths of the Voda Sea.

There was only one option—Full frontal assault. Someone else would have to be the last line of defense.

With renewed gusto, Snap pressed forward, moving himself up through the ranks.

The craw wyrm had been right, one day was as good to die on as any other. For that matter, a single second of that day would do just fine.

* * * * *

The sounds of battle and death were not even noticed by the feasting triumvirate.

"I've never tasted such wonderful serpent stew," Borg belched out, his forked tongue wiping the juice from the corners of his mouth.

"Thank you, my comrade with the gourmet gullet," Strother replied. The dwarf bowed and flourished his ladle. "I've always said that among the long line of Borg orcs—"

"Of which I am the ninth."

"Of which you are indeed the ninth," the dwarf assented, "you are undoubtedly the one with the best taste."

"Oh, I don't know about that," Elam argued with a leer. "Let me have a bite of your arm so that I can find out."

"Not that type of taste," Borg corrected warily.

"Just kidding," Elam replied with a chuckle, "but you know how we could really improve this already delicious soup?"

"How?"

"Why, add more serpents!"

Strother looked out past the generator, to the crater beyond. A craw wyrm was covered in serpents, and a forest giant toppled to the ground, his girth squashing a contingent of elf archers.

"Things look good on the battlefield. I guess every third serpent for stew wouldn't hurt," the dwarf agreed.

* * * * *

All around Snap was carnage.

True, dead serpents outnumbered dead comrades-in-arms, but the battle raged on. Behemoth's and other massive creatures of the forest began to fall, one right after another, worn down by the sheer number of attacks.

Even a one-legged brownie could lick a snake . . . but what about an unending wave of snakes?

The smell of death filled the crater, and the second wave was losing ground.

Still Snap pressed on—through the blood and over the bodies.

Every serpent that got in his way was quickly dispatched with the teeth of his razor sharp jaws.

To tarry was to die. The image of the dead emerald dragon was firmly engraved in his mind.

Snap pressed on.

* * * * *

"You know what I like best about the serpent stew?" Elam asked.

"The serpents," Borg agreed.

"Indeed," Strother conceded, patting his swelling belly. He couldn't remember when it had last been so full. Still, the goblin and orc were outeating him, and this wouldn't do. He quickly surmised what his problem was and set about correcting it.

"To blast with the stew," the dwarf announced. "Why should I have to spend time stewing? Let's just eat them raw!"

Elam looked over the generator and grabbed a fresh one.

"Victory is almost at hand," the goblin announced. "Every other serpent should do just fine."

"Agreed!" the other two conceded.

Elam quickly cut the serpent in three and divvied up the pieces.

"I almost hate to think about having to turn this little thing off," Strother admitted.

"Elf meat is sweeter," Borg pointed out.

"And a lot more meaty," Elam added.

"Indeed," Strother replied, his mouth full and his mind and belly making up for lost time.

* * * * *

The dragon named Snap pushed forward, pausing only a moment to look beyond the next pile of corpses and to the wall.

He could now clearly see the breach.

Indeed, it was the source of the serpents!

And they seemed to be coming out more slowly.

Maybe his comrades could hold or even regain their lost ground.

He had to try.

* * * * *

Belch.

"Says you."

"How's the battle going?"

"Something green is just within reach. Anyone want dessert?"

* * * * *

An orcish hand reached out at Snap, but the dragon darted ahead and right below it, into what seemed to be a dark tunnel in the breach.

* * * * *

"Damn it! It got away!"

"What was it?"

"A twig dragon, I think."

"Not worth the bother."

"Not even a mouthful."

"Where did it go?"

"Into the generator."

"Into the generator?"

* * * * *

Snap pressed onward and came head to head with a serpent that he quickly dispatched—biting off its head and swallowing it whole.

The rest of its body thrashed, as headless serpents are wont to do. Still Snap pressed on, using the serpent corpse first as a battering ram before him and then as a buffer. Another serpent tried to push its way through the hole.

With one last shove, Snap made the serpent corpse into a plug.

* * * * *

"Something went in."

"And now nothing is coming out!"

"The twig dragon is stopping up the works."

"Why is the generator beginning to smoke?"

"They usually do that before they explode."

"Explode!"

* * * * *

The enchanted metal of the magical machine quickly overheated. Gears whined. Tubes blazed. The whole thing exploded, spewing the lowly twig dragon and a host of serpent corpses out through the gap. It blew itself apart, sending a wave of magical shrapnel across the rocky plateau.

The ugly triumvirate, realizing an explosion was imminent, had hightailed it down among jagged rock formations and back to safety. As a result, they did not see the rock slide triggered by the artifact engine's noisy self-destruction. Sand, gravel, and boulders tightly sealed the breach in the crater wall, restoring it to its previous impenetrability.

* * * * *

"That was a close call," Borg admitted.

"You said a mouthful," Elam agreed.

"Indeed!" Strother assented.

"So where are our provisions?" a new voice joined the chorus.

The ugly triumvirate turned around to face the goblin press gang, who looked very hungry and not very pleased.

"Well . . ." Borg began to explain.

The orc in charge, a brutish fellow three times the size of Borg, raised his claw to signal silence.

"Save it for the sergeant," he ordered. "I just hope he assigns you to me. Tomorrow we set off for the slough of zombies. Nothing puts me in the mood for battling undead better than kicking the butts of new recruits."

If it weren't for the fear that gripped their entire bodies, the three might have noticed that they were once again hungry. All of the serpents, consumed and otherwise, had vanished with the demise of the Dirk's dastardly generator.

* * * * *

Snap came to in the hand of a druid priestess who ministered to the wounded of the Battle of the Breach.

"You have done well, little twig dragon," she cooed. "The fey have reported your bravery to the king. Adamkin wants to give you a medal."

"Is Cometia saved?" the twig dragon asked.

"Indeed," she replied. "You stopped the serpents and sealed the breach."

"I did?"

"Indeed."

* * * * *

Once upon a time Cometia was attacked.
Because of a crack, the crust was breached.
Because of the breach, the crater was invaded.
Because of the invasion, lives were lost.
But all was not doomed. . . .
Because of a twig dragon, an engine was jammed.
Because the engine jammed, the plague was abated.
Because the plague abated, the invasion was stopped.
Because the invasion stopped, the breach was sealed.
Because of a twig dragon, paradise was restored,
And peace returned to Cometia.
All because of a twig dragon.

Keldon Staredown
Scott McGough

The Parley

High in the northern mountains of Keld, Warlord Astor stopped a mere hundred feet from his goal. Fully armed and armored, with nothing but icy air and a clear line of sight between him and the cave, he fell motionless. This was the place he had come to see. This was where the dragon was. But something was definitely wrong.

He had studied dragons but never encountered one before. Nevertheless, he knew he was looking at one's nest: there were scorch marks and long furrows carved into the rocks, and the snow around the cave entrance had been repeatedly crushed down and planed flat by a heavy, dragging weight. It looked as if something slightly bigger than the cave's entrance had dragged itself out of the mountain's hollow peak, spitting fire and venom as it came. Argivians said that if you looked for a dragon's nest and couldn't find it, you were either very blind, or very wise.

Astor thought Argivians talked too much. He could feel something about this nest was not right: the smell, the density of the air, the patterns of energy only a Keldon warrior chief could see. Though he had seen barely nineteen winters, he was still a full-fledged warlord. He was connected to the harsh landscape of Keld, able to sense the ebb and flow of potential violence that permeated his homeland. Here, the waves were diffuse and uncertain, though they ought to have been stark and solid, like Keld itself. Something was out of place, and his surroundings were out of balance.

Behind Astor, his translator, Ysenga, struggled over the last rise of rock. Astor wondered if she had heard the old Argivian saying about finding a dragon's nest. He also wondered if she knew its Keldon corollary: By the time you find a dragon, it has certainly found you.

Ten paces behind Ysenga came his warhost: thirty foot-soldiers led by three commanders, all ready, willing, and eager to fight and die at the barest nod from their warlord. The grim, gray-skinned warriors moved in tight formation. Astor grunted in satisfaction. These men were as they should be. Their energy was crisp and determined. They themselves were focused and alert. Astor reveled in their collective hunger for combat, inhaling their trust in his leadership like a swimmer about to submerge.

The translator staggered to his side. Though Astor was still growing, he towered over Ysenga. She was in all ways ill-equipped for the wilds of Keld: slight build, pale skin, short red hair, pale blue eyes. She shivered in the wind and squinted in the glare from the snow. Her breath came in great, gasping clouds of fog that hung in the air long after they left her body.

Astor remained silent and still.

Ysenga gratefully planted her feet in the deep snow, leaned on her staff, and focused all her attention on breathing. She filled her lungs slowly and evenly to avoid choking on the frigid air.

Astor continued to stare at the entrance to the cave.

Over the past seven days, there had been strange lights in the sky and strange rumblings in the mountains. An armed convoy had gone missing in the Northern Wastes, which were under his protection. When he investigated, Astor had sensed uncertainty in the region. Now, he could see the disturbance centered around this cave. The resident dragon's good behavior had been guaranteed by ritual, oath, and hostage. If she was in fact marauding, Astor was here to remind her who the true masters of Keld were.

"When I speak," he said suddenly to Ysenga, "you will translate what I say, only what I say, and exactly what I say." He was gratified to see her flash of exasperation and annoyance at such basic advice. Astor was pleased. He respected her confidence.

Nonetheless, he leaned in, mere inches from her face. Deep inside his helm, his eyes smoldered.

"Acknowledge," he said softly, and there was no mistaking the threat in his tone.

"Yes, sir," she said immediately. Ysenga was not a native Keldon, and she still didn't understand the delicate brutality of the warhost's chain of command. She understood languages, however, and she was quickly learning that how a warlord spoke conveyed far more than what he actually said.

She had been sent to Astor as a special attaché to his 'host—a gift of sorts from his female mentor, the Doyenne Tajamin. Tajamin was one of the fiercest individuals in Keld, and one of the most powerful members of the ruling council. Astor was proud to call her his ally and had offered sincere thanks for the translator's services. In private, however, he cursed Tajamin as one curses a meddlesome aunt. The doyenne employed all of the translators that spoke dragon-tongue. Thus she guaranteed that any conflict between Keldon and dragon came from proper enmity rather than miscommunication . . . and served her interests as well as Keld's.

Astor nudged Ysenga and jerked his head toward the cave. She nodded wearily.

"Yes, sir."

Astor snarled, distracted. " 'Understood' is sufficient, translator."

"Yes . . . understood."

Astor began to move, bounding with long, loping strides over the heavy snow. Ysenga fell in behind him. She swore softly, unable to keep up and clearly terrified of falling too far behind.

In the flattened clearing around the entrance, Astor motioned for Ysenga to stand beside a charred black rock. Stepping up onto the rock himself, Astor cupped both hands and bellowed, "Hoy, dragon!" down into the cave, in the rough common tongue of his people. He planted his hands on his hips, within easy reach of the twin short *kugri* blades he kept strapped at his waist. A broadsword rode on his back.

Ysenga hesitated until Astor fixed her with a steely gaze.

"Translate," he prompted.

Struggling for the words, Ysenga turned and stammered in the hissing, shrieking cadence of dragon tongue, "Hail . . . Mighty One. We . . . crave an audience."

An angry buzzing hum issued from the cave, but there was no reply.

"Kavalex." Astor called the dragon by name. "Show yourself. I say you have violated the ancient compact. Keld will have satisfaction, or," he produced a melon-sized dragon egg from his leather satchel and held it high, "your progeny becomes my omelet."

Ysenga's eyes bulged, but her voice stayed even and clear as she screeched out the translation.

There was definite movement from inside the cave. A huge, ponderous scraping sound emerged, and the scaly crest of a dragon's head appeared.

Ysenga started to edge back, but Astor froze her with another glare and a hand on his kugri.

"You risk more by running," he said in High Keld. Ysenga remained where she was. Astor dropped the egg back into the satchel.

A narrow crested head rose into full view, framed by the entrance to the cave. The eyes stared, and the tongue lolled clumsily out of the tapered snout. As the face leaned from the cave, it overbalanced and crashed onto the flattened snow, rolling end over end until the horns snagged on a broken rock. The head had been torn off the neck hours ago, perhaps even days. There was no blood left to stain the ground.

"Kavalex is not home," an eerie, mocking voice called from inside the cave. It spoke in Common Keld.

The head that now appeared in the entrance was very

much alive. It was long, rounded, and massive, like an over-
turned rowboat. Its huge eyes were aglow with gleeful malice
and blue eldritch energy. Dozens of serrated, hand-sized
teeth gleamed in its mouth. Snakelike, the live dragon
pushed its head through the entrance, its eyes fixed on
Astor. It worked its long neck and flexible torso through.
Once its front limbs were entirely clear, it popped its shoulders back into joint, spread its wings, and let out a small roar
that drove Ysenga's hands over her ears.

Astor stood resolute, his arms grimly crossed over his
chest. The dragon was at least eighteen feet long, and he
added another ten for the tail still hidden in the cave.
There was no way to gauge its weight. Flying dragons had
evolved lightweight skeletons and musculature, and were
often aided by innate or acquired enchantments that kept
them aloft. Astor sensed no heat coming off it, but instead
a lazy, swirling eddy that pulled energy toward it like a
draining basin.

Here was the source of the energy disruption. Here was
the unseen factor in the basic equation of Keld. A blue-
scaled dragon had supplanted Kavalex and was calming the
tides of power instead of churning them.

Half in and half out of the cave, the new dragon looked
down at Astor and Ysenga. Its eyes opened wider as it hissed.

"Greetings, little ape," the dragon said cheerfully. "I
am Skouras from across the sea. I like very much these
mountains of yours. So calm, so peaceful. So cold. I think
I will be staying here for quite some time." As he spoke,
Skouras's head wove on his sinuous neck, listing slowly to
the right, to the left, forward and back.

"Greetings, rubber neck. You speak our language well. I am
Astor the Upstart, warlord of Keld, steward of the Northern

Wastes." From the side of his mouth, he muttered to Ysenga, "Run. He understands me, and I him. Run. Now."

Skouras hissed and sneered. "Languages are a hobby of mine. I was speaking to Kavalex in this clumsy tongue of yours, right before I took her head. Strange how she never spoke it to any of you."

Kavalex had been far larger than Skouras, Astor thought, and she could breathe fire, as a proper dragon should. Skouras must have surprised her. Perhaps he talked her to death.

Skouras continued. "She promised me, by the way, that I could expect to see a platoon of you ill-mannered brutes before the snows came. And here you are." The dragon craned its long neck and brought its head down to Astor's level, holding his eyes from thirty feet away. "How amusing. Are you mad, little warrior, or simply unintelligent?"

"Both, I think." Astor felt the first stirrings of a wild fury burrowing into his brain, and he welcomed it. Behind him his warriors felt it, too, and he knew they were straining for the order to attack. "And you need not worry about the snows," Astor added. "They aren't due for weeks, and you will be dead long before the first flake ever touches the ground."

"Sir?" Ysenga whispered miserably. She hadn't moved. Astor kept his eyes fixed on the dragon's. "Sir," she repeated, louder and more urgently. "I can't move."

Skouras maintained eye contact with Astor but spoke to Ysenga. "Child," he said, "I think you should do as your master commands. Run. It won't save you." He ruffled his wings absently. "But it will let us finish this delightful conversation in peace."

Furious, Astor snarled in High Keld, "Go now, translator." His voice rose. "Warriors—"

Skouras slammed his forelimbs into the frozen ground, creating a tremor that shook rocks free from the slopes below and bowled Astor backward off his perch.

Before he landed, Astor barked out the rest of his attack command. In perfect unison, his warhost drew their weapons and charged. Astor jumped back to his feet, gorging himself on their fury, feeding them with his own, and he drew his broadsword. A huge wave of violence swelled up between Astor and the dragon. It would crest soon, and Astor howled in the ripe joy of not knowing which way it would break.

He led his troops straight toward Skouras and the stolen nest.

With a cruel smile and without taking his eyes off Astor, Skouras opened his wings and threw himself into the sky.

The Rout

Like all Keldons, Astor had been fighting since his arms were strong enough to raise his infant fists. He had cut down scores of enemy troops; he had scarred and wounded dozens of insubordinate warriors; he had even killed two fellow warlords who dared challenge his authority. Outside of his mentors Olvresk and Tajamin, there wasn't a doyen or doyenne on the council who didn't fear his full potential.

In a single battle, high in the northern mountains of Keld, Skouras the dragon nearly took it all away from him.

A full warhost should have been able to defeat a dragon, even a large, unfamiliar dragon like Skouras. Astor's warriors should have been able to spear him from the sky, to hack him down to the point where Astor himself could deliver the killing blow by either magic or steel. The unique bond that linked Keldon warriors to their warlord in killing frenzy should have made them all strong enough to pierce the dragon's hide, fast enough to dodge his reaping claws, and angry enough to ignore their instinctual fear of such a dangerous creature.

Should have, should have, should have.

Astor accepted full responsibility. Under Doyenne Tajamin's baleful eye, he had studied hundreds of Keldon campaigns and skirmishes. At Doyen Olvresk's side, he had fought against hundreds, even thousands of Keld's enemies. Nine times out of ten, Keld won the day through sheer and sudden overwhelming force. Keld's warriors covered ground more quickly than her enemy's, killed faster and more brutally than they could be killed. All the unfamiliar terrain and old soldier's tricks in the world couldn't keep your blood in your veins once a Keldon got his hands on you.

But Astor had come prepared to fight one dragon, and hadn't altered his thinking or his attack strategy enough when faced with Skouras. The malicious dragon from across the sea had kept the young warlord off-balance and out of tune with his 'host from the moment the battle began. The wave of battle Astor was riding never actually broke.

As Astor recovered his footing after Skouras's ground tremor, Ysenga stayed where she was, rooted, eyes wide. She was not in the direct path of the charging warhost, so Astor ignored her. Sometimes in battle, a single moment can stretch to impossible lengths. For Astor, that moment came while he and his 'host were charging forward and Skouras was swooping down to meet them. He held his enemy's eyes every step of the way.

Unlike previous transcendent moments, however, this one was not caused by the warrior's haze, or impending death, or even the rush of imminent victory. Instead, it was an actual physical sensation, a nauseous lurch in his guts that grew into body-wide numbness that deadened both his senses and his connection to his 'host. Astor could see and hear himself roaring, running, and swinging his blade, but he was straining against the very air to do so. It felt like he swam through tree sap or climbed a rope with stones chained to his feet. Astor became more of a spectator than a warlord, and his tightly disciplined 'host became a mere collection of crazed, flailing individuals.

Skouras scornfully flew over Astor and landed heavily in the middle of the advancing 'host. The impact of his body alone claimed seven. His claws, jaws, and tail immediately killed or maimed a dozen more.

Ten seconds into the battle, and more than half of Astor's troops were gone. He struggled to turn and join the melee, but his limbs were dead, leaden and unresponsive. He tried to shout orders, but in the time it took him to inhale Skouras killed three more of his 'host. The dragon found the warlord's eyes again. Skouras smiled at him.

Astor's roar was an explosion of pure hatred and frustration. It rose above the killing field, eclipsing the curses of the wounded and the incessant hissing of the dragon. As his war cry echoed and reechoed off the nearby cliffs, Astor blinked. The heavy blanket around him grew lighter.

Ysenga stumbled forward, then caught herself and struggled back, down the ridge and away from the battle as Astor had ordered.

Heat and hatred built up behind Astor's eyes as he muttered the words to the Bogardan fire bolt spell. His left hand burst into flame but did not burn. From his fist erupted a solid column of fire.

Skouras's hissing grew angrier. He flung a half-dismembered warrior directly into the fire bolt and sprang skyward once more. The end of his tail and his left hind leg were caught in the fire, but it did little more than jar him off course as he rose. The scales that had caught the blast were blackened but undamaged.

Astor remembered the egg. It was a weapon, as well as a hostage. Infused with enough raw magic, it would explode like fifty pounds of black powder. Astor concentrated, gathering heat from deep below his feet and from the battle around him. He pulled out the egg, clamped it between both hands, and released it to float freely between them. He glared, channeling energy into it. The egg began to rotate. Once it glowed white-hot and spun like a top, he heaved the egg back over his shoulder. It bounced once and disappeared down the gullet of Skouras's cave. A huge gout of flame blew outward, shaking the ground.

"Hoy, Skouras!" Astor shouted savagely. "Kavalex's hoard is on fire! How much of it burns? How much of it melts? Hurry, rubber neck, while there's still treasure to rescue!"

Skouras was as greedy as Astor suspected. He roared in fury and came to ground, snatching up more warriors in each foreleg and in his mouth. He rained their pieces down on the others as he drove toward Astor and the cave.

"Ground him," Astor yelled. As Skouras charged past him, he drove the point of his broadsword into the dragon's side. "Let light through his wings."

Skouras snapped both his wings out wide, hurling Astor backward and decapitating another warrior. From behind, a spearman hurled his weapon, sinking it deep into the joint where Skouras's left wing met his body.

The dragon roared, more outraged than hurt. He turned

and undulated his long neck toward the javelin thrower. His closed mouth slammed dead center into the warrior's chest, bursting the man like a melon under a mallet.

His muzzle dripping, Skouras stole a glance at the cave, which now belched smoke and an angry, molten hiss. Skouras snarled, looked back at Astor, and narrowed his huge eyes.

In perfect imitation of Astor's voice, Skouras said, "Go, now," in High Keld, exactly as Astor had said to Ysenga.

Astor stared at the dragon, amazed as well as furious. "Fall back over that ridge," he called to his warriors, "back down the mountain. Find the translator and wait for me."

"Done," six scattered voices instantly replied.

Skouras hissed furiously, speaking in Common Keld once more. "Go on and run, little ape. I'll have more fun hunting you down than I would slaughtering you all here.

"This is my mountain now. And tomorrow, I'll take another. In a month, there won't be a Keldon alive between here and the sea." Skouras held Astor's eyes, all arrogance and amusement.

Astor grinned, and Skouras's confident smirk faltered.

"Prove it," Astor said. He spat at Skouras, sneered, and bounded over the ridge. Ahead of him, farther down the slope, he could see his warriors and beyond them, his translator.

As they headed for the forest, they kept close watch on the empty skies above the battlefield until they reached tree line and disappeared into the tall evergreens.

The Outcasts

On any good map of Keld, the village of Letha lay two days' march south of the Parman border, nestled between two of the most forbidding peaks on the continent. Keldon warriors joked that in order to find Letha, you had to be born there, and most of those born there had either fled or frozen to death trying to get out.

Astor had never been to Letha, but as steward of the region, he had memorized several excellent maps and was able to lead the remainder of his forces straight from the battleground at Skouras's cave to the silent, sleeping village.

Letha overlooked the coldest, most treacherous, and least-traveled passage north. The ice never melted, the winds never ceased, and in springtime the nearby mountains shrugged off their snowy shrouds at the merest whisper. In all, its buildings covered less than half an acre, and its permanent population numbered fewer than fifty. In truth, Letha was little more than a way station for travelers to and from the Border Citadel, ten days' march to the west.

In Keld, one lived as either a doyen's warrior or a doyenne's agent—or as an outcast in villages like Letha. The failed, the forgotten, and the forsaken were driven away from Keld's brutal culture by internal shame or external threats. Keldon prisoners of war also wound up in Letha, until they died or earned a place in the warrior nation's strict hierarchy of dominance. In the meantime, they simply languished like Letha itself—frozen, isolated, and ignored.

The predawn silence in Letha was almost palpable, but not unbreakable. Astor peered up at the watchtower sentry, who had observed the progress of the war band toward the village and nervously kept one hand on his poleaxe and the other on the alarm bell's rope.

The six warriors who followed Astor stopped as one behind him. Ysenga stood in the center of the unit, her eyes unfocused but her spine stiff.

"Blow your horn, sentry," Astor called in Common Keld. "Assemble your neighbors. There is killing to be done."

The sentry paused and snorted derisively. "I think you've taken a wrong turn, Commander. There's nothing here worth killing."

There was a brief and terrible pause. Then Astor called out, "You mean, besides you?"

In the darkness, Astor could not see the sentry clearly enough to cow him. Judging by his distracted tone, the man's survival instincts had been dulled by life in the doldrums of Letha. It was time to sharpen them.

"Who are you?" the sentry asked, his voice cracking.

Astor hooked a thumb under his faceplate and flipped his helm off onto the ground behind him. He gave the sentry a clear view of his stern gray face, long black hair that was frozen and matted with blood, and eyes ringed in black kohl and sparking like a blacksmith's forge.

"I am Astor," he called, his voice powerful and even. "Warlord of Keld. Steward of the Northern Wastes. Bearer of Three Blades. The Upstart." Astor lashed out, jutting his arm palm-first at the sentry. A head-sized fireball formed while his hand was in motion. It shot upward, slamming into the tower, erupting through the floorboards, and knocking the sentry back onto the rails.

"Sentry," Astor continued, "will you blow your horn now, or shall I tear out your lungs and use them to blow it for you?"

Astor continued to glare at the sentry, now lost in a cloud of smoke. Between the harsh laughter of his warriors and the frantic, incessant howl of the assembly horn, he would have wagered that Letha had never heard so much noise before sunrise.

Ten minutes later, Astor surveyed the assembled residents

of Letha. He spat angrily and turned to the primus, who governed the village, and the enforcer, who saw that the primus's orders were obeyed.

"Is this all?"

The primus, an elderly Keldon woman named Felal, nodded. "Fifteen men, twelve women. We're under strength at the moment. We sent our two best guides and a party of eight to the Border Citadel three days ago. They should be back in two weeks."

Astor pointedly looked at Felal, at her two personal bodyguards, and at the enforcer behind her.

"Eighteen men," he corrected, indicating the enforcer and Felal's bodyguards. "Thirteen women. Plus my six, my translator, and myself."

"With respect, warlord, I will be of little use to you. I left Port City many years ago to escape the noise of the council. I say I am unfit to serve you. This situation may be desperate—"

"Primus," Astor said seriously, "obey me and keep silent. We have much to do and no time to do it."

Felal nodded. "Understood. I can get the noncombatants hidden safely in the basement of the granary. The others should be able to help defend—"

"You misunderstand, Primus. From this moment forward, there are no noncombatants. We will not be 'defending' anything."

Felal looked pained. "Understood. But—"

"You misunderstand, Primus," Astor repeated, with an edge of menace. "There is a marauding dragon less than a day's march from here. I attacked him. He slaughtered most of my warhost. And," Astor's face went dark, "he is coming here."

"Uhh . . . understood."

Astor waited for Felal to add "but" again so he could cut her throat where she stood.

"Warlord Astor," Ysenga interposed. She had said very little during the trek down the mountain. She kept very close to Astor, however.

Astor kept his eyes fixed on the trembling primus. "You have something to add, translator?"

"I have something to translate. When the primus says 'Uhh . . . understood,' what she actually means is that Skouras already defeated a full 'host of thirty-odd warriors. There are fewer Lethans than that, and they can't fight half as well as the men Skouras has already killed."

Astor fixed her with a stern glare. Ysenga paled, but she defiantly held her head straight, her eyes focused on Astor's chin.

"Is that an accurate translation of your concerns, Primus? Or shall I trade this translator in for one that keeps to the words that have actually been said?"

"She is correct, Warlord. I am at your service, as is all of Letha. But we are not warriors. With six months of drills, I think we could march in formation. But we will never replace your warhost. Doubly so against the dragon who killed them."

Astor smiled coldly. "You are both correct," he said. "None of this pathetic rabble will ever be warriors." The primus's face remained an impassive mask, but Astor could tell she was not encouraged by his sudden candor.

"Warlord," Felal began. "You said—"

"I said there would be no noncombatants. I did not say there would be warriors.

"Lethans," he called out and suddenly stepped forward.

His warhost had lined the villagers up into one long bleary-eyed row. They watched Astor closely. Collectively, they were ready to rabbit, and he could feel it.

"Your village is dead," he went on. "From the moment I arrived, it ceased to exist. By sunset, any who remain here will also be dead.

"Knarr," he bellowed, and a huge Keldon warrior armed with a battle-axe stepped forward. "Muster these sheep," Astor commanded in High Keld.

"Done," Knarr said. He slung his axe across his back as he strode down the line of Lethans. "Everyone who owns a weapon, step forward. Everyone who has seen combat, step forward again. Everyone else—"

"That's enough," Letha's enforcer barked. Like the tower sentry, he carried a long poleaxe. Unlike the sentry, he held it ready, pointed at Knarr, but not so much that he couldn't quickly reorient it on Astor.

"—stand where you are," Knarr continued. He pointed at one of his fellow 'host warriors. "Take the armed ones around to collect their weapons. Assemble—"

"I said, that's enough!" the enforcer hollered. He and Knarr stared at each other. The enforcer's pike was steady.

"Hoy, dead man" Astor called. He stood easy, relaxed, his hands empty at his sides.

The enforcer turned his eyes and his weapon on Astor. "This is insane," he sputtered. He was a huge, blond brute from the icy fjords of Vosok, three thousand miles away. His Common Keld was rough, but understandable. "I am sworn to protect these people from all threats external or otherwise, including other Keldons. You will not lead them into certain death."

"Them," Astor said, "or you?"

The enforcer clenched his teeth. "Both."

"And you will not *allow* me to do this?"

"No. I won't."

Astor unsheathed his kugri blades. "A moment ago, you had no choice in the matter. Now you have even less."

"With respect, Warlord," the enforcer said, his tone belying his words, "you attacked a dragon and lost. He is coming to kill you for it. Tell me again how this concerns the people of Letha. Tell me again why we shouldn't drive you out to die somewhere else."

Astor approached the enforcer, step by deliberate step.

"We were taken from our homes by you savages." The enforcer's face had gone red, frenzied spittle flying from his lips. "When we refused to die in your army or serve in your countinghouses, we were sent here. We are not Keldons, Warlord. We never will be. We will not fight and die for the nation that enslaved us."

There were murmurs of agreement from the crowd. Astor stopped exactly one pace outside the reach of the enforcer's poleaxe.

"If I kill you now," the enforcer said, "even your soldiers will cheer. Your incompetence almost got them killed. Why should any of us follow you further?"

Astor looked to Ysenga, to Knarr, to the rest of his surviving troops. They laughed. Knarr shook his head in disbelief. Ysenga turned away from the scene.

Astor was younger, smaller, and less experienced than Letha's enforcer. But he was a warlord, and he could see the patterns of heat and rage dancing around the Vosok's body. Astor measured the man's eyes, boring into his brain, gauging the heft of his fighting spirit. Astor sneered.

"Watch closely," he said to the assembly.

The enforcer growled and thrust his polearm forward.

Astor swatted the axe head aside with his left blade and chopped it off the pole with his right.

He wielded his kugri, a chopping blade, thicker at its tip to produce deep wounds with a minimum of force. Astor's came to a sharp point so that he could thrust it like a dagger or hack with it like a machete.

The enforcer quickly jerked his truncated weapon back and spun it like a quarterstaff. He charged forward with a giant overhand swing, intending to stave Astor's skull in, or at least crush him to the ground.

Astor dropped the blade in his right hand and caught the pole with a bone-rattling *thwap*. He hauled on his end of the pole, but the enforcer maintained his grip. Astor brought his left arm over and chopped another three feet off the pole. He held onto the new length he had taken, spinning it casually like a baton.

The enforcer charged again.

With his blade, Astor grounded the Vosok's pole. He lashed the length of wood in his hand across the enforcer's face with a backhand so powerful it snapped the makeshift weapon in two.

The enforcer grunted as the back of his head slammed into the frozen dirt. Astor was on him before the crowd could gasp.

The blade sank deep between the enforcer's ribs. Astor viciously twisted it, and there was a loud, wet snap. The enforcer's eyes went wide. His lungs let out a long, protracted wheeze as they emptied for the last time.

Astor wiped the blade on the enforcer's tunic and went back to retrieve its twin.

"I am not your enemy," he said to the assembly as he sheathed his weapons. He looked meaningfully at Primus

Felal and the bodyguards beside her. "Skouras is your enemy. He offers you a victim's death and nothing more."

"Unlike a warlord," Felal snarled.

"Bring her here," Astor said.

Two of his warhost seized Felal and pulled her forward, her feet dragging uselessly on the ground.

To Felal, but loud enough so that everyone could hear, Astor said, "Keld is not your enemy. Keld offers you life. Violent life, in fire and blood. Life with the glorious chance to take your enemies with you."

Astor struck off Felal's left ear. She yelped, and Astor's warriors let her fall to her knees.

"The next Lethan who speaks out of turn dies in pieces." He wiped his kugri on the collar of Felal's robe as she knelt and cradled her head.

He stepped back, and his voice grew louder still. "I might kill you. Keld might kill you. Skouras *will* kill you." He shrugged. "Choose."

Astor turned his back on the crowd and stalked back toward Ysenga.

While Felal knelt, both her personal bodyguards and the tower sentry joined the ranks of villagers being sorted by Knarr.

"Bullag." A leaner, more feral member of Astor's warhost came forward. "Get her," he pointed back to Felal with his thumb, "to tell you where the food is. Everyone eats. Warriors first."

"Done." Bullag roughly pulled Felal to her feet, and Astor strode on.

"Ysenga," he snapped, and the translator jumped. She had been staring at the carnage in Astor's wake.

"Sir! I mean—"

Astor raised a hand, silencing her. "Find out if any of these stump-bred colos know anything about dragons. Something specific would be best, but anything at all is useful."

"Done."

"Bring what you find to that public house over yonder. We're having a war council. I'll be waiting."

"Understood."

"On my mark!" Astor bellowed, and a square full of people froze as six berserker warriors waited for their next command.

"No one leaves this square until I return," Astor called. "Any tongue that wags between now and then comes out by the roots."

"Done," said six warriors in unison. There was no laughter, but there was a strong element of joy in their response that made all the Lethans in earshot shudder.

Astor did not share their joy. He made for the tavern for one last opportunity to consider his circumstances and the dwindling chance that he might survive them.

The Shaping

"None of them knows anything," Ysenga reported. "They didn't even know that Kavalex lived so close, much less that she had been replaced."

"What a surprise," Astor grumbled. He took a long quaff from a jug of a thick, red spirit called ogre's blood. Outside, Knarr was drafting the Lethans into units and Bullag was feeding the units, one at a time.

Ysenga cleared her throat. "Warlord?" she asked tentatively.

"Translator."

"I, uh . . . I would like to offer my opinion."

"Then offer it. That's why you're here." He waved his hand expansively at the empty stools next to him.

Ysenga uncomfortably slid into one, leaving two empty between her and Astor. "Earlier, at Skouras's cave, you told me to run."

"And you didn't." Astor had not bothered with a glass, and he slid the jug of ogre's blood closer to her.

"No, I didn't. Because I couldn't. And not because I was frightened."

Astor stared at her icily.

Ysenga took a small sip, winced, and swallowed it. "Okay, I was frightened. At first. But to be honest, I was . . . I am more afraid of you than I am of Skouras."

"As it should be. That's something I have to ingrain in those meat puppets out there before Skouras arrives."

"Er . . . yes. But you're not . . . I don't think you see my point."

Astor took another sip. "Then you should drive it home."

Ysenga fortified herself with another, longer draught. "You felt it, too, Warlord. Something about Skouras's voice, or his eyes. I felt paralyzed."

Astor eyed her approvingly. "Yes. I did feel a . . . heaviness."

"It felt like magic."

"Agreed."

"It felt like influence magic. Subjugation. Like he was slowing us down somehow, from the inside, without ever touching us."

Astor nodded. "How do you suppose he killed Kavalex?"

"The same way he tried to kill you. He paralyzed her and then tore her apart."

"I agree." Astor took a mammoth gulp. "He also spoke

to us in Common Keld. According to Skouras, Kavalex understood Common Keld but refused to speak it. I think Skouras read Common Keld in her mind. As you said, 'from the inside.' "

"That would fit. If he's using influence magic, then he knows how to navigate through someone's thoughts and disrupt them."

Astor grimaced. "He also knows how to navigate the Northern Wastes. He will be upon us soon. We didn't have time to cover our tracks. Once he's assessed the damage that exploding egg did to his hoard, he'll be coming for us. I think he only let us go so that we would lead him to a place worth ransacking. The joke's on him, though—we led him here."

Ysenga took another nip off the jug, choked it down, and took another. She slid the jug back over to Astor and said, "Forgive me, sir, but do you have a plan? I mean, besides waiting for Skouras to find us and then stabbing and burning him till he dies?"

Astor snorted, amused. "I do. Though stabbing and burning him till he dies are a large part of it."

"Then . . . will you take off my ear if I ask what it is? I am at your service," she added quickly, "and your warriors are ready to follow your lead. But right now, the Lethans are only more afraid of you than of the dragon because he's not here. When he comes, won't they panic? Won't they fail you? I'm not a warlord . . . but wouldn't it be better if you gave them something to fight for, as well as against?"

Astor stared at her. "You are not a warlord," he said seriously, "but you are right. It'd be best to use all of the resources I have."

"Then let them help you."

Astor shook his head. "I can kill Skouras with what's

left of my warhost. The only way the Lethans can help is as a distraction."

"How? How can you kill him with six warriors when you couldn't with thirty?"

"Keld will kill him," Astor said simply. "There is enough fire in the land below to cripple him and enough snow and rocks on the peaks above to bury him. I will use them both. I will bring Letha and two entire mountains down around his ears."

"And what of the Lethans? What of me? What of Astor the Upstart, for that matter? Is Skouras worth all of us?"

"Keld is worth all of us. And more."

"Prove it," Ysenga said in High Keld. Astor blinked. "Show them how to survive, for the glory of Keld. Shape them into something that can stop Skouras and go on to fight again."

Astor felt an idea forming in his mind, one sparked by Ysenga's choice of words. Doyen Olvresk had trained him in Bogardan fire magic as well as warfare, and the Bogardans had a saying: Anyone can read a spell—it takes a master to *shape* one. To Ysenga's visible horror, Astor smiled, the deep, profound grin of a gambler who's just put his entire stake down on a single roll of the bones.

"Translator," he said formally. "If we both survive the next few hours, you will no longer be a specialist on loan from Tajamin. You will be my personal advisor, reporting directly to me."

Ysenga's eyes panicked. "But Doyenne Tajamin—"

"Is far, far away. If she wants you back, she can come collect you." Astor waited patiently for a moment. "You may express your gratitude now."

"Oh—uh, thank you, Warlord."

Astor stood up, jamming the cork back into the jug of

ogre's blood. "I was going to send you out of harm's way, to get word back to Olvresk and Tajamin and the rest of the council. But your idea is so compelling, I'll keep you here to help me implement it."

"Ah. I mean, good."

"I'll need you to teach me a few words in dragon-tongue, of course. And I'll need you by my side until Skouras is cold. But for now, I think some sort of explanation to the Lethans is in order." He took his helmet off the bar and tucked it under his arm. "And a demonstration," he added. He thumped Ysenga roughly on the shoulder, half-knocking her off her stool.

"Come. It's time to whip my new 'warhost' into a frenzy, so they can help me kill a dragon. I may need you to translate."

Knarr was waiting for them in the square. He stood at the head of one line of Lethans, and Bullag stood twenty feet away at the head of another, far smaller line.

"All are fed," Knarr reported. "These," he pointed at the villagers nearest to him, "await your orders. Those," he pointed at Bullag's group, "do not."

Astor's lip curled. "'Do not?'"

Knarr nodded. "They cannot or will not fight."

Astor eyed the smaller group. He was pleased to see Felal and the tower sentry in Knarr's line. "Separate them, Bullag," he growled. "Tell me who 'can't' and why."

Bullag marched down his line, pulling villagers out and shoving them toward Astor as he went.

"Wounded," Bullag offered as he propelled a limping Keldon male forward. He continued to tick off the Lethans' excuses as he yanked them out of the group. "Old. Half-blind. Untrained. Child." He shrugged, halfway between boredom and disgust. There were five remaining in the line of unwilling Lethans.

With a half-mumbled curse, Astor stepped forward. To the villagers Bullag had pulled out, he growled, "Get in the other line. 'Can't' fight is meaningless. If you are willing, I will make you able." He stepped closer to the others.

"If you can stand, you can fight," he said. "You are all on your feet. Yet you will not fight?"

"We will not," said a defiant Keldon female at the front of the line.

"Then you will die," Astor said evenly.

"We would rather die now than at the hands of a dragon."

Astor glared at her, and she dropped her eyes. The others had never even raised their heads.

"Go on," he said, irritated. "Run." He half-turned away. "Skouras is coming here. We," he indicated the rest of the villagers, "are going to stop him. But this village will be destroyed. If you value your lives at all, run. Enjoy the final few hours that you have."

The defiant Keldon nodded, unimpressed. "We shall, warlord." Keeping her eyes on Astor, she took a few tentative steps down the road out of town. When Astor did not cut her down, she began walking steadily out of the village. Astor watched her and her four trembling accomplices go.

"Anyone else?" Astor did not turn his head to look at the villagers behind him. No one else moved.

"That one's a guide," Bullag said from beside Astor. "She convinced them that she could get them safely to the Border Citadel."

"Wish them luck," Astor sneered. He turned and faced the remaining Lethans.

"Torches," he snapped. "Unlit. All around." All six of his

warriors set about collecting appropriate pieces of wood, or tearing them off whatever was handy. Soon everyone in the square had a length of wood and a curious expression.

"Single file," Astor said. To Knarr, he added, "You and the other five get to the far end." The villagers and warriors all lined up. Astor stopped Ysenga from joining the line. "By my side," he reminded her. She nodded.

Astor stepped up to the first Lethan in line, Primus Felal. He stood close to her, his eyes fierce, and she carefully kept her eyes down.

"You cannot hold my eyes." Astor spoke softly, so that even the person directly to Felal's left could not make out what he said.

"No, Warlord."

"Skouras did. He looked me full in the face and sapped my strength. His eyes are deeper than mine, colder. And he can drink up even more than I can serve." Astor lifted her face to his with a finger on her chin. "But he has not seen your eyes. He has not seen what your eyes look like, through mine."

Felal looked uncomfortably from side to side. "Warlord. I don't underst—"

"Would you like to see through my eyes?" Astor whispered. "Would you like to see the look on Skouras's face when we destroy him? See it firsthand?"

Startled, Felal met his gaze. As she did, a huge spark leapt from Astor's crackling eyes to hers. Her head jerked back, and a reddish-black smoke wafted up into the frozen morning air. She gasped, and a predator's grin split her face.

"Burn," Astor ordered, and the end of Felal's torch exploded into bright, yellow flame. She raised it high over her head and howled.

Astor extended his hand. "Join me," he said. Felal took

his hand. He pulled her forward, out of line and into position behind him.

Astor stepped over to the next villager. "You cannot hold my eyes. . . ."

Behind him, he could hear Felal's furious breathing, deep and ragged. To his left, Ysenga wore a determined look of hope, as if Astor could not succeed unless she were willing it as hard as she could. In front of him, another score of Lethans waited for the spark that would ignite their torches and their fighting spirits. Above him, high among the freezing clouds, Skouras soared ever closer.

And all around him, the dead air and silent aura that permeated Letha began to boil.

The Staredown

As the sun sank behind the mountains, Skouras arrived. At top speed, with his claws clenched across his chest as if cradling something, he tucked his great head and slammed into the four-story primus's mansion. He struck with all the force of an exploding bomb. The top two floors simply disintegrated. Debris spread clear across the town square. The remainder of the building collapsed in on itself.

"Hoy, little ape," Skouras jeered in Common Keld, scanning the square for Astor. "I had hoped your last stand would take place on a slightly grander site. No matter. You'll be just as dead when I'm through."

Astor watched him from a rocky ridge overlooking the town. Behind and below him stood the forces he had assembled—twenty-odd civilians, six warriors, and one translator-cum-advisor. He almost laughed.

Instead, he concentrated on the single-room guardhouse that lay directly between himself and Skouras. They had placed ten casks of heating oil inside. Astor began muttering softly to himself, his open hand out at arm's length. He turned to glance at his "warriors."

"Watch closely," he said. A ripple of rough laughter rolled past him. He smiled. He turned back to the guardhouse.

"Burn," he said, clenching his hand into a tight fist. The entire building went up with a blast that sent Skouras reeling backward and briefly lit up the entire square.

Skouras regained his balance and skidded to a halt. Swearing in dragon-tongue, he lashed out with his tail and reduced another single-room edifice to toothpicks and splinters.

"Well played," Skouras hissed. "But nowhere near enough. Perhaps you lack incentive, Warlord." Skouras uncoupled his hands and waved one of them out in a wide, backhanded arc. Several round objects flew from his grasp, like seeds from a farmer's hand.

"Your scouts will not be bringing back reinforcements anytime soon," Skouras taunted. The heads of the Lethans who had refused to join Astor thudded to the ground and rolled into the gutter.

A deep, rumbling growl rose up behind Astor, but he waved it down. He stared at another building they had mined, one much farther from Skouras.

"Burn," Astor repeated, and pumped his fist. The second building went up in a great burst of heat and noise. Skouras shrank back slightly and then laughed.

"How loud and bright we are. How fiery," he said. "Are you trying to kill me by giving me a headache?"

Skouras's taunt trailed off as Astor gestured on the ridge. The flames from the second explosion were not burning out.

Instead, under Astor's direction, they were swirling, merging, coalescing into a ball. The ball of fire hung there, spinning, and Skouras looked at it curiously, perched on the tips of his claws, his wings spread in case the tiny, whirling sun suddenly lunged at him.

The ball of flame deformed as it spun, becoming more oblate. At its center, two brighter spots of flame appeared. Below them, a hole opened up and widened. The flames continue to sculpt themselves until they began crudely to resemble the face of the man who controlled them.

"Mine is the only head you need to worry about," Astor growled. The blazing effigy-head boomed out the words exactly as Astor spoke them. High up on the ridge, Astor hacked and spit. Down in the town square, his puppet-head did the same, hurling a gobbet of fire past Skouras's ear.

The dragon turned, suddenly pivoting away from the fiery vision in front of him. Though Astor was certain Skouras could not see him on the ridge, the dragon glared directly at the warlord.

"There you are," he hissed. He sprang into the air, veering off to plow straight through the flaming head and burst it like a balloon. With two flaps of his great wings, he covered the distance between himself and Astor and crashed down onto the trees in front of the ridge.

Astor and Skouras locked eyes over ten feet of frigid air. Skouras snorted and licked his lips hungrily.

"Time to die, Warlord."

Astor felt his stomach drop once more as the deadening effect of Skouras's eyes took hold. His vision blurred. Skouras's hiss drowned out the sounds of Letha burning. The air slowed, and the cold deepened. With a titanic effort of will, Astor raised a thick length of wood over his head.

Unconcerned, Skouras hunkered down, stretching his neck to bring his paralysis stare closer to Astor's face. He licked his lips again, hissing all the while.

"Burn," Astor said, gripping the torch so tightly that it began to splinter. His torch ignited. Behind him, Ysenga's torch also burst into flame, high over her head. Then Knarr's. Then Felal's. Then Bullag's.

One after the other, the Lethans' and warriors' torches exploded into life until the entire ridge was aglow in flickering firelight. Astor could feel Skouras's distraction, but the dragon did not break off. He continued to pry into Astor's mind, forcing his way in past the flame in Astor's eyes and miring his brain with his sickening influence.

"On my mark," Astor said in High Keld. The heat they were generating clashed with the void that flowed out from Skouras. A hot wind whipped up, and the snows alternately melted and refroze.

Drowning in Skouras's gaze, Astor reached out and touched the flames beneath his feet once more. He felt the molten ocean of energy that infused the bedrock of Keld, teased it, drew it out and upward to him. Astor then took the growing furor behind him: the anger the Lethans felt for their ruined homes and threatened lives; the rabid desire of his warhost to bathe in enemy blood; the earnest wish of Ysenga to see Skouras dead so she could discover more of the world that Astor offered her; and the vengeful protectiveness deep within himself, steward of this place and one of the rightful rulers of this violent nation.

The transcendent moment stretched. Astor heard nothing as Skouras's eyes swallowed him whole. The dragon's eyes were far deeper than his, so very much older and more profound.

Astor was a single star in an endless black void, the faintest spark in an ocean of ice. He was drowning in the dragon's eyes.

Astor brought his arm down. "Now," he said.

In unison, in the elite tongue of their adoptive homeland, thirty-two voices cried, "Burn!" With his eyes still deep into Skouras's, Astor himself cried a single word in the native tongue of dragons. The call overlapped the command shouted by his followers.

"Kneel," he ordered.

A gargantuan wave of energy screamed out of the Lethans, out of the ground itself, and blasted into Astor. He was no longer the single source of light, but a doorway through which a thousand lights flowed. Not a mere spark, nor a flame, but an inferno, channeled into a coherent beam of rage.

Skouras screamed. His mind surrounded Astor's, smothered him, pressed down from above, below, and around. Astor struck back through the heavy fog. His mind was smaller than Skouras's, younger and less profound but also hotter. Skouras had tried to swallow an angry wasp, and was discovering too late that its sting was lethal. The focused fury of Keld and its people erupted out of Astor's eyes and slammed into the dragon's. It blasted his head backward on his sinuous neck, shattering his great nostrils, scouring his eye sockets out and charring his forebrain from the inside.

Skouras's body shuddered. He clawed and twitched feebly. Smoke wafted from his ruined face. Then he fell clumsily backward, his brain dead and his body jerking, crushing trees and rocks alike as he rolled and slid helplessly down the ridge.

A primal cheer went up from the Lethans, one that died

stillborn as Astor turned his furious gaze upon them. He drew his broadsword. Everyone on the ridge held his or her breath.

Astor offered the sword to the assembly, hilt-first.

"Everybody cuts," he jerked his head toward the still-twitching body of Skouras the dragon. "But the head belongs to me."

"Done," thirty-two Keldons replied. Astor's six original warriors sprang forward, eager to be first, hungry to wet their own blades.

Ysenga came to Astor and took his sword.

"Doyen," she said reverently, and thrust Astor's sword high. "Astor!"

"Not doyen," Astor corrected gently. "Not yet."

But the chant of his name had taken root and began to spread across the ridge. Down below, his warriors picked up the chant and joined in as they hacked off scales, claws, and bits of tail as trophies. All around them, virtually unnoticed, Letha continued to burn.

"The head belongs to me," Astor said again, though it was nearly dawn before he was able to claim his prize.

The Toast

The red-sashed herald arrived ten days later, mounted on a snow-white colos. The watchtower sentry announced him, and Astor stood ready for his dispatch at the center of what used to be Letha. Ten warriors and Ysenga stood by him. Around them, the rest of Letha's former residents were busily breaking down their belongings and packing up their essentials.

"Warlord," the herald stopped and bowed his head. His

mount was dragging a heavy cart behind him, but its cargo was concealed beneath thick blankets.

"Herald," Astor replied.

"I bring you word from the citadel of Doyen Olvresk." He held out a simple metal scroll case. Astor took it and examined its contents.

"Your message is delivered, herald," Astor said once he had finished reading. "Help yourself to provisions before you return. Tell Olvresk his orders will be carried out."

"Warlord." The herald unharnessed his colos, and one of Astor's warhost stepped forward and escorted them both away.

"Advisor," he called. Ysenga stepped forward. He offered her the scroll, and she took it.

"Olvresk is annoyed that Kavalex is dead. He spent a great deal of time . . . negotiating their bargain."

Astor slapped the cart like an old and trusted friend. "The doyen also sends us a cask of his finest ale," he continued. "And 'Olvresk's finest' is saying something. He bids me and my warriors drink it in honor of Kavalex, a respected foe and a valued ally.

"He also orders anyone who drinks it to then pass water over the ashes of the scum who killed her." Astor grinned, pulled back the blankets covering the cask, and punched his kugri blade through the wooden top.

"On my mark," he called, and everyone in earshot came to attention.

"The line forms behind me," he called. "Bring cups, mugs, and tankards. Anything that can hold liquid. We have one more task to accomplish before we strike out for my citadel."

Astor tipped the punctured cask over, bent, and drank deeply from the wide stream as it poured. When he was full, he motioned for Ysenga to step in and take his place. In turn, Knarr readied himself to take her place when she was done.

They began chanting his name once more as they lined up. They were still chanting half an hour later, when the cask was empty and not a single drop had been spilled.

About the Authors

Bram Stoker and Aurora Award winner **Edo van Belkom** is the author of the DRAGONLANCE® novel *Lord Soth*, and the horror/mystery *Teeth*. Some of his over 175 short stories have been gathered into the collections *Death Drives a Semi* and *Six-Inch Spikes*. His books of nonfiction include *Northern Dreamers*, a book of interviews, and two how-to writing guides, *Writing Horror* and *Writing Erotica*. His website is located at www.vanbelkom.com.

A veteran of fifteen long years in the gaming industry trenches, **Edward Bolme's** previous work includes the award-winning supplement *Six-guns and Sorcery* and the novel *Title Deleted for Security Reasons*. At various times he has kept a heron in his

About the Authors

bathtub, had chewed-up bread spit in his ear, and been served with a warrant for his arrest for not mowing his lawn. In spite of all this, he still considers himself a pretty normal guy. Really.

Tom Dupree is a former rock critic, wire service reporter, advertising creative director, and public relations man. His work has also appeared in a number of science fiction, fantasy, and horror anthologies, including Wizards of the Coast's FORGOTTEN REALMS® collections *Realms of Magic* and *Realms of the Arcane*. He lives in New York City with his wife, Linda.

Denise R. Graham lives in the desert southwest with her husband Ron. In addition to telling big fat lies in the form of stories and novels, she enjoys reading, weight lifting, and running amok.

Award-winning children's magazine editor and writer **Allison Lassieur** has published more than two dozen books about history, world cultures, current events, Native Americans, space, and health. She has written for magazines such as *National Geographic World*, *Highlights for Children*, *Scholastic News*, and *Disney Adventures*, and also writes fiction short stories, puzzle books, role-playing game books, and computer-game materials. Her first fantasy novel was published by Wizards of the Coast in 2000. In addition to writing, Ms. Lassieur enjoys reading, spinning, and recreating historical textiles. She lives and works in Easton, Pennsylvania.

While not on the road touring with the heavy-metal band Blood Red Steel, **Jess Lebow** divides his time between feeding the homeless at local soup kitchens and working toward a world-wide Marxist revolution. He currently resides in Seattle, Washington, and no, he did not smash any windows during the WTO rallies last year.

Scott McGough tends to move around a lot. He's lived in New Jersey, Baltimore, San Pedro, and most recently, Seattle, where he's spent the past ten years with his wife Elena, two cats, and two psychotic lumps of muscle (a.k.a., dogs). In his spare time, he enjoys single malt whiskey, swearing at bothersome inanimate objects, and watching any movie with monsters in it.

Vance Moore was born in Sunnyside, Washington during 1967. He learned to read at an early age and devoured the childhood classics of the fantastic—Dr. Seuss, fairy tales, Dr. Dolittle, Oz. He lives in Washington State and complains about the weather. He has two short stories and a novel published by Wizards of the Coast. He is currently working on a new MAGIC: THE GATHERING® novel.

Tim Ryan's favorite haunts are museums, bookstores, and the labyrinths of the Manhattan subway system, which he battles every day. He is an avid reader, an aspiring writer, and a competitive gamer.

Born in Wisconsin in 1967, **Steven Schend** fell into the world of fantasy quite quickly, growing up on L. Frank Baum's Oz books, Edgar Rice Burroughs's Tarzan and Barsoom novels, and Ray Harryhausen movies. He now calls Seattle home, a place that attracts writers at least with easy access to good coffee. For ten years, Steven worked with TSR, Inc., and Wizards of the Coast as an editor, developer,

About the Authors

and designer on a multitude of projects. Steven has written scores of magazine articles and game products, though he hopes to match that track record with his current stint as a fiction author and freelance novelist.

Paul B. Thompson is the author of ten novels, including *Sundipper*, *Thorn and Needle*, *Nemesis*, *Red Sands*, and six DRAGONLANCE® novels, written in collaboration with Tonya Carter Cook. The latest of these, *Children of the Plains*, begins a new trilogy know collectively as The Barbarians. In addition to his novels, Thompson has written numerous short stories and nonfiction articles. "Deathwings" is his third story for MAGIC: THE GATHERING® anthologies. He lives in Chapel Hill, North Carolina, with his wife Elizabeth.

Brian M. Thomsen was one of the founding editors of Warner Books' science fiction/fantasy program (where he edited two Hugo-Award-winning books and numerous other award nominees) and spent five years as the head of TSR's book and periodicals program. He himself has been nominated for a Hugo, has served as a World Fantasy Award judge, and is the author of two novels for TSR (*Once Around the Realms* and *The Mage in the Iron Mask*, both in the FORGOTTEN REALMS® line) and over thirty short stories. His most recent publications as an editor are two anthologies in collaboration with Marty Greenberg for DAW Books (*Oceans of Space* and *Oceans of Magic*). As a writer, he was the co-author of Julius Schwartz's memoirs (*Man of Two Worlds*), and he is currently working on a critical anthology entitled *The American Fantasy Tradition*. He resides in Brooklyn with his wife Donna and two loving cats (Sparky and Minx).